IN THE MAD MOUNTAINS

Praise for *In the Mad Mountains*

"Joe Lansdale squares up to the Great Old Ones—and taps into rich veins of awe and wit, with always a backbeat thrum of cosmic terror. You'll never look at the howling void in the black heart of the universe the same way again."

—Kim Newman, author of the *Anno Dracula* series

"Lansdale's trick: Doing it better, with a wider array of voices, including those of Poe and Twain and the classic American folk tale and his own Texas noir sensibility. This collection is a box of cursed yet delicious chocolates. Take a bite of every one!"

—Nick Mamatas, author of *Move Under Ground* and *I Am Providence*

"Horror royalty Joe Lansdale's take on cosmic horror and the Cthulhu Mythos is everything you'd hope for—bloody, profane, grimly humorous, and as vivid as Technicolor hell splashed on a 20-foot tall silver screen."

—Laird Barron, author of *Not a Speck of Light*

"Lansdale proves once again with *In the Mad Mountains*, as he has over his long and triumphant career, to be a master of every genre he touches."

—Rae Wilde, author of *Merciless Waters* and *I Can Fix Her*

"Exploring the darkest corners of the human psyche, here is a lethally entertaining journey through Joe Lansdale's twisted landscape, where ancient evils lurk and sanity hangs by a rapidly fraying thread."

—Paul Finch, author of *Never Seen Again*

"A consistently entertaining, varied, horrifying, and vividly told collection."

—*Umney's Alley*

Selected Works by Joe R. Lansdale

Hap and Leonard

Savage Season (1990)
Mucho Mojo (1994)
The Two-Bear Mambo (1995)
Bad Chili (1997)
Rumble Tumble (1998)
Veil's Visit: A Taste of Hap and Leonard
    (with Andrew Vachss, 1999)
Captains Outrageous (2001)
Vanilla Ride (2009)
Hyenas (2011)
Devil Red (2011)

Dead Aim (2013)
Honky Tonk Samurai (2016)
Hap and Leonard (2016)
Rusty Puppy (2017)
Blood and Lemonade (2017)
The Big Book of Hap and Leonard (2018)
Jack Rabbit Smile (2018)
The Elephant of Surprise (2019)
Of Mice and Minestrone (2020)
Born for Trouble (2022)
Sugar in the Bones (2024)

Other Novels

Act of Love (1981)
Dead in the West (1986)
The Magic Wagon (1986)
The Nightrunners (1987)
The Drive-In (1988)
Cold in July (1989)
Batman: Captured by the Engines (1991)
Tarzan: The Lost Adventure
    (with Edgar Rice Burroughs, 1995)
The Boar (1998)
Freezer Burn (1999)
Waltz of Shadows (1999)
The Big Blow (2000)
The Bottoms (2000)
A Fine Dark Line (2002)

Sunset and Sawdust (2004)
Lost Echoes (2007)
Leather Maiden (2008)
Flaming Zeppelins (2010)
All the Earth, Thrown to Sky (2011)
Edge of Dark Water (2012)
The Thicket (2013)
Paradise Sky (2015)
Fender Lizards (2015)
Bubba and the Cosmic Bloodsuckers
    (2017)
Jane Goes North (2020)
More Better Deals (2020)
Moon Lake (2021)
Donut Legion (2022)

Collections

By Bizarre Hands (1989)
Electric Gumbo (1994)
Writer of the Purple Rage (1994)
High Cotton (2000)
Bumper Crop (2004)
Mad Dog Summer and Other Stories
    (2004)
The Shadows, Kith and Kin (2007)
Sanctified and Chicken Fried (2009)
The Best of Joe R. Lansdale (2010)

Bleeding Shadows (2013)
Miracles Ain't What They Used to Be
    (2016)
Terror Is Our Business
    (with Kasey Lansdale, 2018)
Driving to Geromino's Grave
    and Other Stories (2018)
Things Get Ugly (2023)
The Senior Girls Bayonet Drill Team
    and Other Stories (2024)

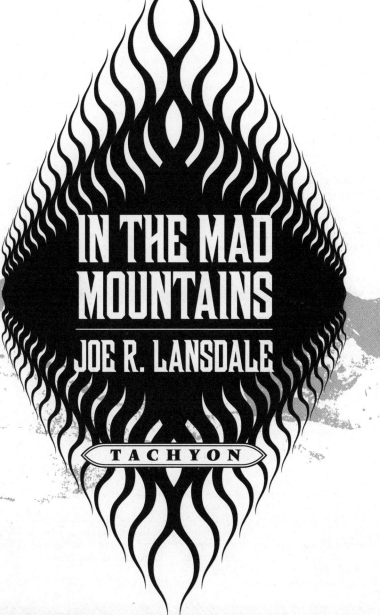

IN THE MAD MOUNTAINS

JOE R. LANSDALE

TACHYON

TACHYON PUBLICATIONS LLC
1459 18TH STREET #139
SAN FRANCISCO, CA 94107
415.285.5615
WWW.TACHYONPUBLICATIONS.COM
TACHYON@TACHYONPUBLICATIONS.COM

SERIES EDITOR: JACOB WEISMAN
EDITOR: RICHARD KLAW

PRINT ISBN: 978-1-61696-424-5
DIGITAL ISBN: 978-1-61696-425-2

PRINTED IN THE UNITED STATES BY
VERSA PRESS, INC.

FIRST EDITION: 2024
9 8 7 6 5 4 3 2 1

For Terrill Lee Lankford—wrong book, right time.

Introduction by Joe R. Lansdale

THESE MAY NOT be all the stories I've written inspired by H. P. Lovecraft, but they are, to my way of thinking, the best. I may write others, but truthfully, I believe I am through.

Don't trust me on that. I'm a moody sort of writer, and the Lovecraftian mood may strike me again. But at this moment in time, I feel that I'm done.

Here's an odd note: I really don't much care for Lovecraft's writing. It always seemed as unnecessarily difficult as trying to remove a Himalayan snowbank with a garden trowel and a bucket of hot water.

What I liked about Lovecraft were his ideas of the Old Ones. That science-fictional horror he created. I find that vastly appealing.

Not liking his writing style does not diminish his impact on the field of horror and science fiction for me, and many may find his rococo use of language exciting. I don't.

For me, it's all about Cthulhu and that whole gaggle of Old Ones. They're fun. A little creepy. Unsettling. They wait just outside our realm, tapping at the walls that separate us from them, and there's always someone trying to assist them in their endeavor for a nebulous reward.

Really, guys?

I mean, they seem so trustworthy, these horrible beings from beyond.

Many of the ideas in Lovecraft's creations were suggested, in my view, by better writers, like Arthur Machen and Algernon Blackwood. But it was Lovecraft's approach to this unseen realm and what lurked there that caught on.

That says something valuable. He had a vision so strong that it leapt over his massive walls of sometimes-unintelligible prose and entered into the human consciousness as if those alien entities might actually exist.

I certainly hope they do not.

More importantly for this collection, I hope I have done his influence justice.

I've always loved Robert Johnson's music and the story about how he sold his soul to the devil at midnight at the crossroads so he could be granted the wish of being a fantastic guitar player. Of course, Johnson had to give up his soul. The story was probably borrowed from another blues musician and is about as true as using Fruit Loops for life preservers, no matter who claims it. But it's a cool story. It fit the whole concept of "The Music of Erich Zann," about a guy who played music to hold back something dark and ravenous that lived on the other side of this dimension. I combined the ideas, gave it a Southern flavor, and went for it. I'm also a big fan of hard-boiled novels and private-eye stories. I added that in, set the story in the fifties, and this came out. I like it. Hope you do.

THE BLEEDING SHADOW

I WAS DOWN at the Blue Light Joint that night, finishing off some ribs and listening to some blues, when in walked Alma May. She was looking good too. Had a dress on and it fit her the way a dress ought to fit every woman in the world. She was wearing a little flat hat that leaned to one side, like an unbalanced plate on a waiter's palm. The high heels she had on made her legs look tight and way all right.

The light wasn't all that good in the joint, which is one of its appeals. It sometimes helps a man or woman get along in a way the daylight wouldn't stand, but I knew Alma May enough to know light didn't matter. She'd look good wearing a sack and a paper hat.

There was something about her face that showed me right off she was worried, that things weren't right. She was glancing left and right, like she was in some big city trying to cross a busy street and not get hit by a car.

I got my bottle of beer, left out from my table, and went over to her.

Then I knew why she'd been looking around like that. She said, "I was looking for you, Richard."

"Say you were," I said. "Well you done found me."

The way she stared at me wiped the grin off my face.

"Something wrong Alma May?"

"Maybe. I don't know. I got to talk, though. Thought you'd be here, and I was wondering you might want to come by my place."

"When?"

"Now."

"All right."

"But don't get no business in mind," she said. "This isn't like the old days. I need your help, and I need to know I can count on you."

"Well, I kind of like the kind of business we used to do, but all right, we're friends. It's cool."

"I hoped you'd say that."

"You got a car?" I said.

She shook her head. "No. I had a friend drop me off."

I thought, *friend*? Sure.

"All right then," I said, "let's strut on out."

I guess you could say it's a shame Alma May makes her money turning tricks, but when you're the one paying for the tricks, and you are one of her satisfied customers, you feel different. Right then, anyway. Later, you feel guilty. Like maybe you done peed on the *Mona Lisa*. 'Cause that gal, she was one fine dark-skin woman who should have got better than a thousand rides and enough money to buy some eats and make some coffee in the morning. She deserved something good. Should have found and married a man with a steady job that could have done all right by her.

But that hadn't happened. Me and her had a bit of something once, and it wasn't just business, money changing hands after she got me feeling good. No, it was more than that, but we couldn't work it out.

She was in the life and didn't know how to get out. And as for deserving something better, that wasn't me. What I had were a couple of nice suits, some two-tone shoes, a hat and a gun—.45 caliber automatic, like they'd used in the war a few years back.

Alma May got a little on the dope, too, and though she shook it, it had dropped her down deep. Way I figured, she wasn't never climbing out of that hole, and it didn't have nothing to do with dope now. What it had to do with was time. You get a window open now and again, and if you don't crawl through it, it closes. I know. My window had closed some time back. It made me mad all the time.

We were in my Chevy, a six-year-old car, a forty-eight model. I'd had it reworked a bit at a time: new tires, fresh windshield, nice seat covers and so on. It was shiny and special.

We were driving along, making good time on the highway, the lights racing over the cement, making the recent rain in the ruts shine like the knees of old dress pants.

"What you need me for?" I asked.

"It's a little complicated," she said.

"Why me?"

"I don't know. . . . You've always been good to me, and once we had a thing goin'."

"We did," I said.

"What happened to it?"

I shrugged. "It quit goin'."

"It did, didn't it? Sometimes I wish it hadn't."

"Sometimes I wish a lot of things," I said.

She leaned back in the seat and opened her purse and got out a cigarette and lit it, then rolled down the window. She remembered I didn't like cigarette smoke. I never had got on the tobacco. It took your wind and it stunk and it made your breath bad too. I hated when it got in my clothes.

"You're the only one I could tell this too," she said. "The only one that would listen to me and not think I been with the needle in my arm. You know what I'm sayin'?"

"Sure, baby, I know."

"I sound to you like I been bad?"

"Naw. You sound all right. I mean, you're talkin' a little odd, but not like you're out of your head."

"Drunk?"

"Nope. Just like you had a bad dream and want to tell someone."

"That's closer," she said. "That ain't it, but that's much closer than any needle or whisky or wine."

Alma May's place is on the outskirts of town. It's the one thing she got out of life that ain't bad. It's not a mansion. It's small, but it's tight and bright in the daylight, all painted up canary yellow color with deep blue trim. It didn't look bad in the moonlight.

Alma May didn't work with a pimp. She didn't need one. She was well known around town. She had her clientele. They were all safe, she told me once. About a third of them were white folks from on the other side of the tracks, up there in the proper part of Tyler Town. What she had besides them was a dead mother and a runaway father, and a brother, Tootie, who liked to travel around, play blues and suck that bottle. He was always needing something, and Alma May, in spite of her own demons, had always managed to make sure he got it.

That was another reason me and her had to split the sheets. That brother of hers was a grown-ass man, and he lived with his mother and let her tote his water. When the mama died, he sort of went to pieces. Alma May took Mama's part over, keeping Tootie in whisky and biscuits, even bought him a guitar. He lived off her whoring money, and it didn't bother him none. I didn't like him. But I will say this. That boy could play the blues.

When we were inside her house, she unpinned her hat from her hair and sailed it across the room and into a chair.

She said, "You want a drink?"

"I ain't gonna say no, long as it ain't too weak, and be sure to put it in a dirty glass."

She smiled. I watched from the living room doorway as she went and got a bottle out from under the kitchen sink, showing me how tight that dress fit across her bottom when she bent over. She pulled some glasses off a shelf, come back with a stiff one. We drank a little of it, still standing, leaning against the door frame between living room and kitchen. We finally sat on the couch. She sat on the far end, just to make sure I remembered why we were there. She said, "It's Tootie."

I swigged down the drink real quick, said, "I'm gone."

As I went by the couch, she grabbed my hand. "Don't be that way, baby."

"Now I'm baby," I said.

"Hear me out, honey. Please. You don't owe me, but can you pretend you do?"

"Hell," I said and went and sat down on the couch.

She moved, said, "I want you to listen."

"All right," I said.

"First off, I can't pay you. Except maybe in trade."

"Not that way," I said. "You and me, we do this, it ain't trade. Call it a favor."

I do a little detective stuff now and then for folks I knew, folks that recommended me to others. I don't have a license. Black people couldn't get a license to shit broken glass in this town. But I was pretty good at what I did. I learned it the hard way. And not all of it was legal. I guess I'm a kind of private eye. Only I'm really private. I'm so private I might be more of a secret eye.

"Best thing to do is listen to this," she said. "It cuts back on some explanation."

There was a little record player on a table by the window, a stack of records. She went over and opened the player box and turned it on.

The record she wanted was already on it. She lifted up the needle and set it right, stepped back and looked at me.

She was oh so fine. I looked at her and thought maybe I should have stuck with her, brother or no brother. She could melt butter from ten feet away, way she looked.

And then the music started to play.

It was Tootie's voice. I recognized that right away. I had heard him plenty. Like I said, he wasn't much as a person, willing to do anything so he could lay back and play that guitar, slide a pocket knife along the strings to squeal out just the right sound, but he was good at the blues, of that, there ain't no denying.

His voice was high and lonesome, and the way he played that guitar, it was hard to imagine how he could get the sounds out of it he got.

"You brought me over here to listen to records?" I said.

She shook her head. She lifted up the needle, stopped the record, and took it off. She had another in a little paper cover, and she took it out and put it on, dropped the needle down.

"Now listen to this."

First lick or two, I could tell right off it was Tootie, but then there came a kind of turn in the music, where it got so strange the hair on the back of my neck stood up. And then Tootie started to sing, and the hair on the back of my hands and arms stood up. The air in the room got thick and the lights got dim, and shadows come out of the corners and sat on the couch with me. I ain't kidding about that part. The room was suddenly full of them, and I could hear what sounded like a bird, trapped at the ceiling, fluttering fast and hard, looking for a way out.

Then the music changed again, and it was like I had been dropped down a well, and it was a long drop, and then it was like those shadows were folding around me in a wash of dirty water. The room stunk of something foul. The guitar no longer sounded like a guitar, and Tootie's voice was no longer like a voice. It was like someone dragging a razor over concrete while trying to yodel with a throat full of glass. There was something inside the music; something that squished and scuttled and honked and raved, something unsettling, like a snake in a satin glove.

"Cut it off," I said.

But Alma May had already done it.

She said, "That's as far as I've ever let it go. It's all I can do to move to cut it off. It feels like it's getting more powerful the more it plays. I don't want to hear the rest of it. I don't know I can take it. How can that be, Richard? How can that be with just sounds?"

I was actually feeling weak, like I'd just come back from a bout with the flu and someone had beat my ass. I said, "More powerful? How do you mean?"

"Ain't that what you think? Ain't that how it sounds? Like it's getting stronger?"

I nodded. "Yeah."

"And the room—"

"The shadows?" I said. "I didn't just imagine it?"

"No," she said. "Only every time I've heard it, it's been a little different. The notes get darker, the guitar licks, they cut something inside me, and each time it's something different and something deeper. I don't know if it makes me feel good or it makes me feel bad, but it sure makes me feel."

"Yeah," I said, because I couldn't find anything else to say.

"Tootie sent me that record. He sent a note that said: 'Play it when you have to.' That's what it said. That's all it said. What's that mean?"

"I don't know, but I got to wonder why Tootie would send it to you in the first place. Why would he want you to hear something makes you almost sick? And how in hell could he do that, make that kind of sound, I mean?"

She shook her head. "I don't know. Someday, I'm gonna play it all the way through."

"I wouldn't," I said.

"Why?"

"You heard it. I figure it only gets worse. I don't understand it, but I know I don't like it."

"Yeah," she said, putting the record back in the paper sleeve. "I know. But it's so strange. I've never heard anything like it."

"And I don't want to hear anything like it again."

"Still, you have to wonder."

"What I wonder is what I was wondering before. Why would he send this shit to you?"

"I think he's proud of it. There's nothing like it. It's . . . original."

"I'll give it that," I said. "So, what do you want with me?"

"I want you to find Tootie."

"Why?"

"Because I don't think he's right. I think he needs help. I mean, this . . . it makes me think he's somewhere he shouldn't be."

"But yet, you want to play it all the way through," I said.

"What I know is I don't like that. I don't like Tootie being associated with it, and I don't know why. Richard, I want you to find him."

"Where did the record come from?"

She got the sleeve and brought it to me. I could see through the little donut in the sleeve where the label on the record ought to be. Nothing but disk. The package itself was like wrapping paper you put meat in. It was stained.

"I think he paid some place to let him record," I said. "Question is, what place? You have an address where this came from?"

"I do." She went and got a large manila envelope and brought it to me. "It came in this."

I looked at the writing on the front. It had as a return address the Hotel Champion. She showed me the note. It was on a piece of really cheap stationery that said THE HOTEL CHAMPION and had a phone number and an address in Dallas. The stationery looked old and it was sun-faded.

"I called them," she said, "but they didn't know anything about him. They had never heard of him. I could go look myself, but . . . I'm a little afraid. Besides, you know, I got clients, and I got to make the house payment."

I didn't like hearing about that, knowing what kind of clients she meant, and how she was going to make that money. I said, "All right. What you want me to do?"

"Find him."

"And then what?"

"Bring him home."

"And if he don't want to come back?"

"I've seen you work, bring him home to me. Just don't lose that temper of yours."

I turned the record around and around in my hands. I said, "I'll go take a look. I won't promise anything more than that. He wants to come, I'll bring him back. He doesn't, I might be inclined to break his leg and bring him back. You know I don't like him."

"I know. But don't hurt him."

"If he comes easy, I'll do that. If he doesn't, I'll let him stay, come back and tell you where he is and how he is. How about that?'

"That's good enough," she said. "Find out what this is all about. It's got me scared, Richard."

"It's just bad sounds," I said. "Tootie was probably high on some- thing when he recorded it, thought it was good at the time, sent it to you because he thought he was the coolest thing since Robert Johnson."

"Who?"

"Never mind. But I figure when he got over his hop, he probably didn't even remember he mailed it."

"Don't try and tell me you've heard anything like this. That listening to it didn't make you feel like your skin was gonna pull off your bones, that some part of it made you want to dip in the dark and learn to like it. Tell me it wasn't like that? Tell me it wasn't like walking out in front of a car and the headlights in your face, and you just wanting to step out there even though it scared the hell out of you and you knew it was the devil or something even worse at the wheel. Tell me you didn't feel something like that."

I couldn't. So I didn't say anything. I just sat there and sweated, the sound of that music still shaking down deep in my bones, boiling my blood.

"Here's the thing," I said. "I'll do it, but you got to give me a photograph of Tootie, if you got one, and the record so you don't play it no more."

She studied me a moment. "I hate that thing," she said, nodding at the record in my hands, "but somehow I feel attached to it. Like getting rid of it is getting rid of a piece of me."

"That's the deal."

"All right," she said, "Take it, but take it now."

Motoring along by myself in the Chevy, the moon high and bright, all I could think of was that music, or whatever that sound was. It was stuck in my head like an axe. I had the record on the seat beside me, had Tootie's note and envelope, the photograph Alma May had given me.

Part of me wanted to drive back to Alma May and tell her no, and never mind. Here's the record back. But another part of me, the dumb part, wanted to know where and how and why that record had been made. Curiosity, it just about gets us all.

Where I live is a rickety third-floor walk-up. It's got the stairs on the outside, and they stop at each landing. I was at the very top.

I tried not to rest my hand too heavy on the rail as I climbed, because it was about to come off. I unlocked my door and turned on the light and watched the roaches run for cover.

I put the record down, got a cold one out of the ice box. Well, actually it was a plug in. A refrigerator. But I'd grown up with ice boxes, so calling it that was hard to break. I picked up the record again and took a seat.

Sitting in my old arm chair with the stuffings leaking out like a busted cotton sack, holding the record again, looking at the dirty brown sleeve, I noticed the grooves were dark and scabby looking, like something had gotten poured in there and had dried tight. I tried to determine if that had something to do with that crazy sound. Could something in the grooves make that kind of noise? Didn't seem likely.

I thought about putting the record on, listening to it again, but I couldn't stomach the thought. The fact that I held it in my hand made me uncomfortable. It was like holding a bomb about to go off.

I had thought of it like a snake once. Alma May had thought of it like a hit-and-run car driven by the devil. And now I had thought of it like a bomb. That was some kind of feeling coming from a grooved-up circle of wax.

Early next morning, with the .45 in the glove box, a razor in my coat pocket, and the record up front on the seat beside me, I tooled out toward Dallas, and the Hotel Champion.

I got into Big D around noon, stopped at a café on the outskirts where there was colored, and went in where a big fat mama with a pretty face and a body that smelled real good made me a hamburger and sat and flirted with me all the while I ate it. That's all right. I like women, and I like them to flirt. They quit doing that, I might as well lay down and die.

While we was flirting, I asked her about the Hotel Champion, if she knew where it was. I had the street number of course, but I needed tighter directions.

"Oh, yeah, honey, I know where it is, and you don't want to stay there. It's deep in the colored section, and not the good part, that's what I'm trying to tell you, and it don't matter you brown as a walnut yourself. There's folks down there will cut you and put your blood in a paper cup and mix it with whisky and drink it. You too good-looking to get all cut up and such. There's better places to stay on the far other side."

I let her give me a few hotel names, like I might actually stay at one or the other, but I got the address for the Champion, paid up, giving her a good tip, and left out of there.

The part of town around the Hotel Champion was just as nasty as the lady had said. There were people hanging around on the streets, and leaning into corners, and there was trash everywhere. It wasn't exactly a place that fostered a lot of pride.

I found the Hotel Champion and parked out front. There was a couple fellas on the street eyeing my car. One was skinny. One was big. They were dressed up with nice hats and shoes, just like they had jobs. But if they did, they wouldn't have been standing around in the middle of the day eyeing my Chevy.

I pulled the .45 out of the glove box and stuck it in my pants, at the small of my back. My coat would cover it just right.

I got out and gave the hotel the gander. It was nice-looking if you were blind in one eye and couldn't see out the other.

There wasn't any doorman, and the door was hanging on a hinge. Inside I saw a dusty stairway to my left, a scarred door to my right.

There was a desk in front of me. It had a glass hooked to it that went to the ceiling. There was a little hole in it low down on the counter that had a wooden stop behind it. There were fly specks on the glass, and there was a man behind the glass, perched on a stool, like a frog on a lily pad. He was fat and colored and his hair had blue blanket wool in it. I didn't take it for decoration. He was just a nasty sonofabitch.

I could smell him when he moved the wooden stop. A stink like armpits and nasty underwear and rotting teeth. Floating in from somewhere in back, I could smell old cooking smells, boiled pigs' feet and pigs' tails that might have been good about the time the pig lost them, but now all that was left was a rancid stink. There was also a reek like cat piss.

I said, "Hey, man, I'm looking for somebody."

"You want a woman, you got to bring your own," the man said. "But

I can give you a number or two. Course, I ain't guaranteeing anything about them being clean."

"Naw. I'm looking for somebody was staying here. His name is Tootie Johnson."

"I don't know no Tootie Johnson."

That was the same story Alma May had got.

"Well, all right, you know this fella?" I pulled out the photograph and pressed it against the glass.

"Well, he might look like someone got a room here. We don't sign in and we don't exchange names much."

"No? A class place like this?"

"I said he might look like someone I seen," he said. "I didn't say he definitely did."

"You fishing for money?"

"Fishing ain't very certain," he said.

I sighed and put the photograph back inside my coat and got out my wallet and took out a five-dollar bill.

Frog Man saw himself as some kind of greasy high roller. "That's it? Five dollars for prime information?"

I made a slow and careful show of putting my five back in my wallet. "Then you don't get nothing," I said.

He leaned back on his stool and put his stubby fingers together and let them lay on his round belly. "And you don't get nothing neither, jackass."

I went to the door on my right and turned the knob. Locked. I stepped back and kicked it so hard I felt the jar all the way to the top of my head. The door flew back on its hinges, slammed into the wall. It sounded like someone firing a shot.

I went on through and behind the desk, grabbed Frog Man by the shirt and slapped him hard enough he fell off the stool. I kicked him in the leg and he yelled. I picked up the stool and hit him with it across the chest, then threw the stool through a doorway that led into a kitchen. I heard something break in there and a cat made a screeching sound.

"I get mad easy," I said.

"Hell, I see that," he said, and held up a hand for protection. "Take it easy, man. You done hurt me."

"That was the plan."

The look in his eyes made me feel sorry for him. I also felt like an asshole. But that wouldn't keep me from hitting him again if he didn't answer my question. When I get perturbed, I'm not reasonable.

"Where is he?"

"Do I still get the five dollars?"

"No," I said, "now you get my best wishes. You want to lose that?"

"No. No, I don't."

"Then don't play me. Where is he, you toad?"

"He's up in room 52, on the fifth floor."

"Spare key?"

He nodded at a rack of them. The keys were on nails and they all had little wooden pegs on the rings with the keys. Numbers were painted on the pegs. I found one that said 52, took it off the rack.

I said, "You better not be messing with me."

"I ain't. He's up there. He don't never come down. He's been up there a week. He makes noise up there. I don't like it. I run a respectable place."

"Yeah, it's really nice here. And you better not be jerking me."

"I ain't. I promise."

"Good. And let me give you a tip. Take a bath. And get that shit out of your hair. And those teeth you got ain't looking too good. Pull them. And shoot that fucking cat, or at least get him some place better than the kitchen to piss. It stinks like a toilet in there."

I walked out from behind the desk, out in the hall, and up the flight of stairs in a hurry.

I rushed along the hallway on the fifth floor. It was covered in white linoleum with a gold pattern in it; it creaked and cracked as I walked along. The end of the hall had a window, and there was a stairwell on that end too. Room 52 was right across from it.

I heard movement on the far end of the stairs. I had an idea what that was all about. About that time, two of the boys I'd seen on the street showed themselves at the top of the stairs, all decked out in their nice hats and such, grinning.

One of them was about the size of a Cadillac, with a gold tooth that shown bright when he smiled. The guy behind him was skinny with his hand in his pocket.

I said, "Well, if it isn't the pimp squad."

"You funny, nigger," said the big man.

"Yeah, well, catch the act now. I'm going to be moving to a new locale."

"You bet you are," said the big man.

"Fat ass behind the glass down there, he ain't paying you enough to mess with me," I said.

"Sometimes, 'cause we're bored, we just like messin'."

"Say you do?"

"Uh-huh," said the skinny one.

It was then I seen the skinny guy pull a razor out of his pocket. I had one too, but razor work, it's nasty. He kept it closed.

Big guy with the gold tooth flexed his fingers, and made a fist. That made me figure he didn't have a gun or a razor; or maybe he just liked hitting people. I know I did.

They come along toward me then, and the skinny one with the razor flicked it open. I pulled the .45 out from under my coat. "You ought to put that back in your pocket," I said, "save it for shaving."

"Oh, I'm fixing to do some shaving right now," he said.

I pointed the .45 at him.

The big man said, "That's one gun for two men."

"It is," I said, "but I'm real quick with it. And frankly, I know one of you is gonna end up dead. I just ain't sure which one right yet."

"All right then," said the big man, smiling. "That'll be enough." He looked back at the skinny man with the razor. The skinny man put the razor back in his coat pocket and they turned and started down the stairs.

I went over and stood by the stairway and listened. I could hear them walking down, but then all of a sudden, they stopped on the stairs. That's the way I had it figured.

Then I could hear the morons rushing back up. They weren't near as sneaky as they thought they was. The big one was first out of the chute, so to speak; come rushing out of the stairwell and onto the landing. I brought the butt of the .45 down on the back of his head, right where the skull slopes down. He did a kind of frog hop and bounced across the hall and hit his head on the wall, and went down and laid there like his intent all along had been a quick leap and a nap.

Then the other one was there, and he had the razor. He flicked it, and then he saw the .45 in my hand.

"Where did you think this gun was gonna go?" I said. "On vacation?"

I kicked him in the groin hard enough he dropped the razor, and went to his knees. I put the .45 back where I got it. I said, "You want some, man?"

He got up, and come at me. I hit him with a right and knocked him clean through the window behind him. Glass sprinkled all over the hallway.

I went over and looked out. He was lying on the fire escape, his head against the railing. He looked right at me.

"You crazy, cocksucker. What if there hadn't been no fire escape?"

"You'd have your ass punched into the bricks. Still might."

He got up quick and clamored down the fire escape like a squirrel. I watched him till he got to the ground and went limping away down the alley between some overturned trash cans and a slinking dog.

I picked up his razor and put it in my pocket with the one I already had, walked over and kicked the big man in the head just because I could.

I knocked on the door. No one answered. I could hear sounds from inside. It was similar to what I had heard on that record, but not quite, and it was faint, as if coming from a distance.

No one answered my knock, so I stuck the key in the door and opened it and went straight away inside.

I almost lost my breath when I did.

The air in the room was thick and it stunk of mildew and rot and things long dead. It made those boiled pigs' feet and that shitting cat and that rotten-tooth bastard downstairs smell like perfume.

Tootie was lying on the bed, on his back. His eyes were closed. He was a guy usually dressed to the top, baby, but his shirt was wrinkled and dirty and sweaty at the neck and arm pits. His pants were nasty too. He had on his shoes, but no socks. He looked like someone had set him on fire and then beat out the flames with a two-by-four. His face was like a skull, he had lost so much flesh, and he was as bony under his clothes as a skeleton.

Where his hands lay on the sheet, there were bloodstains. His guitar was next to the bed, and there were stacks and stacks of composition notebooks lying on the floor. A couple of them were open and filled with writing. Hell, I didn't even know Tootie could write.

The wall on the far side was marked up in black and red paint; there were all manner of musical notes drawn on it, along with symbols I had never seen before; swiggles and circles and stick-figure drawings. Blood was on the wall too, most likely from Tootie's bleeding fingers. Two open paint cans, the red and the black, were on the floor with brushes stuck up in them. Paint was splattered on the floor and had dried in humped-up blisters. The guitar had bloodstains all over it.

A record player, plugged in, setting on a nightstand by the bed, was playing that strange music. I went to it right away and picked up the needle and set it aside. And let me tell you, just making my way across the room to get hold of the player was like wading through mud with my ankles tied together. It seemed to me as I got closer to the record, the louder it got, and the more ill I felt. My head throbbed. My heart pounded.

When I had the needle up and the music off, I went over and touched Tootie. He didn't move, but I could see his chest rising and falling. Except for his hands, he didn't seem hurt. He was in a deep sleep. I picked up his right hand and turned it over and looked at it. The fingers were cut deep, like someone had taken a razor to the tips. Right off, I figured that was from playing his guitar. Struck me, that to get the sounds he got out of it, he really had to dig in with those fingers. And from the looks of this room, he had been at it non-stop, until recent.

I shook him. His eyes fluttered and finally opened. They were bloodshot and had dark circles around them.

When he saw me, he startled, and his eyes rolled around in his head like those little games kids get where you try to shake the marbles into holes. After a moment, they got straight, and he said, "Ricky?"

That was another reason I hated him. I didn't like being called Ricky.

I said, "Hello, shithead. Your sister's worried sick."

"The music," he said. "Put back on the music."

"You call that music?" I said.

He took a deep breath, rolled out of the bed, nearly knocking me aside. Then I saw him jerk, like he'd seen a truck coming right at him. I turned. I wished it had been a truck.

Let me try and tell you what I saw. I not only saw it, I felt it. It was in the very air we were breathing, getting inside my chest like mice wearing barbed-wire coats. The wall Tootie had painted and drawn all that crap on shook.

And then the wall wasn't a wall at all. It was a long hallway, dark as original sin. There was something moving in there, something that slithered and slid and made smacking sounds like an anxious old drunk about to take his next drink. Stars popped up; greasy stars that didn't remind me of anything I had ever seen in the night sky; a moon the color of a bleeding fish eye was in the background, and it cast a light on something moving toward us.

"Jesus Christ," I said.

"No," Tootie said. "It's not him."

Tootie jumped to the record player, picked up the needle, and put it on. There came that rotten sound I had heard with Alma May, and I knew what I had heard when I first came into the room was the tail end of that same record playing, the part I hadn't heard before.

The music screeched and howled. I bent over and threw up. I fell back against the bed, tried to get up, but my legs were like old pipe cleaners. That record had taken the juice out of me. And then I saw it.

There's no description that really fits. It was . . . a thing. All blanket wrapped in shadow with sucker mouths and thrashing tentacles and centipede legs mounted on clicking hooves. A bulb-like head plastered all over with red and yellow eyes that seemed to creep. All around it, shadows swirled like water. It had a beak. Well, beaks.

The thing was coming right out of the wall. Tentacles thrashed toward me. One touched me across the cheek. It was like being scalded with hot grease. A shadow come loose of the thing, fell onto the floorboards of the room, turned red and raced across the floor like a gush of blood. Insects and maggots squirmed in the bleeding shadow, and the record hit a high spot so loud and so goddamn strange, I ground my teeth, felt as if my insides were being twisted up like wet wash. And then I passed out.

When I came to, the music was still playing. Tootie was bent over me.

"That sound," I said.

"You get used to it," Tootie said, "but the thing can't. Or maybe it can, but just not yet."

I looked at the wall. There was no alleyway. It was just a wall plastered in paint designs and spots of blood.

"And if the music stops?" I said.

"I fell asleep," Tootie said. "Record quits playing, it starts coming."

For a moment I didn't know anything to say. I finally got off the floor and sat on the bed. I felt my cheek where the tentacle hit me. It throbbed and I could feel blisters. I also had a knot on my head where I had fallen.

"Almost got you," Tootie said. "I think you can leave and it won't come after you. Me, I can't. I leave, it follows. It'll finally find me. I guess here is as good as any place."

I was looking at him, listening, but not understanding a damn thing.

The record quit. Tootie started it again. I looked at the wall. Even that blank moment without sound scared me. I didn't want to see that thing again. I didn't even want to think about it.

"I haven't slept in days, until now," Tootie said, coming to sit on the bed. "You hadn't come in, it would have got me, carried me off, taken my soul. But, you can leave. It's my lookout, not yours. . . . I'm always in some kind of shit, ain't I, Ricky?"

"That's the truth."

"This though, it's the corker. I got to stand up and be a man for once. I got to fight this thing back, and all I got is the music. Like I told you, you can go."

I shook my head. "Alma May sent me. I said I'd bring you back."

It was Tootie's turn to shake his head. "Nope. I ain't goin'. I ain't done nothin' but mess up Sis's life. I ain't gonna do it."

"First responsible thing I ever heard you say," I said.

"Go on," Tootie said. "Leave me to it. I can take care of myself."

"If you don't die of starvation, or pass out from lack of sleep, or need of water, you'll be just fine."

Tootie smiled at me. "Yeah. That's all I got to worry about. I hope it is one of them other things kills me. 'Cause if it comes for me. . . . Well, I don't want to think about it."

"Keep the record going, I'll get something to eat and drink, some coffee. You think you can stay awake a half hour or so?"

"I can, but you're coming back?"

"I'm coming back," I said.

Out in the hallway I saw the big guy was gone. I took the stairs.

When I got back, Tootie had cleaned up the vomit, and was looking through the notebooks. He was sitting on the floor and had them stacked all around him. He was maybe six inches away from the record player. Now and again he'd reach up and start it all over.

Soon as I was in the room, and that sound from the record was snugged up around me, I felt sick. I had gone to a greasy spoon down the street, after I changed a flat tire. One of the boys I'd given a hard time had most likely knifed it. My bet was the lucky son-of-a-bitch who had fallen on the fire escape.

Besides the tire, a half dozen long scratches had been cut into the paint on the passenger's side, and my windshield was knocked in. I got back from the café, I parked what was left of my car behind the hotel, down the street a bit, and walked a block. Car looked so bad now, maybe nobody would want to steal it.

I sat one of the open sacks on the floor by Tootie.

"Both hamburgers are yours," I said. "I got coffee for the both of us here."

I took out a tall cardboard container of coffee and gave it to him, took the other one for myself. I sat on the bed and sipped. Nothing tasted good in that room with that smell and that sound. But Tootie, he ate like a wolf. He gulped those burgers and coffee like it was air.

When he finished with the second burger, he started up the record again, leaned his back against the bed.

"Coffee or not," he said, "I don't know how long I can stay awake."

"So what you got to do is keep the record playing?" I said.

"Yeah."

"Lay up in bed, sleep for a few hours. I'll keep the record going. You're rested, you got to explain this thing to me, and then we'll figure something out."

"There's nothing to figure," he said. "But, god, I'll take you up on that sleep."

He crawled up in the bed and was immediately out.

I started the record over.

I got up then, untied Tootie's shoes and pulled them off. Hell, like him or not, he was Alma May's brother. And another thing, I wouldn't wish that thing behind the wall on my worst enemy.

I sat on the floor where Tootie had sat and kept restarting the record as I tried to figure things out, which wasn't easy with that music going. I got up from time to time and walked around the room, and then I'd end up back on the floor by the record player, where I could reach it easy.

Between changes, I looked through the composition notebooks. They were full of musical notes mixed with scribbles like the ones on the wall. It was hard to focus with that horrid sound. It was like the air was full of snakes and razors. Got the feeling the music was pushing at something behind that wall. Got the feeling too, there was something on the other side, pushing back.

It was dark when Tootie woke up. He had slept a good ten hours, and I was exhausted with all that record changing, that horrible sound. I had a headache from looking over those notebooks, and I didn't know any more about them than when I first started.

I went and bought more coffee, brought it back, and we sat on the bed, him changing the record from time to time, us sipping.

I said, "You sure you can't just walk away?"

I was avoiding the real question for some reason. Like, what in hell is that thing, and what is going on? Maybe I was afraid of the answer.

"You saw that thing. I can walk away, all right. And I can run. But wherever I go, it'll find me. So, at some point, I got to face it. Sometimes I make that same record sound with my guitar, give the record a rest. Thing I fear most is the record wearing out."

I gestured at the notebooks on the floor. "What is all that?"

"My notes. My writings. I come here to write some lyrics, some new blues songs."

"Those aren't lyrics, those are notes."

"I know," he said.

"You don't have a music education. You just play."

"Because of the record, I can read music, and I can write things that don't make any sense to me unless it's when I'm writing them, when I'm listening to that music. All those marks, they are musical notes, and the other marks are other kinds of notes, notes for sounds that I couldn't make until a few days back. I didn't even know those sounds were possible. But now, my head is full of the sounds and those marks and all manner of things, and the only way I can rest is to write them down. I wrote on the wall 'cause I thought the marks, the notes themselves, might hold that thing back and I could run. Didn't work."

"None of this makes any sense to me," I said.

"All right," Tootie said, "this is the best I can explain something that's got no explanation. I had some blues boys tell me they once come to this place on the South Side called Cross Road Records. It's a little record shop where the streets cross. It's got all manner of things in it, and it's got this big colored guy with a big white smile and bloodshot eyes that works the joint. They said they'd seen the place, poked their heads in, and even heard Robert Johnson's sounds coming from a player on the counter. There was a big man sitting behind the counter, and he waved them in, but the place didn't seem right, they said, so they didn't go in.

"But, you know me. That sounded like just the place I wanted to go. So, I went. It's where South Street crosses a street called Way Left.

"I go in there, and I'm the only one in the store. There's records everywhere, in boxes, lying on tables. Some got labels, some don't. I'm looking, trying to figure out how you told about anything, and this big fella with the smile comes over to me and starts to talk. He had breath like an unwiped butt, and his face didn't seem so much like black skin as it did black rock.

"He said, 'I know what you're looking for.' He reached in a box, and pulled out a record didn't have no label on it. Thing was, that whole box didn't have labels. I think he's just messing with me, trying to make a sale. I'm ready to go, 'cause he's starting to make my skin crawl. Way he moves ain't natural, you know. It's like he's got something wrong with his feet, but he's still able to move, and quick like. Like he does it between the times you blink your eyes.

"He goes over and puts that record on a player, and it starts up, and it was Robert Johnson. I swear, it was him. Wasn't no one could play like him. It was him. And here's the thing. It wasn't a song I'd ever heard by him. And I thought I'd heard all the music he'd put on wax."

Tootie sipped at his coffee. He looked at the wall a moment, and then changed the record again.

I said, "Swap out spots, and I'll change it. You sip and talk. Tell me all of it."

We did that, and Tootie continued.

"Well, one thing comes to another, and he starts talking me up good, and finally I ask him how much for the record. He looks at me, and he says, 'For you, all you got to give me is a little blue soul. And when you come back, you got to buy something with a bit more of it till it's all gone and I got it. Cause you will be back.'

"I figured he was talking about me playing my guitar for him, 'cause I'd told him I was a player, you know, while we was talking. I told him I had my guitar in a room I was renting, and I was on foot, and it would take me all day to get my guitar and get back, so I'd have to pass on that deal. Besides, I was about tapped out of money. I had a place I was supposed to play that evening, but until then, I had maybe three dollars and some change in my pocket. I had the rent on this room paid up all week, and I hadn't been there but two days. I tell him all that, and he says, 'Oh, that's all right. I know you can play. I can tell about things like that. What I mean is, you give me a drop of blood and a promise, and you can have that record.' Right then, I started to walk out, 'cause I'm thinking, this guy is nutty as fruit cake with an extra dose of nuts, but I want that record. So, I tell him, sure, I'll give him a drop of blood. I won't lie none to you, Ricky, I was thinking about nabbing that record and making a run with it. I wanted it that bad. So a drop of blood, that didn't mean nothin'.

"He pulls a record needle out from behind the counter, and he comes over and pokes my finger with it, sudden like, while I'm still trying to figure how he got over to me that fast, and he holds my hand and lets blood drip on—get this—the record. It flows into the grooves.

"He says, 'Now, you promise me your blues-playing soul is mine when you die.'

"I thought it was just talk, you know, so I told him he could have it. He says, 'When you hear it, you'll be able to play it. And when you play it, sometime when you're real good on it, it'll start to come, like a rat easing its nose into hot dead meat. It'll start to come.'

"'What will?' I said. 'What are you talking about?'

"He says, 'You'll know.'

"Next thing I know, he's over by the door, got it open and he's smiling at me, and I swear, I thought for a moment I could see right through him. Could see his skull and bones. I've got the record in my hand, and I'm walking out, and as soon as I do, he shuts the door and I hear the lock turn.

"My first thought was, I got to get this blood out of the record grooves, 'cause that crazy bastard has just given me a lost Robert Johnson song for nothing. I took out a kerchief, pulled the record out of the sleeve, and went to wiping. The blood wouldn't come out. It was in the notches, you know.

"I went back to my room here, and I tried a bit of warm water on the blood in the grooves, but it still wouldn't come out. I was mad as hell, figured the record wouldn't play, way that blood had hardened in the grooves. I put it on and thought maybe the needle would wear the stuff out, but as soon as it was on the player and the needle hit it, it started sounding just the way it had in the store. I sat on the bed and listened to it, three or four times, and then I got my guitar and tried to play what was being played, knowing I couldn't do it, 'cause though I knew that sound wasn't electrified, it sounded like it was. But, here's the thing. I could do it. I could play it. And I could see the notes in my head, and my head got filled up with them. I went out and bought those notebooks, and I wrote it all down just so my head wouldn't explode, 'cause every time I heard that record, and tried to play it, them notes would cricket-hop in my skull."

All the while we had been talking, I had been replaying the record.

"I forgot all about the gig that night," Tootie said. "I sat here until morning playing. By noon the next day, I sounded just like that record. By late afternoon, I started to get kind of sick. I can't explain it, but I was feeling that there was something trying to tear through somewhere, and it scared me and my insides knotted up.

"I don't know any better way of saying it than that. It was such a strong feeling. Then, while I was playing, the wall there, it come apart the way you seen it, and I seen that thing. It was just a wink of a look. But there it was. In all its terrible glory.

"I quit playing, and the wall wobbled back in place and closed up. I thought, Damn, I need to eat or nap, or something. And I did. Then I was back on that guitar. I could play like crazy, and I started going off on that song, adding here and there. It wasn't like it was coming from me, though. It was like I was getting help from somewhere.

"Finally, with my fingers bleeding and cramped and aching, and my voice gone raspy from singing, I quit. Still, I wanted to hear it, so I put on the record. And it wasn't the same no more. It was Johnson, but the words was strange, not English. Sounded like some kind of chant, and I knew then that Johnson was in that record, as sure as I was in this room, and that that chanting and that playing was opening up a hole for that thing in the wall. It was the way that fella had said. It was like a rat working its nose through red hot meat, and now it felt like I was the meat. Next time I played the record, the voice on it wasn't Johnson's. It was mine.

"I had had enough, so I got the record and took it back to that shop. The place was the same as before, and like before, I was the only one in there. He looked at me, and comes over, and says, 'You already want to undo the deal. I can tell. They all do. But that ain't gonna happen.'

"I gave him a look like I was gonna jump on him and beat his ass, but he gave me a look back, and I went weak as kitten.

"He smiled at me, and pulls out another record from that same box, and he takes the one I gave him and puts it back, and says, 'You done made a deal, but for a lick of your soul, I'll let you have this. See, you done opened the path, now that rat's got to work on that meat. It don't take no more record or you playing for that to happen. Rat's gotta eat now, no matter what you do.'

"When he said that, he picks up my hand and looks at my cut-up fingers from playing, and he laughs so loud everything in the store shakes, and he squeezes my fingers until they start to bleed.

"'A lick of my soul?' I asked.

"And then he pushed the record in my hand, and if I'm lying, I'm dying, he sticks out his tongue, and it's long as an old rat snake and black as a hole in the ground, and he licks me right around the neck. When he's had a taste, he smiles and shivers, like he's just had something cool to drink."

Tootie paused to unfasten his shirt and peel it down a little. There was a spot halfway around his neck like someone had worked him over with sandpaper.

"'A taste,' he says, and then he shoves this record in my hand, which is bleeding from where he squeezed my fingers. Next thing I know, I'm looking at the record, and it's thick, and I touch it, and its two records, back to back. He says, 'I give you that extra one cause you tasted mighty good, and maybe it'll let you get a little more rest that way, if you got a turntable drop. Call me generous and kind in my old age.'

"Wasn't nothing for it but to take the records and come back here. I didn't have no intention of playing it. I almost threw it away. But by then, that thing in the wall, wherever it is, was starting to stick through. Each time the hole was bigger and I could see more of it, and that red shadow was falling out on the floor. I thought about running, but I didn't want to just let it loose, and I knew, deep down, no matter where I went, it would come too.

"I started playing that record in self-defense. Pretty soon, I'm playing it on the guitar. When I got scared enough, got certain enough that thing was coming through, I played hard, and that hole would close, and that thing would go back where it come from. For a while.

"I figured though, I ought to have some insurance. You see, I played both them records, and they was the same thing, and it was my voice, and I hadn't never recorded or even heard them songs before. I knew then, what was on those notes I had written, what had come to me was the counter song to the one I had been playing first. I don't know if that was just some kind of joke that record store fella had played on me, but I knew it was magic of a sort. He had give me a song to let it in and he had give me another song to hold it back. It was amusing to him, I'm sure.

"I thought I had the thing at bay, so I took that other copy, went to the Post Office, mailed it to Alma, case something happened to me. I guess I thought it was self-defense for her, but there was another part was proud of what I had done. What I was able to do. I could play anything now, and I didn't even need to think about it. Regular blues, it was a snap. Anything on that guitar was easy, even things you ought not to be able to play on one. Now, I realize it ain't me. It's something else out there.

"But when I come back from mailing, I brought me some paint and brushes, thought I'd write the notes and such on the wall. I did that, and I was ready to pack and go roaming some more, showing off my new skills, and all of a sudden, the thing, it's pushing through. It had gotten stronger 'cause I hadn't been playing the sounds, man. I put on the record, and I pretty much been at it ever since.

"It was all that record fella's game, you see. I got to figuring he was the devil, or something like him. He had me playing a game to keep that thing out, and to keep my soul. But it was a three-minute game, six if I'd have kept that second record and put it on the drop. If I was playing on the guitar, I could just work from the end of that record back to the front of it, playing it over and over. But it wore me down. Finally, I started playing the record nonstop. And I have for days.

"The fat man downstairs, he'd come up for the rent, but as soon as he'd use his key and crack that door, hear that music, he'd get gone. So here I am, still playing, with nothing left but to keep on playing, or get my soul sucked up by that thing and delivered to the record store man."

Tootie minded the record, and I went over to where he told me the record store was with the idea to put a boot up the guy's ass, or a .45 slug in his noggin. I found South Street, but not Way South. The other street that should have been Way South was called Back Water. There wasn't a store either, just an empty, unlocked building. I opened the door and went inside. There was dust everywhere, and I could see where some tables had been, 'cause their leg marks was in the dust. But anyone or anything that had been there was long gone.

I went back to the hotel, and when I got there, Tootie was just about asleep. The record was turning on the turntable without any sound. I looked at the wall, and I could see the beak of that thing, chewing at it. I put the record on, and this time, when it come to the end, the thing was still chewing. I played it another time, and another, and the thing finally went away. It was getting stronger.

I woke Tootie up, said, "You know, we're gonna find out if this thing can outrun my souped-up Chevy."

"Ain't no use," Tootie said.

"Then we ain't got nothing to lose," I said.

We grabbed up the record and his guitar, and we was downstairs and out on the street faster than you can snap your fingers. As we passed where the toad was, he saw me and got up quick and went into the kitchen and closed the door. If I'd had time, I'd have beat his ass on general principles.

When we walked to where I had parked my car, it was sitting on four flats and the side windows was knocked out and the aerial was snapped off. The record Alma May had given me was still there, lying on the seat. I got it and put it against the other one in my hand. It was all I could do.

As for the car, I was gonna drive that Chevy back to East Texas like I was gonna fly back on a sheet of wet newspaper.

Now, I got to smellin' that smell. One that was in the room. I looked at the sky. The sun was kind of hazy. Green even. The air around us trembled, like it was scared of something. It was heavy, like a blanket. I grabbed Tootie by the arm, pulled him down the street. I spied a car at a curb that I thought could run, a V-8 Ford. I kicked the back side window out, reached through and got the latch.

I slid across the seat and got behind the wheel. Tootie climbed in on the passenger side. I bent down and worked some wires under the dash loose with my fingers and my razor, hot-wired the car. The motor throbbed and we was out of there.

It didn't make any kind of sense, but as we was cruising along, behind us it was getting dark. It was like chocolate pudding in a big wad rolling after us. Stars was popping up in it. They seemed more like eyes than stars. There was a bit of a moon, slightly covered over in what looked like a red fungus.

I drove that Ford fast as I could. I was hitting the needle at a hundred and ten. Didn't see a car on the highway. Not a highway cop, not an old lady on the way to the store. Where the hell was everybody?

The highway looped up and down like the bottom was trying to fall out from under us.

To make it all short, I drove hard and fast, and stopped once for gas, having the man fill it quick. I gave him a bill that was more than the gas was worth, and he grinned at me as we burned rubber getting away. I don't think he could see what we could see—that dark sky with that thing in it. It was like you had to hear the music to see the thing existed, or for it to have any effect in your life. For him, it was daylight and fine and life was good.

By the time I hit East Texas, there was smoke coming from under that stolen Ford's hood. We came down a hill, and it was daylight in front of us, and behind us the dark was rolling in; it was splittin', making a kind of corridor, and there was that beaked thing, that . . . . whatever it was. It was bigger than before and it was squirming its way out of the night sky like a weasel working its way under a fence. I tried to convince myself it was all in my head, but I wasn't convinced enough to stop and find out.

I made the bottom of the hill, in sight of the road that turned off to Alma May's. I don't know why I felt going there mattered, but it was something I had in my mind. Make it to Alma May's, and deliver on my agreement, bring her brother into the house. Course, I hadn't really thought that thing would or could follow us.

It was right then the car engine blew in an explosion that made the hood bunch up from the impact of thrown pistons.

The car died and coasted onto the road that led to Alma May's house. We could see the house, standing in daylight. But even that light was fading as the night behind us eased on in.

I jerked open the car door, snatched the records off the back seat, and yelled to Tootie to start running. He nabbed his guitar, and a moment later, we were both making tracks for Alma May's.

Looking back, I saw there was a moon back there, and stars too, but mostly there was that thing, full of eyes and covered in sores and tentacles and legs and things I can't even describe. It was like someone had thrown critters and fish and bugs and beaks and all manner of disease into a bowl and whipped it together with a whipping spoon.

When we got to Alma May's, I beat on the door. She opened it, showing a face that told me she thought I was knocking too hard, but then she looked over my shoulder and went pale, almost as if her skin was white. She had heard the music, so she could see it too.

Slamming the door behind us, I went straight to the record player. Alma May was asking all kinds of questions, screaming them out, really. First to me, then to Tootie. I told her to shut up. I jerked one of the records out of its sleeve, put it on the turntable, lifted the needle, and—

—the electricity crackled and it went dark. There was no playing anything on that player. Outside, the world was lit by that blood-red moon.

The door blew open. Tentacles flicked in, knocked over an end table. Some knickknacks fell and busted on the floor. Big as the monster was, it was squeezing through, causing the door frame to crack; the wood breaking sounded like someone cracking whips with both hands.

Me and Alma May, without even thinking about it, backed up. The red shadow, bright as a campfire, fled away from the monster and started flowing across the floor, bugs and worms squirming in it.

But not toward us.

It was running smooth as an oil spill toward the opposite side of the room. I got it then. It didn't just want through to this side. It wanted to finish off that deal Tootie had made with the record store owner. Tootie had said it all along, but it really hit me then. It didn't want me and Alma at all.

It had come for Tootie's soul.

There was a sound so sharp I threw my hands over my ears, and Alma May went to the floor. It was Tootie's guitar. He had hit it so hard, it sounded electrified. The pulse of that one hard chord made me weak in the knees. It was a hundred times louder than the record. It was beyond belief, and beyond human ability. But, it was Tootie.

The red shadow stopped, rolled back like a tongue.

The guitar was going through its paces now. The thing at the doorway recoiled slightly, and then Tootie yelled, "Come get me. Come have me. Leave them alone."

I looked, and there in the faint glow of the red moonlight through the window, I saw Tootie's shadow lift that guitar high above his head by the neck, and down it came, smashing hard into the floor with an explosion of wood and a springing of strings.

The bleeding shadow came quickly then. Across the floor and onto Tootie. He screamed. He screamed like someone having the flesh slowly burned off. Then the beast came through the door as if shot out of a cannon.

Tentacles slashed, a million feet scuttled, and that beaks came down, ripping at Tootie like a savage dog tearing apart a rag doll. Blood flew all over the room. It was like a huge strawberry exploded.

Then another thing happened. A blue mist floated up from the floor, from what was left of Tootie, and for just the briefest of moments, I saw Tootie's face in that blue mist; the face smiled a toothless kind of smile, showing nothing but a dark hole where his mouth was. Then, like someone sniffing steam off soup, the blue mist was sucked into the beaks of that thing, and Tootie and his soul were done with.

The thing turned its head and looked at us. I started to pull my .45, but I knew there wasn't any point to it. It made a noise like a thousand rocks and broken automobiles tumbling down a cliff made of gravel and glass, and it began to suck back toward the door. It went out with a snapping sound, like a wet towel being popped. The bleeding shadow ran across the floor after it, eager to catch up; a lapdog hoping for a treat.

The door slammed as the thing and its shadow went out, and then the air got clean and the room got bright.

I looked where Tootie had been.

Nothing.

Not a bone.

Not a drop of blood.

I raised the window and looked out.

It was morning.

No clouds in the sky.

The sun looked like the sun.

Birds were singing.

The air smelled clean as a newborn's breath.

I turned back to Alma May. She was slowly getting up from where she had dropped to the floor.

"It just wanted him," I said, having a whole different kind of feeling about Tootie than I had before. "He gave himself to it. To save you, I think."

She ran into my arms and I hugged her tight. After a moment, I let go of her. I got the records and put them together. I was going to snap them across my knee. But I never got the chance. They went wet in my hands, came apart and hit the floor and ran through the floorboards like black water, and that was all she wrote.

Mark Twain's Huckleberry Finn *is one of my favorite novels. I love Huck's voice and the comradery that he and Jim have. I also like the idea of an island that only appears from time to time. Wanting to write something based on that idea has been with me for a long time. There are stories about islands at sea, in lakes and rivers, that can only be accessed at certain times of the year, or during peculiar weather circumstances. Of course, I was also influenced by* Brigadoon, *a fanciful stage musical and film about a lost and hard to locate place in the Scottish Highlands. Brigadoon only appears out of the mist every one hundred years. Toss in* Lost Horizon's *Shangri-La high in the Himalayas, and you have some idea of the sources. Unlike Brigadoon or Shangri-La, my mysterious island is no paradise. My little river island also collects unpleasant oddities in the form of characters and creatures from literature and history, as well as the dark fantasies of Lovecraft. Bad things ensue.*

DREAD ISLAND

THIS HERE STORY is a good'n, and just about every word of it is true. It's tempting to just jump to the part about where we seen them horrible things, and heads was pulled off and we was in a flying machine and such. But I ain't gonna do it, 'cause Jim says that ain't the way to tell a proper yarn.

Anyhow, this here story is as true as that other story that was written down about me and Jim. But that fella wrote it down made all the money and didn't give me or Jim one plug nickel of it. So I'm going to try and tell this one myself like it happened, and have someone other than that old fart write it down for me, take out most of the swear words and such, and give you a gussied-up version that I can sell and get some money.

Jim says when you do a thing like that, trying to make more of something than it is, it's like you're taking a drunk in rags and putting a hat on him and giving him new shoes with ties in them, and telling everybody he's from uptown and has solid habits. But anyone looks at him, they're still gonna see the rags he's wearing and know he's a drunk 'cause of the stagger and the smell. Still, lots of drunks are more interesting than bankers, and they got good stories, even if you got to stand downwind to hear them in comfort.

If I get somebody to write it down for me, or I take a crack at it, is yet to be seen. All I know right now is it's me talking and you listening, and you can believe me or not, because it's a free country. Well, almost a free country, unless your skin ain't white. I've said it before: I know it ain't right in the eyes of God to be friends with a slave, or in Jim's case, an ex-slave that's got his free papers. But even if it ain't right, I don't care. Jim may be colored, but he has sure fire done more for me than God. I tried praying maybe a dozen times, and the only thing I ever got out of it was some sore knees. So, if I go to hell, I go to hell.

Truth is, I figure heaven is probably filled with dogs, 'cause if you get right down to it, they're the only ones deserve to be there. I don't figure a cat or a lawyer has any chance at all.

Anyway, I got a story to tell, and keep in mind—and this part is important—I'm trying to tell mostly the truth.

Now, any old steamboater will tell you that come the full moon, there's an island out there in the wide part of the Mississippi. You're standing on shore, it's so far out it ain't easy to see. But if the weather's just right, and you got some kind of eye on you, you can see it. It don't last but a night—the first night of the full moon—and then it's gone until next time.

Steamboats try not to go by it, 'cause when it's there, it has a current that'll drag a boat in just like a fella with a good stout line pulling in a fish. I got word about it from half a dozen fellas that knew a fella that knew a fella that had boated past it and been tugged by them currents. They said it was all they could do to get away. And there's plenty they say didn't get away, and ain't never been heard of again.

Another time, me and Tom Sawyer heard a story about how

sometimes you could see fires on the island. Another fella, who might have been borrowing the story from someone else, said he was out fishing with a buddy, and come close to the island, and seen a post go up near the shore, and a thing that wasn't no kind of man was fastened to it. He said it could scream real loud, and that it made the hairs on the back of his neck stand up. He said there was other things dancing all around the post, carrying torches and making a noise like yelling or some such. Then the currents started pulling him in, and he had to not pay it any more mind, because he and his buddy had to row for all they was worth to keep from being sucked onto the island.

When we got through hearing the story, first thing Tom said was, "Someday, when the moon is right, and that island is there, I'm gonna take a gun and a big bowie knife, and I'm going to go out there. I'll probably also have to pack a lunch."

That danged old island is called Dread Island, and it's always been called that. I don't know where it got that name, but it was a right good one. I found that out because of Tom and Joe.

Way this all come about was me and Jim was down on the bank of the river, night fishing for catfish. Jim said there was some folks fished them holes by sticking their arms down in them so a catfish would bite. It wasn't a big bite, he said, but they clamped on good and you could pull them out that way, with them hanging on your arm. Then you could bust them in the head, and you had you something good to eat. He also said he wouldn't do that for nothing. The idea of sticking his hand down in them holes bothered him to no end, and just me thinking on it didn't do me no good either. I figured a gator or a moccasin snake was just as likely to bite me, and a fishing line with a hook on it would do me just as good. Thinking back on that, considering I wouldn't put my hand in a hole for fear something might bite it, and then me going out to Dread Island, just goes to show you can talk common sense a lot more than you can act on it.

But anyway, that ain't how this story starts. It starts like this.

So, there we was, with stinky bait, trying to catch us a catfish, when I seen Becky Thatcher coming along the shoreline in the moonlight.

Now Becky is quite a nice looker, and not a bad sort for a girl; a breed I figure is just a step up from cats. Jim says my thinking that way is because I'm still young and don't understand women's ways. He also explained to me their ways ain't actually understandable, but they sure do get a whole lot more interesting as time goes on.

I will say this. As I seen her coming, her hair hanging, and her legs working under that dress, the moonlight on her face, I thought maybe if she wasn't Tom's girl, I could like her a lot. I'm a little ashamed to admit that, but there you have it.

Anyway, she come along, and when she saw us, she said, "Huck. Jim. Is that you?"

I said, "Well, if it ain't, someone looks a whole lot like us is talking to you."

She come over real swift-like then. She said, "I been looking all over for you. I figured you'd be here."

"Well," I said, "we're pretty near always around somewhere or another on the river."

"I was afraid you'd be out on your raft," she said.

"We don't like to go out on the water the night Dread Island is out there," I said.

She looked out over the water, said, "I can't see a thing."

"It looks just like a brown line on top of the water, but it's sharp enough there in the moonlight," I said. "If you give a good look."

"Can you see it too, Jim?" she asked.

"No, Miss Becky, I ain't got the eyes Huck's got."

"The island is why I'm looking for you," she said. "Tom has gone out there with Joe. He's been building his courage for a long time, and tonight, he got worked up about it. I think maybe they had some liquid courage. I went to see Tom, and he and Joe were loading a pail full of dinner into the boat. Some cornbread and the like, and they were just about to push off. When I asked what they were doing, Tom told me they were finally going to see Dread Island and learn what was on it. I didn't know if he was serious. I'm not even sure there is an island, but you tell me you can see it, and well . . . I'm scared he wasn't just talking, and really did go."

"Did Tom have a big knife with him?" I asked.

"He had a big one in a scabbard stuck in his belt," she said. "And a pistol."

"What do you think, Jim?" I asked.

"I think he's done gone out there, Huck," Jim said. "He said he was gonna, and now he's got that knife and gun and dinner. I think he's done it."

She reached out and touched my arm and a shock run through me like I'd been struck by lightning. It hurt and felt good at the same time, and for a moment there, I thought I'd go to my knees.

"Oh my God," she said. "Will they be all right?"

"I reckon Tom and Joe will come back all right," I said, but I wasn't really that sure.

She shook her head. "I'm not so certain. Could you and Jim go take a look?"

"Go to Dread Island?" Jim said. "Now, Miss Becky, that ain't smart."

"Tom and Joe went," she said.

"Yes, ma'am," Jim said, like she was a grown woman, "and that proves what I'm saying. It ain't smart."

"When did they go?" I said.

"It was just at dark," she said. "I saw them then, and they were getting in the boat. I tried to talk Tom out of it, because I thought he was a little drunk and shouldn't be on the water, but they went out anyway, and they haven't come back."

I figured a moment. Nightfall was about three or four hours ago.

I said, "Jim, how long you reckon it takes to reach that island?"

"Couple of hours," Jim said, "or something mighty close to that."

"And a couple back," I said. "So what say we walk over to where Tom launched his boat and take a look. See if they done come in. They ain't, me and Jim will go take a gander for him."

"We will?" Jim said.

I ignored him.

Me and Jim put our lines in the water before we left, and figured on checking them later. We went with Becky to where Tom and Joe had pushed off in their boat. It was a pretty far piece. They hadn't come back, and when we looked out over the water, we didn't see them coming neither.

Becky said, "Huck, I think I see it. The island, I mean."

"Yeah," I said, "there's a better look from here."

"It's just that line almost even with the water, isn't it?" she said.

"Yep, that's it."

"I don't see nothing," Jim said. "And I don't want to."

"You will go look for him?" Becky said.

"We'll go," I said.

"We will?" Jim said again.

"Or I can go by myself," I said. "Either way."

"Huck," Jim said, "you ought not go out there. You ain't got no idea what's on that island. I do. I heard more stories than you have, and most of it's way worse than an entire afternoon in church and having to talk to the preacher personal-like."

"Then it's bad," I said, and I think it was pretty obvious to Becky that I was reconsidering.

Becky took my arm. She pulled herself close. "Please, Huck. There's no one else to ask. He's your friend. And then there's Joe."

"Yeah, well, Joe, he's sort of got his own lookout far as I'm concerned," I said. I admit I said this 'cause I don't care for Joe Harvey much. I ain't got no closer friend than Jim, but me and Tom was friends too, and I didn't like that he'd asked Joe to go with him out there to Dread Island

and not me. I probably wouldn't have gone, but a fella likes to be asked.

"Please, Huck," she said, and now she was so close to me I could smell her, and it was a good smell. Not a stink, mind you, but sweet like strawberries. Even there in the moonlight, her plump, wet lips made me want to kiss them, and I had an urge to reach out and stroke her hair. That was something I wasn't altogether understanding, and it made me feel like I was coming down sick.

Jim looked at me, said, "Ah, hell."

Our raft was back where we had been fishing, so I told Becky to go on home and I'd go look for Tom and Joe, and if I found them, I'd come back and let her know or send Tom to tell her, if he hadn't been ate up by alligators or carried off by mermaids. Not that I believed in mermaids, but there was them said they was out there in the river. But you can't believe every tall tale you hear.

All the while we're walking back to the raft, Jim is trying to talk me out of it.

"Huck, that island is all covered in badness."

"How would you know? You ain't never been. I mean, I've heard stories, but far as I know, they're just stories."

I was talking like that to build up my courage; tell the truth, I wasn't so sure they was just tall tales.

Jim shook his head. "I ain't got to have been. I know someone that's been there for sure. I know more than one."

I stopped walking. It was like I had been stunned with an ox hammer. Sure, me and Tom had heard a fella say he had been there, but when something come from Jim, it wasn't usually a lie, which isn't something I can say for most folks.

"You ain't never said nothing before about that, so why now?" I said. "I ain't saying you're making it up 'cause you don't want to go. I ain't saying that. But I'm saying, why tell me now? We could have conversated on it before, but now you tell me."

Jim grabbed my elbow, shook me a little, said, "Listen here, Huck. I ain't never mentioned it before because if someone tells you that you ought not to do something, then you'll do it. It's a weakness, son. It is."

I was startled. Jim hadn't never called me "son" before, and he hadn't never mentioned my weakness. It was a weakness me and Tom shared, and it wasn't something I thought about, and most of the time I just figured I did stuff 'cause I wanted to. But with Jim saying that, and grabbing my arm, calling me "son," it just come over me all of a sudden that he was right. Down deep, I knew I had been thinking about going to that island for a long time, and tonight just set me a purpose. It was what them preachers call "a revelation."

"Ain't nobody goes over there in they right mind, Huck," Jim said. "That ole island is all full of haints, they say. And then there's the Brer People."

"Brer People," I said. "What in hell is that?"

"You ain't heard nothing about the Brer People? Why I know I ain't told you all I know, but it surprises me deep as the river that you ain't at least heard of the Brer People. They done come on this land from time to time and do things, and then go back. Them fellas I know been over there and come back, both of them colored, they ain't been right in they heads since. One of them lost a whole arm, and the other one, he lost his mind, which I figure is some worse than an arm."

"You sure it's because they went out to Dread Island?"

"Well, they didn't go to Nantucket," Jim said, like he had some idea where that was, but I knew he didn't. It was just a name he heard and locked onto.

"I don't know neither them to be liars," Jim said, "and the one didn't lose his senses said the Brer People was out there, and they was lucky to get away. Said the island was fading when they got back to their boat. When it went away, it darn near pulled them after it. Said it was like a big ole twister on the water, and then it went up in the sky and was gone."

"A twister?"

"What they said."

I considered a moment. "I guess Brer People or not, I got to go."

"You worried about that Miss Becky," Jim said, "and what she thinks?"

"I don't want her upset."

"I believe that. But you thinking you and her might be together. I know that's what you thinking, 'cause that's what any young, red-blooded white boy be thinking about Miss Becky. I hope you understand now, I ain't crossing no color lines in my talk here, I'm just talking to a friend."

"Hell, I know that," I said. "And I don't care about color lines. I done decided if I go to hell for not caring about that, at least you and me will be there to talk. I figure too that danged ole writer cheated us out of some money will be there too."

"Yeah, he done us bad, didn't he?"

"Yeah, but what are these Brer People?"

We had started walking again, and as we did, Jim talked.

"Uncle Remus used to tell about them. He's gone now. Buried for some twenty years, I s'pect. He was a slave. A good man. He knew things ain't nobody had an inkling about. He come from Africa, Huck. He was a kind of preacher man, but the gods he knew, they wasn't no god of the Bible. It wasn't no Jesus he talked about, until later when he had to talk about Jesus, cause the massas would beat his ass if he didn't. But he knew about them hoodoo things. Them animals that walked like men. He told about them even to the whites, but he made like they was little stories. I heard them tales when I was a boy, and he told them to me and all the colored folks in a different way."

"You ain't makin' a damn bit of sense, Jim."

"There's places where they show up. Holes in the sky, Uncle Remus used to say. They come out of them, and they got them some places where they got to stay when they come out of them holes. They can wander some, but they got to get back to their spot a'fore their time runs out. They got 'strictions. That island, it's got the same 'strictions."

"What's ''strictions'?"

"Ain't exactly sure, but I've heard it said. I think it means there's rules of a sort."

By this time we had come to the raft and our fishing lines, which we checked right away. Jim's had a big ole catfish on it.

Jim said, "Well, if we gonna go to that dadburn island, we might as well go with full bellies. Let's get out our gear and fry these fish up."

"You're going then?" I said.

Jim sighed. "I can't let you go out there by yourself. Not to Dread Island. I did something like that, I couldn't sleep at night. Course, I didn't go, I would at least be around to be without some sleep."

"Go or don't go, Jim, but I got to. Tom is my friend, and Becky asked me. If it was you, I'd go."

"Now, Huck, don't be trying to make me feel bad. I done said I'd go."

"Good then."

Jim paused and looked out over the river.

"I still don't see it," Jim said, "and I'm hoping you just think you do."

We cooked up those catfish and ate them. When we was done eating, Jim got his magic hairball out of the ditty bag he carried on a rope around his waist. He took a gander at it, trying to divine things. That hairball come from the inside of a cow's stomach, and Jim said it had more mystery in it than women, but was a lot less good to look at. He figured he could see the future in it, and held stock by it.

Jim stuck his big thumbs in it and moved the hair around and eyeballed it some, said, "It don't look good, Huck."

"What's that hairball telling you?" I was looking at it, but I didn't see nothing but a big ole wad of hair that the cow had licked off its self and left in its stomach before it got killed and eat up; it smelled like an armpit after a hard day of field work.

Jim pawed around some more, then I seen his face change.

He said, "We go out there, Huck, someone's gonna die."

"You ain't just saying that about dying 'cause you don't want to go, are you?" I said.

He shook his head. "I'm saying it, 'cause that's what the hairball says."

I thought on that a moment, then said, "But that don't mean it's me or you dying, does it?"

Jim shook his head again. "No. But there ain't no solid way of telling."

"It's a chance we have to take," I said.

Jim stood for a moment just looking at me, shoving that hairball back into his pants pocket.

"All right," he said. "If that's how it is, then put this in your left shoe."

He had whittled a little cross, and it was small enough I could slide it down the side of my shoe and let it press up against the edge of my foot. Jim put a cross in his shoe too. We didn't normally have no shoes, but some Good Samaritans gave them to us, and we had taken to wearing them now and again. Jim said it was a sure sign we was getting civilized, and the idea of it scared me to death. Civilizing someone meant they had to go to jobs; and there was a time to show up and a time to leave; and you had to do work in between the coming and leaving. It was a horrible thing to think about, yet there I was with shoes on. The first step toward civilization and not having no fun anymore.

I said, "Is that cross so Jesus will watch over us?"

"A cross has got them four ends to it that show the four things make up this world. Fire, wind, earth, and water. It don't do nothing against a regular man, but against raw evil, it's supposed to have a mighty big power."

"But you don't know for sure?" I said.

"No, Huck, I don't. There ain't much I know for sure. But I got these too."

Jim held up two strings, and each of them had a big nail tied to it.

"These supposed to be full of power against evil," he said.

"Ain't the nails on account of Jesus?" I said. "Them being stuck in his hands and feet and such. I think I was told that in Sunday school. It's something like a cymbal."

"A cymbal? Like you hit in a band?"

"You know, I ain't sure, but I think that's what I was told."

"I don't see it being about no cymbals," Jim said. "Iron's got magic in it, that's all I know. It had magic in it before anyone ever heard of any Jesus. It's just iron to us, but to them haints, well, it's a whole nuther matter. Here. Loop this here string over your neck and tie the other end back to the nail. Make you a necklace of it. That ought to give you some protection. And I got some salt here in little bags for us. You never know when you might have the devil on your left, which is where he likes to stay, and if you feel him there, you can toss salt over your left shoulder, right into his eye. And we can use some of it on something to eat, if we got it."

"Finally," I said, "something that sounds reasonable."

When I had the nail around my neck, the cross in my shoe, and the bag of salt in my pocket, and my pocketknife shoved down tight in my back pocket, we pushed off the raft. Moment later we was sailing out across the black night water toward Dread Island.

The water was smooth at first, and the long pushing poles helped us get out in the deep part. When we got out there, we switched to Jim using the tiller, and me handling the sails, which is something we had added as of recent. They worked mighty good, if you didn't shift wrong; and, of course, there had to be wind.

It had been pretty still when we started out, and that had worried me, but before long, a light wind come up. It was just right, filling that canvas and pushing us along.

It didn't seem long before that line of dark in the water was a rise of dark, and then it was sure enough an island. Long and low and covered in fog, thick as the wool on a sheep's ass.

The raft started moving swift on account of it was caught up in a current, and before we knowed it, we was going through the fog and slamming up on the bank of Dread Island. We got out and used the docking rope to drag the raft on shore. It was a heavy rascal out of the water, and I thought I was gonna bust a gut. But we finally got it pulled up on solid ground.

Right then, there wasn't much to see that was worth seeing.

The fog was heavy, but it was mostly around the island. On the island itself it was thin. Off to my right, I could see briars rising up about ten feet high, with dark thorns on them bigger than that nail I had tied around my neck. The tips of them were shiny in the moonlight, and the bit of fog that was off the water twisted in between them like stripped wads of cotton. To the left, and in front of us, was some woods; it was as dark in there as the inside of a dog's gut.

"Well, here we is all ready for a rescue," Jim said. "And we don't even know they here anywhere. They may have done come and gone home. They could have come back while we was frying catfish and I was looking at my hairball."

I pointed to the mud gleaming in the moonlight, showed Jim there was a drag line in it.

"That looks like the bottom of a boat," I said.

Jim squatted down and touched the ground with his fingers. "It sure do, Huck."

We followed the drag line until we come to a patch of limbs. I moved them back, and seen they had been cut and was thrown over the boat to hide it.

"I figure this is their boat," I said. "They're exploring, Jim. They done hid the boat, and gone out there."

"Well, they didn't hide it so good," he said, "'cause it took us about the time it takes a duck to eat a june bug to find it."

We got a big cane knife off the raft, and Jim took that and cut down some limbs, and we covered the raft up with them. It wasn't a better hiding place than Tom and Joe's boat, but it made me feel better to do it.

With Jim carrying the cane knife, and me with a lit lantern, we looked for sign of Tom and Joe. Finally, we seen some footprints on the ground. One was barefoot, and the other had on shoes. I figured Tom, who had been getting civilized too, would be the shoe wearer, and Joe would be the bare footer.

Their sign led off in the woods. We followed in there after them. There was hardly any moon now, and even with me holding the lantern close to the ground, it wasn't no time at all until we lost track of them.

We kept going, and after a while we seen a big old clock on the ground. I held the lantern closer, seen it was inside a skeleton. The skeleton looked like it belonged to an alligator. Inside them alligator bones was human bones, all broke up, along with what was left of a hat with a feather in it, a boot, and a hook of the sort fits on a fella with his hand chopped off.

It didn't make no sense, but I quit thinking about, because I seen something move up ahead of us.

I wasn't sure what I had seen, but I can tell you this, it didn't take but that little bit of a glance for me to know I didn't like the looks of it.

Jim said, "Holy dog turd, was that a man with a rabbit's head?"

I was glad he said that. I had seen the same darn shadowy thing, but was thinking my mind was making it up.

Then we saw movement again, and that thing poked its head out from behind a tree. You could see the ears standing up in the shadows. I could see some big white buckteeth too.

Jim called out, "You better come out from behind that tree, and show yourself good, or I'm gonna chop your big-eared head off with this cane knife."

That didn't bring the thing out, but it did make it run. It tore off through them woods and underbrush like its tail was on fire.

And it actually had a tail. A big cotton puff that I got a good look at, sticking out of the back of a pair of pants.

I didn't figure we ought to go after it. Our reason for being here was to find Tom and Joe and get ourselves back before the light come up. Besides, even if that thing was running, that didn't give me an idea about chasing it down. I might not like it if I caught it.

So, we was standing there, trying to figure if we was gonna shit or go blind, and that's when we heard a whipping sound in the brush. Then we seen torches. It didn't take no Daniel Boone to figure that it was someone beating the bushes, driving game in front of it. I reckoned the game would be none other than that thing we saw, so I grabbed Jim's arm and tugged him back behind some trees, and I blowed out the light. We laid down on our bellies and watched as the torches got closer, and they was bright enough we could see what was carrying them.

Their shadows come first, flickering in the torchlight. They was shaped something odd, and the way they fell on the ground, and bent around trees, made my skin crawl. But the shadows wasn't nothing compared to what made them.

Up front, carrying a torch, was a short fella wearing blue pants with rivets up the side, and he didn't have on no shirt. His chest was covered in a red fur and he had some kind of pack strapped to his back. His head, well, it wasn't no human head at all. It was the head of a fox. He was wearing a little folded hat with a feather in it. Not that he really needed that feather to get our attention. The fact that he was walking on his hind paws, with shoes on his feet, was plenty enough.

With him was a huge bear, also on hind legs, and wearing red pants that come to the knees. He didn't have no shoes on, but like the fox, he wasn't without a hat. Had a big straw one like Tom Sawyer liked to wear. In his teeth was a long piece of some kind of weed or another. He was working it from one side of his mouth to the other. He was carrying a torch.

The other four was clearly weasels, only bigger than any weasels I had ever seen. They didn't have no pants on at all, nor shoes neither, but they was wearing some wool caps. Two of the weasels had torches, but the other two had long switch limbs they was using to beat the brush.

But the thing that made me want to jump up and grab Jim and run back toward the raft was this big nasty shape of a thing that was with them. It was black as sin. The torch it was carrying flickered over its body and made it shine like fresh-licked licorice. It looked like a big baby, if a baby could be six foot tall and four foot wide. It was fat in the belly and legs. It waddled from side to side on flat, sticky feet that was picking up leaves and pine needles and dirt. It didn't have no real face or body; all of it was made out of that sticky black mess. After a while, it spit a stream that hit in the bushes heavy as a cow pissing on a flat rock. That stream of spit didn't miss me and Jim by more than ten feet. Worse, that thing turned its head in our direction to do the spitting, and when it did, I could see it had teeth that looked like sugar cubes. Its eyes was as blood-red as two bullet wounds.

I thought at first it saw us, but after it spit, it turned its head back the way it had been going, and just kept on keeping on; it and that fox and that bear and them weasels. The smell of its spit lingered behind, and it was like the stink of turpentine.

After they was passed, me and Jim got up and started going back through the woods the way we had come, toward the raft. Seeing what we seen had made up our minds for us, and discussion about it wasn't necessary, and I knowed better than to light the lantern again. We just went along and made the best of it in the darkness of the woods.

As we was about to come out of the trees onto the beach, we seen something that froze us in our tracks. Coming along the beach was more of them weasels. Some of them had torches, some of them had clubs, and they all had hats. I guess a weasel don't care for pants, but dearly loves a hat. One of them was carrying a big, wet-looking bag.

We slipped back behind some trees and watched them move along for a bit, but was disappointed to see them stop by the water. They was strung out in a long line, and the weasel with the bag moved in front of the line and the line sort of gathered around him in a horseshoe shape. The weasel put the bag on the ground, opened it, and took out something I couldn't recognize at first. I squatted down so I could see better between their legs, and when I did, I caught my breath. They was passing a man's battered head among them, and they was each sitting down and taking a bite of it, passing it to the next weasel, like they was sharing a big apple.

Jim, who had squatted down beside me, said, "Oh, Huck, chile, look what they doing."

Not knowing what to do, we just stayed there, and then we heard that beating sound we had heard before. Off to our left was a whole batch of torches moving in our direction.

"More of them," Jim said.

Silent, but as quick as we could, we started going away from them. They didn't even know we was there, but they was driving us along like we was wild game 'cause they was looking for that rabbit, I figured.

After a bit, we picked up our pace, because they was closing. As we went more quickly through the woods, two things happened. The woods got thicker and harder to move through, and whatever was behind us started coming faster. I reckoned that was because now they could hear us. It may not have been us they was looking for, but it was darn sure us they was chasing.

It turned into a full-blowed run. I tossed the lantern aside, and we tore through them woods and vines and undergrowth as hard as we could go. Since we wasn't trying to be sneaky about it, Jim was using that cane knife to cut through the hard parts; mostly we just pushed through it.

Then an odd thing happened. We broke out of the woods and was standing on a cliff. Below us, pretty far down, was a big pool of water that the moon's face seemed to be floating on. Across from the pool was more land, and way beyond that was some mountains that rose up so high the peaks looked close to the moon.

I know. It don't make no sense. That island ought not to have been that big. It didn't fit the facts. Course, I reckon in a place where weasels and foxes and bears wear hats, and there's a big ole thing made of a sticky, black mess that spits turpentine, you can expect the facts to have their problems.

Behind us, them weasels was closing, waving torches, and yipping and barking like dogs.

Jim looked at me, said, "We gonna have to jump, Huck. It's all there is for it."

It was a good drop and wasn't no way of knowing what was under that water, but I nodded, aimed for the floating moon and jumped.

It was a quick drop, as it usually is when you step off nothing and fall. Me and Jim hit the water side by side and went under. The water was as cold as a dead man's ass in winter. When we come up swimming and spitting, I lifted my head to look at where we had jumped from. At the edge of the cliff was now the pack of weasels, and they was pressed up together tighter than a cluster of chiggers, leaning over and looking down.

One of them was dedicated, 'cause he jumped with his torch in his hand. He come down right in front of us in the water, went under, and when he come up he still had the torch, but of course it wasn't lit. He swung it and hit Jim upside the head.

Jim had lost the cane knife in the jump, so he didn't have nothing to hit back with. He and the weasel just sort of floated there eyeing one another.

There was a chittering sound from above, as all them weasels rallied their man on. The weasel cocked back the torch again, and swung at me. I couldn't backpedal fast enough, and it caught me a glancing blow on the side of my head. It was a hard enough lick that for a moment, I not only couldn't swim, I wouldn't have been able to tell you the difference between a cow and a horse and a goat and a cotton sack. Right then, everything seemed pretty much the same to me.

I slipped under, but the water, and me choking on it, brought me back. I clawed my way to the surface, and when I was sort of back to myself, I seen that Jim had the weasel by the neck with one hand, and had its torch arm in his other. The weasel was pretty good-sized, but he wasn't as big as Jim, and his neck wasn't on his shoulders as good neither. The weasel had reached its free hand and got Jim's throat and was trying to strangle him; he might as well have been trying to squeeze a tree to death. Jim's fingers dug into the weasel's throat, and there was a sound like someone trying to spit a pea through a tight-rolled cigar, and then the next thing I knowed, the weasel was floating like a turd in a night jar.

Above, the pack was still there, and a couple of them threw torches at us, but missed; they hissed out in the water. We swam to the other side and crawled out. There was thick brush and woods there, and we staggered into it, with me stopping at the edge of the trees just long enough to yell something nasty to them weasels.

The woods come up along a wall of dirt, and thinned, and there was a small cave in the dirt, and in the cave, sleeping on the floor, was that rabbit we had seen. I doubted it was really a rabbit back then, when we first seen it in the shadows, but after the fox and bear and weasels, and Mr. Sticky, it was hard to doubt anything.

The moonlight was strong enough where the trees had thinned that we could see the rabbit had white fur and wore a red vest and blue pants and no shoes. He had a pink nose and pink in his big ears, and he was sleeping. He heard us, and in a move so quick it was hard to see, he come awake and sprang to his feet. But we was in front of the cave, blocking the way out.

"Oh, my," he said.

A rabbit speaking right good American was enough to startle both me and Jim. But as I said, this place was the sort of place where you come to expect anything other than a free boat ride home.

Jim said slowly, "Why, I think I know who you are. Uncle Remus talked about you and your red vest. You Brer Rabbit."

The rabbit hung his head and sort of collapsed to the floor of the cave.

"Brer Rabbit," the rabbit said, "that would be me. Well, Fred actually, but when Uncle Remus was here, he knowed me by that name. I had a family once, but they was all eat up. There was Flopsy and Mopsy and Fred, and Alice and Fred Two and Fred Three, and then there was . . . oh, I don't even remember now, it's been so long ago they was eaten up, or given to Cut Through You."

There was a roll of thunder, and rain started darting down on us. We went inside the cave with Brer Rabbit and watched lightning cut across the sky and slam into what looked like a sycamore tree.

"Lightning," Jim said, to no one in particular. "It don't leave no shadow. You got a torch, it leaves a shadow. The sun makes a shadow on the ground of things it shines on. But lightning, it don't leave no shadow."

"No," Brer Rabbit said, looking up and out of the cave. "It don't, and it never has. And here, on this island, when it starts to rain and the lightning flashes and hits the ground like that, it's a warning. It means time is closing out. But what makes it bad is there's something new now. Something really awful."

"The weasels, you mean," Jim said.

"No," Brer Rabbit said. "Something much worse."

"Well," Jim said, "them weasels is bad enough. We seen them eating a man's head."

"Riverboat captain probably," Brer Rabbit said. "Big ole steamboat got too close and got sucked in. And then there was the lady in the big, silver mosquito."

"Beg your pardon," I said.

"Well, it reminded me of a mosquito. I ain't got no other way to explain it, so I won't. But that head, it was probably all that remains of that captain. It could have been some of the others, but I reckon it was him. He had a fat head."

"How do you know all this?" I said.

Brer Rabbit looked at me, pulled his paw from behind his back, where he had been keeping it, and we saw he didn't have a hand on the end of it. Course, he didn't have a hand on the one showing neither. He had a kind of paw with fingers, which is the best I can describe it, but that other arm ended in a nubbin.

The rabbit dropped his head then, let his arm fall to his side, like everything inside of him had turned to water and run out on the ground. "I know what happened 'cause I was there, and was gonna be one of the sacrifices. Would have been part of the whole thing had I not gnawed my paw off. It was the only way out. While I was doing it, it hurt like hell, but I kept thinking, rabbit meat, it ain't so bad. Ain't that a thing to think? It still hurts. I been running all night. But it ain't no use. I am a shadow of my former self. Was a time when I was clever and smart, but these days I ain't neither one. They gonna catch up with me now. I been outsmarting them for years, but everything done got its time, and I reckon mine has finally come. Brer Fox, he's working up to the Big One, and tonight could be the night it all comes down in a bad way. If ole Cut Through You gets enough souls."

"I'm so confused I feel turned around and pulled inside out," I said.

"I'm a might confused myself," Jim said.

The rain was really hammering now. The lightning was tearing at the sky and poking down hot yellow forks, hitting trees, catching them on fire. It got so there were so many burning that the inside of our cave was lit up for a time like it was daylight.

"This here rain," Brer Rabbit said. "They don't like it. Ain't nobody likes it, 'cause that lightning can come down on your ass sure as it can on a tree. The Warning Rain, we call it. Means that there ain't much time before the next rain comes. The Soft Rain, and when it does, it's that time. Time to go."

"I just thought I was confused before," I said.

"All right," Brer Rabbit said. "It ain't like we're going anywhere now, and it ain't like they'll be coming. They'll be sheltering up somewhere nearby to get out of the Warning Rain. So, I'll tell you what you want to know. Just ask."

"I'll make it easy," I said. "Tell us all of it."

And he did. Now, no disrespect to Brer Rabbit, but once he got going, he was a dad-burn blabbermouth. He told us all we wanted to know, and all manner of business we didn't want to know. I think it's best I just summarize what he was saying, keeping in mind it's possible I've left out some of the important parts, but mostly, I can assure you, I've left out stuff you don't want to hear anyway. We even got a few pointers on how to decorate a burrow, which seemed to be a tip we didn't need.

The rain got so thick it put those burning trees out, and with the moon behind clouds, it was dark in that cave. We couldn't even see each other. All we could do was hear Brer Rabbit's voice, which was a little squeaky.

What he was telling us was, there was gonna be some kind of ceremony. That whoever the weasels could catch was gonna be a part of it. It wasn't no ceremony where there was cake and prizes and games, least not any that was fun. It was gonna be a ceremony in honor of this fella he called Cut Through You.

According to Brer Rabbit, the island wasn't always a bad place. He and his family had lived here, along with all the other brother and sister animals, or whatever the hell they were, until Brer Fox found the stones and the book wrapped in skin. That's how Brer Rabbit put it. The book wrapped in skin.

Brer Fox, he wasn't never loveable, and Brer Rabbit said right up front, he used to pull tricks on him and Brer Bear all the time. They was harmless, he said, and they was mostly just to keep from getting eaten by them two. 'Cause as nice a place as it was then as measured up against now, it was still a place where meat eaters lived alongside them that wasn't meat eaters, which meant them that ate vegetables was the meat eater's lunch, if they got caught. Brer Rabbit said he figured that was just fair play. That was how the world worked, even if their island wasn't exactly like the rest of the world.

It dropped out of the sky come the full moon and ended up in the big wide middle of the Mississippi. It stayed that way for a few hours, and then come the Warning Rain, as he called it, the one we was having now; the one full of lightning and thunder and hard falling water. It meant they was more than halfway through their time to be on the Mississippi, then there was gonna come the Soft Rain. It didn't have no lightning in it. It was pleasant. At least until the sky opened up and the wind came down and carried them away.

"Where does it take you?" I asked.

Brer Rabbit shook his head. "I don't know I can say. We don't seem to know nothing till we come back. And when we do, well, we just pick up right where we was before. Doing whatever it was we was doing. So if Brer Fox has me by the neck, and the time comes, and we all get sucked away, when it blows back, we gonna be right where we was; it's always night and always like things was when we left them."

He said when that funnel of wind dropped them back on the island, sometimes it brought things with it that wasn't there before. Like people from other places. Other worlds, he said. That didn't make no sense at all to me. But that's what he said. He said sometimes it brought live people, and sometimes it brought dead people, and sometimes it brought Brer People with it, and sometimes what it brought wasn't people at all. He told us about some big old crawdads come through once, and how they chased everyone around, but ended up being boiled in water and eaten by Brer Bear, Brer Fox, and all the weasels, who was kind of butt kissers to Brer Fox.

Anyway, not knowing what was gonna show up on the island,
either by way of that Sticky Storm—as he named it 'cause everything
clung to it—or by way of the Mississippi, made things interesting;
right before it got too interesting. The part that was too interesting
had to do with Brer Fox and that Book of Skin.

Way Brer Rabbit figured, it come through that hole in the sky like
everything else. It was clutched in a man's hand, and the man was
deader than a rock, and he had what Brer Rabbit said was a towel or a
rag or some such thing wrapped around his head.

Brer Rabbit said he seen that dead man from a hiding place in the
woods, and Uncle Remus was with him when he did. Uncle Remus
had escaped slavery and come to the island. He fit in good. Stayed
in the burrow with Brer Rabbit and his family, and he listened to all
their stories.

But when the change come, when that book showed up, and stuff
started happening because of it, he decided he'd had enough and tried
to swim back to shore. Things he saw made him think taking his
chance on drowning, or getting caught and being a slave again, was
worth it. I don't know how he felt later, but he sure got caught, since
Jim knew him and had heard stories about Dread Island from him.

"He left before things really got bad," Brer Rabbit said. "And did
they get bad. He was lucky."

"That depends on how you look at it," Jim said. "I done been a
slave, and I can't say it compares good to much of anything."

"Maybe," Brer Rabbit said. "Maybe."

And then he went on with his story.

Seems that when the storm brought that dead man clutching that
book, Brer Fox pried it out of his hands and opened it up and found it
was written in some foreign language, but he could read it. Brer Rabbit
said one of the peculiars about the island is that everyone—except the
weasels, who pretty much got the short end of the stick when it come
to smarts—could read or speak any language there was.

Now, wasn't just the book and the dead man come through, there was the stones. They had fallen out of the sky at the same time. There was also a mass of black goo with dying and dead fish in it that come through, and it splattered all over the ground.

The stones was carved up. The main marking was a big eye, then there was all manner of other scratchings and drawings. And though the Brer Folk could read or speak any language possible, even the language in that book, they couldn't speak or read what was on them stones. It had been put together by folk spoke a tongue none of their mouths would fit around. Least at first.

Brer Fox went to holding that book dear. Everyone on the island knew about it, and he always carried it in a pack on his back. Brer Bear, who was kind of a kiss ass like the weasels, but smarter than they was—and, according to Brer Rabbit, that was a sad thing to think about, since Brer Bear didn't hardly have the sense to get in out of the Warning Rain—helped Brer Fox set them stones up in that black muck. Every time the storm brought them back, that's what they did, and pretty soon they had the weasels helping them.

Fact was, Brer Fox all but quit chasing Brer Rabbit. He instead sat and read by firelight and moonlight, and started chanting, 'cause he was learning how to say that language that he couldn't read before, the language on the stones, and he was teaching Brer Bear how to do the same. And one time, well, the island stayed overnight.

"It didn't happen but that once," Brer Rabbit said. "But come daylight, here we still was. And it stayed that way until the next night come, and finally before next morning, things got back to the way they was supposed to be. Brer Fox had some power from that book and those stones, and he liked it mighty good."

Now and again he'd chant something from the book, and the air would fill with an odor like rotting fish, and then that odor got heavy and went to whirling about them stones; it was an odor that made the stomach crawl and the head fill with all manner of sickness and worry and grief.

Once, while Brer Rabbit was watching Brer Fox chant, while he was smelling that rotten fish stink, he saw the sky crack open, right up close by the moon. Not the way it did when the Sticky Storm come, which was when everything turned gray and the sky opened up and a twister of sorts dropped down and sucked them all up. It was more like the night sky was just a big black sheet, and this thing with one large, nasty, rolling eye and more legs than a spider—and ropey legs at that—poked through and pulled at the night.

For a moment, Brer Rabbit thought that thing—which from Brer Fox's chanting he learned was called Cut Through You—was gonna take hold of the moon and eat it like a flapjack. It had an odd mouth with a beak, and it was snapping all the while.

Then, sudden-like, it was sucked back, like something got hold of one of its legs and yanked it plumb out of sight. The sky closed up and the air got clean for a moment, and it was over with.

After that, Brer Fox and ole One Eye had them a connection. Every time the island was brought back, Brer Fox would go out there and stand in that muck, or sit on a rock in the middle of them carved stones, and call out to Cut Through You. It was a noise, Brer Rabbit said, sounded like something straining at toilet while trying to cough and yodel all at the same time.

Brer Fox and Brer Bear was catching folk and tying them to the stones. People from the Mississippi come along by accident; they got nabbed too, mostly by the weasels. It was all so Brer Fox could have Cut Through You meetings.

Way it was described to me, it was kind of like church. Except when it come time to pass the offering, the sky would crack open, and ole Cut Through You would lean out and reach down and pull folk tied to the stones up there with him.

Brer Rabbit said he watched it eat a bunch a folk quicker than a mule skinner could pop goober peas; chawed them up and spat them out, splattered what was left in that black mud that was all around the stones.

That was what Brer Fox and Brer Bear, and all them weasels, took to eating. It changed them. They went from sneaky and hungry and animal-like, to being more like men. Meaning, said Brer Rabbit, they come to enjoy cruelty. And then Brer Fox built the Tar Baby, used that book to give it life. It could do more work than all of them put together, and it set up the final stones by itself. Something dirty needed to be done, it was Tar Baby done it. You couldn't stop the thing, Brer Rabbit said. It just kept on a-coming and a-coming.

But the final thing Brer Rabbit said worried him was that each time Cut Through You came back, there's more and more of him to be seen, and it turned out there's a lot more of Cut Through You than you'd think; and it was like he was hungrier each time he showed.

Bottom line, as figured by Brer Rabbit, was this: if Brer Fox and his bunch didn't supply the sacrifices, pretty soon they'd be sacrifices themselves.

Brer Rabbit finished up his story, and it was about that time the rain quit. The clouds melted away and the moonlight was back. It was clear out, and you could see a right smart distance.

I said, "You ain't seen a couple of fellas named Tom and Joe, have you? One of them might be wearing a straw hat. They're about my age and size, but not quite as good-looking."

Brer Rabbit shook his head. "I ain't," he said. "But they could be with all the others Brer Fox has nabbed of late. Was they on the riverboat run aground?"

I shook my head.

Jim said, "Huck, you and me, we got to get back to the raft and get on out of this place, Tom and Joe or not."

"That's right," Brer Rabbit said. "You got to. Oh, I wish I could go with you."

"You're invited," I said.

"Ah, but there is the thorn in the paw. I can't go, 'cause I do, come daylight, if I ain't on this island, I disappear, and I don't come back.

Though to tell you true, that might be better than getting ate up by Cut Through You. I'll give it some considering."

"Consider quick," Jim said, "We got to start back to the raft."

"What we got to do," Brer Rabbit said, "is we got to go that way." He pointed.

"Then," he said, "we work down to the shore, and you can get your raft. And I'm thinking I might just go with you and turn to nothing. I ain't got no family now. I ain't got nothing but me, and part of me is missing, so the rest of me might as well go missing too."

Jim said, "I got my medicine bag with me. I can't give you your paw back, but I can take some of the hurt away with a salve I got."

Jim dressed Brer Rabbit's paw, and when that was done, he got some wool string out of that little bag he had on his belt and tied up his hair—which had grown long—in little sheaves, like dark wheat. He said it was a thing to do to keep back witches.

I pointed out witches seemed to me the least of our worries, but he done it anyway, with me taking my pocketknife out of my back pocket to cut the string for him.

When he had knotted his hair up in about twenty gatherings, we lit out for the raft without fear of witches.

Way we went made it so we had to swim across a creek that was deep in places. It was cold water, like that blue hole we had jumped in, and there was fish in it. They was curious and would bob to the top and look at us; their eyes was shiny as wet stones in the moonlight.

On the other side of the creek, we stumbled through a patch of woods, and down a hill, and then up one that led us level with where we had been before. In front of us was more dark woods. Brer Rabbit said beyond the trees was the shoreline, and we might be able to get to our raft if the weasels hadn't found it. Me and Jim decided if they had, we'd try for Tom and Joe's boat and wish them our best. If their boat was gone, then there was nothing left but to hit that Mississippi

breathing in and out, like bellows being worked to start up a fresh fire.

"You ain't looking so good," Brer Rabbit said.

"Yeah," Brer Fox said, "but looks ain't everything. I ain't looking so good, but you ain't doing so good."

Brer Fox slung his pack off his back and opened it. I could see there was a book in there, the one bound up in human skin. You could see there was a face on the cover, eyes, nose, mouth, and some warts. But that wasn't what Brer Fox was reaching for. What he was reaching for was Brer Rabbit's paw, which was stuffed in there.

"Here's a little something you left back at the ceremony spot." He held up the paw and waved it around. "That wasn't nice. I had plans for you. But, you know what? I got a lucky rabbit's foot now. Though, to tell the truth, it ain't all that lucky for you, is it?"

He put the paw in his mouth and clamped down on it and bit right through it and chewed on it some. He gave what was left of it to Brer Bear, who ate it up in one big bite.

"I figured you wouldn't be needing it," Brer Fox said.

"Why, I'm quite happy with this nubbing," Brer Rabbit said. "I don't spend so much time cleaning my nails now."

Brer Fox's face turned sour, like he had bitten into an unripe persimmon. "There ain't gonna be nothing of you to clean after tonight. And in fact, we got to go quick-like. I wouldn't want you to miss the meeting, Brer Rabbit. You see, tonight, he comes all the way through, and then me and my folk, we're gonna serve him. He's gonna go all over the Mississippi, and then all over the world. He's gonna rule, and I'm gonna rule beside him. He told me. He told me in my head."

With those last words, Brer Fox tapped the side of his head with a finger.

"You gonna get ate up like everyone else," Brer Rabbit said. "You just a big ole idiot."

Brer Fox rose up, waved his hand over his head, yelled out, "Bring them. And don't be easy about it. Let's blood them."

What that meant was they dragged us in that net. We was pressed up tight together, and there was all manner of stuff on the ground to stick us, and we banged into trees and such, and it seemed like forever before we broke out of the woods and I got a glimpse at the place we was going.

Right then I knew why it was Brer Rabbit would rather just disappear.

We was scratched and bumped up and full of ticks and chiggers and poison ivy by the time we got to where we was going, and where we was going didn't have no trees and there wasn't nothing pretty about it.

There was this big stretch of black mud. You could see dead fish in it, and some of them was mostly bones, but there were still some flopping about. They were fish I didn't recognize. Some had a lot of eyes and big teeth and were shaped funny.

Standing up in the mud were these big dark slabs of rock that wasn't quite black and wasn't quite brown, but was somewhere between any color you can mention. The moonlight laid on them like a slick of bacon grease, and you could see markings all over them. Each and every one of them had a big ole eye at the top of the slab, and below it were all manner of marks. Some of the marks looked like fish or things with lots of legs, and beaks, and then there was marks that didn't look like nothing but chicken scratch. But, I can tell you this, looking at those slabs and those marks made my stomach feel kind of funny, like I had swallowed a big chaw of tobacco right after eating too many hot peppers and boiled pigs' feet, something, by the way, that really happened to me once.

Standing out there in that black muck was the weasels. On posts all around the muck right where it was still solid ground, there was men and women with their hands tied behind their backs and then tied to rings on the posts. I reckoned a number of them was from the steamboat wreck. There was also a woman wearing a kind of leather cap, and she had on pants just like a man. She was kind of pretty, and where everyone else was hanging their heads, she looked mad as a hornet. As we was pulled up closer to the muck, I saw that Tom and Joe was there, tied to posts, drooping like flowers too long in the hot sun, missing bowie knife, gun, and packed lunch.

When they seen me and Jim, they brightened for a second, then realized wasn't nothing we could do, and that we was in the same situation as them. It hurt me to see Tom like that, all sagging. It was the first time I'd ever seen him about given up. Like us, they was all scratched up and even in the moonlight, you could see they was spotted like speckled pups from bruises.

Out behind them I could see parts of that big briar patch we had seen when we first sailed our raft onto the island. The briars twisted up high, and the way the moonlight fell into them, that whole section looked like a field of coiled ropes and nails. I hadn't never seen a briar patch like that before.

There were some other things out there in the muck that I can't explain, and there was stuff on the sides of where the muck ended. I figured, from what Brer Rabbit had told us, they was stuff from them other worlds or places that sometimes come through on the Sticky Storm. One of them things was a long boat of sorts, but it had wings on it, and it was shiny silver and had a tail on it like a fish. There was some kind of big crosses on the wings, and it was just sitting on wheels over on some high grass, but the wheels wasn't like any I'd ever seen on a wagon or buggy.

There was also this big thing looked like a gourd, if a gourd could be about a thousand times bigger; it was stuck up in the mud with the fat part down, and the thinner part in the air, and it had little fins on it. Written on it in big writing was something that didn't make no sense to me. It said: HOWDY ALL YOU JAPS.

Wasn't a moment or two passed between me seeing all this, then we was being pulled out of the net and carried over to three empty posts. A moment later, they wasn't empty no more. We was tied to the wooden rings on them tight as a fishing knot.

I turned my head and looked at Jim.

He said, "You're right, they ain't no witch problems around here."

"Maybe," I said, "it's because of the string. Who knows how many witches would be around otherwise."

Jim grinned at me. "That's right. That's right, ain't it?"

I nodded and smiled at him. I figured if we was gonna be killed, and wasn't nothing we could do about it, we might as well try and be cheerful.

Right then, coming across that black mud, its feet splattering and sucking in the muck as it pulled them free for each step, was the Tar Baby. Now that he was out under the moonlight, I could see he was stuck all over with what at first looked like long needles, but as he come closer, I saw was straw. He was shot through with it. I figured it was a thing Brer Fox used to help put him together, mixing it with tar he got from somewhere, and turpentine, and maybe some things I didn't want to know about; you could smell that turpentine as he waddled closer, spitting all the while.

He sauntered around the circle of folks that was tied to the posts, and as he did, his plump belly would flare open, and you could see fire in there and bits of ash and bones being burned up along with fish heads and a human skull. Tar Baby went by each of them on the posts and pushed his face close to their faces so he could enjoy how they curled back from him. I knew a bully when I seen one, 'cause I had fought a few, and when I was younger, I was kind of a bully myself, till a girl named Hortense Miller beat the snot out of me, twisted my arm behind my back and made me say "cotton sack," and even then, after I said it, she made me eat a mouthful of dirt and tell her I liked it. She wasn't one to settle an argument easy like. It cured my bully days.

When the Tar Baby come to me and pushed his face close, I didn't flinch. I just looked him in his red eyes like they was nothing, even though it was all I could do to keep my knees from chattering together. He stayed looking at me for a long time, then grunted, left the air around me full of the fog and stink of turpentine. Jim was next, and Jim didn't flinch none either. That didn't set well with Tar Baby, two rascals in a row, so he reached out with a finger and poked Jim's chest. There was a hissing sound and smoke come off Jim. That made me figure he was being burned by the Tar Baby somehow, but when the Tar Baby pulled his chubby, tar finger back, it was him that was smoking.

I leaned out and took a good look and seen the cause of it—the nail on the string around Jim's neck. The Tar Baby had poked it and that iron nail had actually worked its magic on him. Course, problem was, he had to put his finger right on it, but in that moment, I gathered me up a more favorable view of the hoodoo methods.

Tar Baby looked at the end of his smoking finger, like he might find something special there, then he looked at Jim, and his mouth twisted. I think he was gonna do something nasty, but there come a rain all of a sudden. The Soft Rain Brer Rabbit told us about. It come down sweet-smelling and light and warm. No thunder. No lightning. And no clouds. Just water falling out of a clear sky stuffed with stars and a big fat moon; it was the rain that was supposed to let everyone know it wouldn't be long before daylight and the Sticky Storm.

The weasels and Brer Fox and Brer Bear, and that nasty Tar Baby, all made their way quick-like to the tallest stone in the muck. They stood in front of it, and you could tell they was nervous, even the Tar Baby, and they went about chanting. The words were like someone spitting and sucking and coughing and clearing their throat all at once, if they was words at all. This went on for a while, and wasn't nothing happening but that rain, which was kind of pleasant.

"Huck," Jim said, "you done been as good a friend as man could have, and I ain't happy you gonna die, or me neither, but we got to, it makes me happy knowing you gonna go out with me."

"I'd feel better if you was by yourself," I said, and Jim let out a cackle when I said it.

There was a change in things, a feeling that the air had gone heavy. I looked up and the rain fell on my face and ran in my mouth and tasted good. The night sky was vibrating a little, like someone shaking weak pudding in a bowl. Then the sky cracked open like Brer Rabbit had told us about, and I seen there was light up there in the crack. It was light like you'd see from a lantern behind a wax paper curtain. After a moment, something moved behind the light, and then something moved in front of it. A dark shape about the size of the moon; the moon itself was starting to drift low and thin off to the right of the island.

Brer Rabbit had tried to describe it to us, ole Cut Through You, but all I can say is there ain't no real way to tell you how it looked, 'cause there wasn't nothing to measure it against. It was big and it had one eye that was dark and unblinking, and it had a beak of sorts, and there were all these ropey arms; but the way it looked shifted and changed so much you couldn't get a real handle on it.

I won't lie to you. It wasn't like standing up to the Tar Baby. My knees started knocking together, and my heart was beating like a drum and my insides felt as if they were being worked about like they was in a milk churn. Them snaky arms on that thing was clawing at the sky, and I even seen the sky give on the sides, like it was about to rip all over and fall down.

I pressed my back against the post, and when I did, I felt that pocket-knife in my back pocket. It come to me then that if I stuck out my butt a little and pulled the rope loose as possible on the ring I was tied to, I might be able to thumb that knife out of my pocket, so I give it a try.

It wasn't easy, but that thing up there gave me a lot of willpower. I worked the knife with my thumb and long finger, and got it out, and flicked it open, and turned it in my hand, almost dropping it. When that happened, it felt like my heart had leaped down a long tunnel somewhere. But when I knew I still had it, I turned it and went to cutting. Way I was holding it, twisted so that it come back against the rope on the ring, I was doing a bit of work on my wrists as well as the tie. It was a worrying job, but I stayed at it, feeling blood running down my hands.

While I was at it, that chanting got louder and louder, and I seen off to the side of Cut Through You another hole opening up in the sky; inside that hole it looked like a whirlpool, like you find in the river; it was bright as day in that hole, and the day was churning around and around and the sky was widening.

I figured then the ceremony was in a kind of hurry, 'cause Cut Through You was peeking through, and that whirling hole was in competition to him. He wouldn't have nothing to eat and no chanting to hear, if the Sticky Storm took everyone away first.

You see, it was the chanting that was helping Cut Through You get loose. It gave him strength, hearing that crazy language.

From where we was, I could see the pink of the morning starting to lay across the far end of the river, pushing itself up like the bloom of a rose, and that ole moon dipping down low, like a wheel of rat cheese being slowly lowered into a sack.

So, there we were, Cut Through You thrashing around in the sky, the Sticky Storm whirling about, and the sun coming up. The only thing that would have made it worse was if I had had to pee.

Everything started to shake, and I guess that was because Cut Through You and that storm was banging together in some way behind night's curtain, and maybe the sun starting to rise had something to do with it. The Sticky Storm dipped out of that hole and it come down lower. I could see all manner of stuff up there in it, but I couldn't make out none of it. It looked like someone had taken some different mixes of paint and thrown them all together; a few light things on the ground started to float up toward the storm, and when they did, I really understood why Brer Rabbit called it a Sticky Storm; it was like it was flypaper and all that was sucked up got stuck to it like flies.

About then, I cut that rope in two, and pulled my bleeding hands loose. I ran over to Jim and cut him loose.

Brer Fox and the others didn't even notice. They was so busy looking up at Cut Through You. I didn't have the time, but I couldn't help but look up too. It had its head poking all the way through, and that head was so big you can't imagine, and it was lumpy and such, like a bunch of melons had been put in a tow sack and banged on with a boat paddle; it was leaking green goo that was falling down on the ground, and onto the worshipers, and they was grabbing it off the muck, or off themselves, and sticking their fingers in their mouths and licking them clean.

It didn't look like what the Widow Douglas would have called "sanitary," and I could see that them that was eating it was starting to change. Sores, big and bloody, was popping up on them like a rash.

I ran on around the circle to Tom and Joe and cut them loose, and then we all ran back the other way, 'cause as much as I'd like to have helped them on that farther part of the circle, it was too late. On that side the ground was starting to fold up, and their posts was coming loose. It was like someone had taken a sheet of paper and curled one end of it. They was being sucked up in the sky toward that Sticky Storm, and even the black mud was coming loose and shooting up in the sky.

On the other end of the circle, things was still reasonably calm, so I rushed to Brer Rabbit and cut him loose, then that lady with the pants on. Right about then, Cut Through You let out with a bellow so loud it made the freckles on my butt crawl up my back and hide in my hair, or so it felt. Wasn't no need to guess that Cut Through You was mad that he was running out of time, and he was ready to take it out on most anybody. He stuck long ropey legs out of the sky and went to thrashing at Brer Fox and the others. I had the pleasure of seeing Brer Fox getting his head snapped off, and then Brer Bear was next.

The weasels, not being of strong stuff to begin with, started running like rats from a sinking ship. But it didn't do them no good. That Cut Through You's legs was all over them, grabbing their heads and jerking them off, and them that wasn't beheaded was being pulled up in the sky by the Sticky Storm.

I was still on that side of the circle, cutting people loose, and soon as I did, a bunch of them just ran wildly, some right into the storm.

They was yanked up, and went out of sight. All of the island seemed like it was wadding up.

Brer Rabbit grabbed my shoulder, said, "It's every man for his self," and then he darted along the edge of the Sticky Storm, dashed between two whipping Cut Through You legs, and leaped right into that briar patch, which seemed crazy to me. All the while he's running and jumping in the briars, I'm yelling, "Brer Rabbit, come back."

But he didn't. I heard him say, "Born and raised in the briar patch, born and raised," and then he was in the big middle of it, even as it was starting to fold up and get pulled toward the sky.

Now that we was free, I didn't know what to do. There didn't seem no place to go. Even the shoreline was starting to curl up.

Jim was standing by me. He said, "I reckon this is it, Huck. I say we let that storm take us, and not Cut Through You."

We was about to go right into the storm, 'cause the side of it wasn't but a few steps away, when I got my elbow yanked. I turned and it was Tom Sawyer, and Joe with him.

"The lady," Tom said. "This way."

I turned and seen the short-haired lady was at that silver boat, and she was waving us to her. Any port in a storm, so to speak, so we run toward her with Tom and Joe. A big shadow fell over us as we run, and then a leg come popping out of the sky like a whip, and caught Joe around the neck, and yanked his head plumb off. His headless body must have run three or four steps before it went down.

I heard Tom yell out, and stop, as if to help the body up. "You got to run for it, Tom," I said. "Ain't no other way. Joe's deader than last Christmas."

So we come up on the silver boat with the wings, and there was an open door in the side of it, and we rushed in there and closed it. The lady was up front in a seat, behind this kind of partial wheel, looking out through a glass that run in front of her.

The silver bug was humming, and those crosses on the wings was spinning. She touched something and let loose of something else, and we started to bounce, and then we was running along on the grass. I moved to the seat beside her, and she glanced over at me. She was white-faced, but determined-looking.

"That was Noonan's seat," she said.

I didn't know what to say to that. I didn't know if I should get out of it or not, but I'll tell you, I didn't. I couldn't move. And then we was bouncing harder, and the island was closing in on us, and Cut Through You's rope legs was waving around us. One of them got hit by the crosses, which was spinning so fast you could hardly make them out. They hit it, and the winged boat was knocked a bit. The leg come off in a spray of green that splattered on the glass, and then the boat started to lift up. I can't explain it, and I know it ain't believable, but we was flying.

The sun was really starting to brighten things now, and as we climbed up, I seen the woods was still in front of us. The lady was trying to make the boat go higher, but I figured we was gonna clip the top of them trees and end up punched to death by them, but then the boat rose up some, and I could feel and hear the trees brush against the bottom of it, like someone with a whisk broom snapping dust off a coat collar.

With the island curling up all around us and starting to come apart in a spray of color, being sucked up by the Sticky Storm, and that flying boat wobbling and a-rattling, I figured we had done all this for nothing.

The boat turned slightly, like the lady was tacking a sail. I could glance up and out of the glass and see Cut Through You. He was sticking his head out of a pink morning sky, and his legs was thrashing, but he didn't look so big now; it was like the light had shrunk him up. I seen Tar Baby too, or what was left of him, and he was splattering against that big gourd thing with the writing on it, splattering like someone was flicking ink out of a writing pen. He and that big gourd was whipping around us like angry bugs.

Then there was a feeling like we was an arrow shot from a bow, and the boat jumped forward, and then it went up high, turned slightly, and below I seen the island was turning into a ball, and the ball was starting to look wet. Then it, the rain, every dang thing, including ole Cut Through You, who was sucked out of his hole, shot up into that Sticky Storm.

Way we was now, I could still see Tar Baby splashed on that gourd, and the gourd started to shake, then it twisted and went as flat as a tapeworm, and for some reason, it blowed; it was way worse than dynamite. When it blew up, it threw some Tar Baby on the flying boat's glass. The boat started to shake and the air inside and out had blue ripples in it.

And then—

—the island was gone and there was just the Mississippi below us. Things was looking good for a minute, and then the boat started coughing, and black smoke come up from that whirly thing that had cut off one of Cut Through You's legs.

The boat dropped, the lady pulling at that wheel, yanking at doodads and such, but having about as much luck taking us back up as I'd have had trying to lift a dead cow off the ground by the tail.

"We are going down," she said, as if this might not be something we hadn't noticed. "And there is nothing else to do but hope for the best."

Well, to make a long story short, she was right.

Course, hope only goes so far.

She fought that boat all the way down, and then it hit the water and skipped like it was a flat rock. We skipped and skipped, then the whirly gigs flew off, and one of them smashed the glass. I was thrown out of the seat, and around the inside of the boat like a ball.

Then everything knotted up, and there was a bang on my head, and the next thing I know there's water all over. The boat was about half full inside. I suppose that's what brought me around, that cold Mississippi water.

The glass up front was broke open, and water was squirting in around the edges, so I helped it by giving it a kick. It come loose at the edges, and I was able to push it out with my feet. Behind me was

Tom Sawyer, and he come from the back like a farm mule in sight of the barn. Fact was, he damn near run over me going through the hole I'd made.

By the time he got through, there wasn't nothing but water, and I was holding my breath. Jim grabbed me from below, and pushed me by the seat of my pants through the hole. Then it was like the boat was towed out from under me. Next thing I knew I was on top of the water floating by Tom, spitting and coughing.

"Jim," I said, "where's Jim?"

"Didn't see him come up," Tom said.

"I guess not," I said. "You was too busy stepping on my head on your way out of that flying boat."

Tom started swimming toward shore, and I just stayed where I was, dog-paddling, looking for Jim. I didn't see him, but on that sunlit water there come a big bubble and a burst of something black as the tar baby had been. It spread over the water. It was oil. I could smell it.

Next thing, I felt a tug at my leg. I thought it was one of them big catfish grabbing me, but it wasn't. It was Jim. He bobbed up beside me, and I grabbed him and hugged him and he hugged me back.

"I tried to save her, Huck. I did. But she was done dead. I could tell when I touched her, she was done dead."

"You done what you could."

"What about Tom?" Jim said.

I nodded in the direction Tom had gone swimming. We could see his arms going up and down in the water, swimming like he thought he could make the far shore in about two minutes.

Wasn't nothing to do but for us to start swimming after him. We done that for a long time, floating some, swimming some. And I'm ashamed to say Jim had to pull me along a few times, 'cause I got tuckered out.

When we was both about gone under, a big tree come floating by, and we climbed up on it. We seen Tom wasn't too far away, having gotten slower as he got tired. We yelled for him, and he come swimming back. The water flow was slow right then, and he caught up with us pretty quick, which is a good thing, 'cause if he hadn't, he'd have sure enough drowned. We clung and floated, and it was late that afternoon when we finally was seen by some fishermen and pulled off the log and into their boat.

There isn't much left to tell. All I can say is we was tired for three days, and when we tried to tell our story, folks just laughed at us. Didn't believe us at all. Course, can't blame them, as I'm prone toward being a liar.

It finally got so we had to tell a lie for it to be believed for the truth, and that included Tom, who was in on it with us. We had to say Joe drowned, because they wouldn't believe Cut Through You jerked his head off. They didn't believe there was a Cut Through You. Even the folks believed there was a Dread Island didn't believe our story.

Tom and Becky got together, and they been together ever since. Five years have passed, and dang if Tom didn't become respectable and marry Becky. They got a kid now. But maybe they ain't all that respectable. I count eight months from the time they married until the time their bundle of joy come along.

Last thing I reckon I ought to say is every year I go out to the edge of the Mississippi with Jim and toss some flowers on the water in memory of the lady who flew us off the island in that winged boat.

As for Dread Island, well, here's something odd. I can't see it no more, not even when it's supposed to be there.

Jim says it might be my eyes, 'cause when you get older you lose sight of some things you used to could see.

I don't know. But I think it ain't out there no time anymore, and it might not be coming back. I figure it, Brer Rabbit and Cut Through You is somewhere else that ain't like nothing else we know. If that's true, all I got to say is I hope Brer Rabbit is hid up good, far away from Cut Through You, out there in the thorns, out there where he was raised, in the deep parts of that big old briar patch.

This is a Poe pastiche based on his character and first private detective in literature, C. Auguste Dupin. It is told by his companion. It is also inspired by Arthur Conan Doyle's Sherlock Holmes. It was published in an anthology of Poe-inspired stories. I combined Lovecraft and Arthur Machen and the absurdity of the adventure pulps into the mix as well. Toss in a dollop of Philip José Farmer, run it all through the blender in my brain, and this is the result. I liked it so much that I wrote a sequel that is forthcoming.

THE GRUESOME AFFAIR OF THE ELECTRIC BLUE LIGHTNING

From the Files of Auguste Dupin
Translated loosely from the French

THIS STORY CAN only be described as fantastic in nature, and with no exaggeration, it deals with nothing less than the destruction of the world, but before I continue, I should make an immediate confession. Some of this is untrue. I do not mean the events themselves, for they are accurate, but I have disguised the names of several individuals, and certain locations have been reimagined— for lack of a better word—to suit my own conscience. The end of the cosmos and our world as we know it is of considerable concern, of course, but no reason to abandon manners.

These decisions were made primarily due to the possibility of certain actors in this drama being unnecessarily scandalized or embarrassed, even though they are only mentioned in passing and have little to nothing to do with the events themselves. I do not think historians, warehouse owners and the like should have to bear the burden of my story, especially as it will undoubtedly be disbelieved.

There are, however, specific players in my article, story if you prefer, that have their own names to contend with, old as those names may be, and I have not made any effort whatsoever to alter these. This is owed to the fact that these particular personages are well enough recognized by name, and any attempt to disguise them would be a ridiculous and wasted effort.

This begins where many of my true stories begin. I was in the apartment I share with Auguste Dupin, perhaps the wisest and most rational man I have ever known, if a bit of a curmudgeon and a self-centered ass. A touch of background, should you be interested: we share an apartment, having met while looking for the same obscure book in a library, which brought about a discussion of the tome in question, which in turn we decided to share in the reading, along with the price of an apartment, as neither of us could afford the rental of one alone. Dupin is a Chevalier, and had some financial means in the past, but his wealth had somehow been lost—how this occurred, we have by unspoken agreement never discussed, and this suits me, for I would rather not go into great detail about my own circumstances.

In spite of his haughty nature, Dupin is quite obviously of gentlemanly countenance and bearing, if, like myself he is a threadbare gentleman; I should also add, one who in manners is frequently not a gentleman at all. He is also a sometime investigator. This began merely as a hobby, something he did for his own amusement, until I assured him that regular employment might aid in his problems with the rent, and that I could assist him, for a small fee, of course. He agreed.

What I call "The Gruesome Affair of the Electric Blue Lightning" began quite casually, and certainly by accident. I was telling Dupin how I had read that the intense lightning storm of the night before had been so radical, producing such powerful bolts, it had started fires all along the Rue. In fact, the very newspaper that had recorded the article lay before him, and it wasn't until I had finished telling him about the irregular events that I saw it lying there, and admonished him for not revealing to me he had read the article and knew my comments even before disclosing them for his consideration.

"Yes," Dupin said, leaning back in his chair and clasping his fingers together. "But I appreciate your telling of it. It was far more dramatic and interesting than the newspaper article itself. I was especially interested in, and impressed with, your descriptions of the lightning, for yours was a practical explanation, but not an actual recollection, and therefore perhaps faulty."

"Excuse me," I said.

His eyes brightened and his lean face seemed to stretch even longer as he said, "You described to me lightning that you did not see, and in so doing, you described it as it should appear, not as the newspaper depicted it. Or to be more precise, you only said that the fires had been started by a lightning strike. The newspaper said it was a blue-white fulmination that appeared to climb up to the sky from the rooftops of a portion of the warehouse district rather than come down from the heavens. To be more precise, the newspaper was supposedly quoting a man named F, who said he saw the peculiar lightning and the beginnings of the warehouse fire with his own eyes. He swore it rose upward, instead of the other way around. Out of the ordinary, don't you think?"

"A mistake on his part," I said. "I had forgotten all about his saying that. I didn't remember it that way."

"Perhaps," said Dupin, filling his meerschaum pipe and studying the rain outside the apartment window, "because it didn't make sense to you. It goes against common sense. So, you dismissed it."

"I suppose so," I said. "Isn't that what you do in your investigations? Dismiss items that are nonsensical? Use only what you know to be true? You are always admonishing me for filling in what is not there, what could not be, that which faults ratiocination."

Dupin nodded. "That's correct. But, isn't that what you're doing now? You are filling in what is not there. Or deciding quite by your own contemplations that which should not be there."

"You confuse me, Dupin."

"No doubt," he said. "Unlike you, I do not dismiss something as false until I have considered it fully and examined all the evidence. There is also the part of the article where F's statement was validated by a child named P."

"But, the word of a child?" I said.

"Sometimes they have the clearest eyes," Dupin said. "They have not had time to think what they should see, as you have, but only what they have seen. They can be mistaken. Eyewitnesses often are, of course. But it's odd that the child validated the sighting of the other witness, and if what the article says is true, the man and child did not know one another. They were on very distant sides of the event. Due to this—and of course I would question their not knowing one another until I have made a full examination—perhaps more can be made of the child's recollections. I certainly believe we can rule out coincidence of such an observation. The child and the man either colluded on their story, which I find unlikely, because to what purpose would they say such an unbelievable thing? Or, the other possibility is they did in fact see the same event, and their description is accurate, at least as far as they conceive it."

"That lightning rose up from the ground?" I said. "You say that makes more sense than it coming down from the heavens? I would think suggesting Jove threw a bolt of lightning would be just as irrational as to suggest the lightning rose up from the earth!"

"From a warehouse rooftop, not the earth," he said. "And it was blue-white in color?"

"Ridiculous," I said.

"It is peculiar, I admit, but my suggestion is we do not make a judgment on the matter until we know more facts."

"I didn't realize we cared to make a judgment."

"I am considering it."

"This interests you that much? Why would we bother? It's not a true investigation, just the soothing of a curiosity, which, I might add, pays absolutely nothing."

"What interests me are the deaths from the warehouse fire," Dupin said. "Though, since, as you noted, we haven't been hired to examine the facts, that pays the same absence of price."

"Horrid business," I said. "But I believe you are making much of nothing. I know that area, and those buildings are rats' nests just waiting for a spark to ignite them. They are also the squatting grounds for vagrants. Lightning struck the building. It caught ablaze rapidly, and sleeping vagrants were burned to death in the fire. It is as simple as that."

"Perhaps," Dupin said. He leaned back and puffed on his pipe, blowing blue clouds of smoke from between his teeth and from the bowl. "But how do you explain that our own acquaintance the Police Prefect, G, was quoted as saying that they found a singed but still identifiable arm, and that it appeared to have been sawed off at the elbow, rather than burned?"

I had no answer for that.

"Of course, G is often wrong, so in his case I might suspect an error before suspecting one from the witnessing child. G solves most of his crimes by accident, confession, or by beating his suspect until he will admit to having started the French Revolution over the theft of a ham hock. However, when he has solved his cases, if indeed one can actually consider them solved, it is seldom by any true form of detection. I should also note that there has been a rash of grave robbings of late, all of them involving freshly buried bodies."

Now, as he often did, Dupin had piqued my curiosity. I arose, poured the both of us a bit of wine, sat back down and watched Dupin smoke his pipe, the stench of which was cheap and foul as if burning the twilled ticking of an old sweat-stained mattress.

"For me to have an opinion on this matter, I would suggest we make a trip of it tomorrow, to see where this all occurred. Interview those that were spoken to by the newspaper. I know you have contacts, so I would like you to use them to determine the exact location of these witnesses who observed the lightning and the resulting fire. Does this suit you?"

I nodded. "Very well then."

That was the end of our discussion about these unique but, to my mind, insignificant events, for the time being. We instead turned our attention to the smoking of pipes and the drinking of wine. Dupin read while he smoked and drank, and I sat there contemplating that which we had discussed, finding the whole matter more and more mysterious with the thinking. Later, I decided I would like to take a stroll before retiring, so that I might clear my head of the drinking and heavy smoke.

I also had in mind the ideas that Dupin had suggested, and wanted to digest them. I have always found a walk to be satisfying not only to the legs and heart, but to the mind as well; many a problem such as this one I had considered while walking, and though, after talking to Dupin, I still turned out to be mistaken in my thinking, I had at least eliminated a large number of my fallacies of thought before speaking to him.

Outside the apartment, I found the rain had ceased; the wind had picked up, however, and was quite cool, almost chilly. I pulled my collar up against the breeze and, swinging my cane before me, headed in the direction of the lightning fire in the warehouse district along the Rue. I didn't realize I was going there until my legs began to take me. I knew the location well, and no research was required to locate the site of the events, so I thought that for once, having seen the ruins, I might actually have a leg up on Dupin, and what he called his investigative methods of ratiocination.

and swim for it. We had about as much chance of making that swim as passing through the eye of a needle, but it was a might more inviting than Cut Through You. Least that way we had a chance. Me and Jim was both good swimmers, and maybe we could even find a log to push off into the water with us. As for Brer Rabbit, well, he was thinking on going with us and just disappearing when daylight come; that was a thing made me really want to get off that island. If he was willing to go out that way, then that Cut Through You must be some nasty sort of fella. Worse yet, our salt had got all wet and wasn't worth nothing, and we had both lost the cross in our shoes. All we had was those rusty nails on strings, and I didn't have a whole lot of trust in that. I was more comfortable that I still had my little knife in my back pocket.

We was coming down through the woods, and it got so the trees were thinning, and we could see the bank down there, the river churning along furious-like. My heart was starting to beat in an excited way, and about then, things turned to dog doo.

The weasels come down out of the trees on ropes, and a big net come down with them and landed over us. It was weighed down with rocks, and there wasn't no time to get out from under it before they was tugging it firm around us, and we was bagged up tighter than a strand of gut packed with sausage makings.

As we was laying there, out of the woods come Brer Fox and Brer Bear. They come right over to us. The fox bent down, and he looked Brer Rabbit in the eye. He grinned and showed his teeth.

His breath was so sour we could smell it from four feet away; it smelled like death warmed over and gone cold again.

Up close, I could see things I couldn't see before in the night.

He had fish scales running along the side of his face, and when he breathed there were flaps that flared out on his cheeks; they was gills, like a fish.

I looked up at Brer Bear. There were sores all over his body, and bits of fish heads and fish tails poking out of him like moles. He was

I will not name the exact place, due to this area having recently been renovated, and keep in mind these events took place some years back, so there is no need to besmirch the name of the new owners. But for then, it was an area not considered a wisely traveled pathway by night. It was well known for unsavory characters and poor lighting. That being the case, I was fully aware it was not the best of ideas to be about my business in this vicinity, but what Dupin had said to me was gnawing at my thoughts like a terrier at a rug. I felt reasonably confident that my cane would defend me, as I am—if I say so myself—like Dupin, quite skilled in the art of the cane, and if I should be set upon by more than one ruffian, it contained a fine sword that could help trim my attackers' numbers.

I came to where the warehouse section lay, and found the burned buildings instantly, not far from a large allotment of land where other warehouses were still maintained. I stood for a moment in front of the burned section, going over it with eyes and mind. What remained were blackened shells and teetering lumber; the rain had stirred the charred shambles and the stench of it filled and itched my nostrils.

I walked along the pathway in front of it, and tried to imagine where the fire had started, determining that the areas where the structure of the buildings were most ruined might be the source. I could imagine that the fire jumped from those ruined remains to the other buildings, which, though burned beyond use, were still more structurally sound, suggesting that the fire had raged hottest before it reached them.

I was contemplating all of this when from the ruins I heard a noise, and saw a shape rise up from the earth clothed in hat and overcoat. It was some distance away from me, and even as it rose, it paused for a moment, looking down in the manner of a man who has dropped pocket change.

I can't explain exactly why I thought I should engage, but I immediately set off in that direction, and called out to it. As I neared, the shape looked up, seeing me. I took note of the fact that it carried something, clutched tightly to it, and that this undefined individual was in a kind of panic; it began to run. I wondered then if it might be a thief, looking for some surviving relic that could be swapped or sold, and part of its loot had been dropped when it came up from wherever it had been lurking, and before it could be found, I had startled the prowler.

I took it upon myself to call out again, and when I did, the shape ceased to run, turned and looked at me. I was overcome with fear and awe, for I was certain, even though the being stood back in the shadows, wore an overcoat and had the brim of a hat pulled down tight over its face, that staring back at me was some kind of hairy upright ape clutching a bagged burden to its breast.

Unconsciously, I lifted the shaft of my walking stick and revealed an inch of the hidden sword. The beast—for I can think of it no other way—turned, and once more proceeded to run, its hat blowing off as it went. In a flash, it disappeared behind one of the standing warehouses. I remained where I was for a moment, rooted to the spot, and then, overcome with curiosity, I pursued it, running through the burnt lumber, on out into the clearing that led to the street where I had seen the beast standing. As I turned the corner, I found it waiting for me. It had dropped the bag at its feet, and was lifting up a large garbage container that was dripping refuse.

I was granted a glimpse of its teeth and fiery eyes just before it threw the receptacle at me. I was able to duck, just in time, and as the container clattered along the cobblestones behind me, the thing grabbed up its bag, broke and ran toward a warehouse wall. I knew then I had it trapped, but considering that what it had thrown at me was heavier than anything I could lift, perhaps it would be I who was trapped. These thoughts were there, but my forward motion and determination succeeded in trampling my common sense.

As I came near it again, my previous astonishment was nothing compared to what I witnessed now. The creature divested itself of the overcoat, slung the bag over its shoulder, and with one hand grasped a drainpipe and, using its feet to assist, began to climb effortlessly upwards until it reached the summit of the warehouse. I watched in bewilderment as it moved across the rain-misted night-line, then raced out of sight down the opposite side of the warehouse wall, or so I suspected when it was no longer visible.

I darted down an alley, splashing in puddles as I went, and came to the edge of the warehouse where I was certain the ape-man had descended. Before me was a narrow, wet street, the R, but the ape-man was not in sight.

I leaned against the wall of the warehouse, for at this point in time I needed support, the reality of what I had just witnessed finally sinking into my bones. I momentarily tried to convince myself that I had been suffering the effects of the wine Dupin and I had drunk, but knew this was wishful thinking. I drew the sword from the cane, and strolled down the R in search of the ape, but saw nothing, and frankly was glad of it, having finally had time to consider how close I may have come to disaster.

Replacing the sword in its housing, I walked back to the ruins of the warehouse. Using my cane to move burnt lumber about, throwing up a light cloud of damp ash, I examined the spot where I had seen the thing pulling something from the rubble; that's when I found the arm, severed at the elbow, lying on top of the ash. It had no doubt been dropped there after the fire, for it appeared uncharred, not even smoke-damaged. I knelt down and struck a Lucifer against the tip of the cane, then held it close. It was a small arm with a delicate hand. I looked about and saw that nearby were a series of steps that dipped beneath ground level. It seemed obvious this was where the creature had originated when it appeared to rise out of the very earth. It also seemed obvious this opening had been covered by the collapse of the warehouse, and that the creature had uncovered it and retrieved something from below and tucked it away in the large bag it was carrying. The obvious thing appeared to be body parts, for if he had dropped one, then perhaps others existed and were tucked away in its bag.

I lit another Lucifer, went down the narrow steps into the basement, waved my flickering light so that it threw small shadows about. The area below was larger than I would have expected. It was filled with tables and crates, and what I determined to be laboratory equipment— test tubes, beakers, burners, and the like. I had to light several matches to complete my examination—though *complete* is a loose word, considering I could only see by the small fluttering of a meager flame.

I came upon an open metal container, about the size of a coffin and was startled as I dipped the match into its shadowy interior. I found two human heads contained within, as well as an assortment of amputated legs, arms, feet, and hands, all of them submerged in water.

I jerked back with such revulsion that the match went out. I scrambled about for another, only to discover I had used my entire store. Using what little moonlight was tumbling down the basement stairs as my guide, and almost in a panic, I ran up them and practically leapt into the open. There was more moonlight now than before. The rain had passed and the clouds had sailed; it was a mild relief.

Fearing the ape, or whatever it was, might return, and considering what I had found below, I hurried away from there.

I should have gone straight to the police, but having had dealings with the Police Prefect, G, I was less than enthusiastic about the matter. Neither Dupin nor myself were well liked in the halls of the law for the simple reason Dupin had solved a number of cases the police had been unable to, thereby making them look foolish. It was they who came to us in time of need, not us to them. I hastened my steps back to the apartment, only to be confronted by yet another oddity. The moon was turning to blood. Or so it appeared, for a strange crimson cloud, the likes of which I had never before seen, or even heard of, was enveloping the moon, as if it were a vanilla biscuit tucked away in a bloody-red sack. The sight of it caused me deep discomfort.

It was late when I arrived at our lodgings. Dupin was sitting by candle-light, still reading. He had a stack of books next to him on the table, and when I came in he lifted his eyes as I lit the gas lamp by the doorway to further illuminate the apartment. I was nearly breathless, and when I turned to expound on my adventures, Dupin said, "I see you have been to the site of the warehouses, an obvious deduction by the fact that your pants and boots are dusted heavily in ash and soot and are damp from the rain. I see too that you have discovered body parts in the wreckage. I will also conjecture we can ignore having a discussion with the lightning witnesses, for you have made some progress on your own."

My mouth fell open. "How could you know that I discovered body parts?"

"Logic. The newspaper account spoke of such a thing, and you come rushing in the door, obviously excited, even a little frightened. So if a severed arm was found there the other day, it stands to reason that you too discovered something of that nature. That is a bit of speculation, I admit, but it seems a fair analysis."

I sat down in a chair. "It is accurate, but I have seen one thing that you cannot begin to decipher, and it is more fantastic than even severed body parts."

"An ape that ran upright?"

"Impossible!" I exclaimed. "You could not possibly know."

"But I did." Dupin paused a moment, lit his pipe. He seemed only mildly curious. "Continue."

It took me a moment to collect myself, but finally I began to reveal my adventures.

"It was carrying a package of some kind. I believe it contained body parts because I found an arm lying in the burned wreckage, as you surmised. Something I believe the ape dropped."

"Male or female?" Dupin said.

"What?"

"The arm, male or female?"

I thought for a moment.

"I suppose it was female. I didn't give it considerable evaluation, dark as it was, surprised as I was. But I would venture to guess—and a guess is all I am attempting—that it was female."

"That is interesting," Dupin said. "And the ape?"

"You mean was the ape male or female?"

"Exactly," Dupin said.

"What difference does it make?"

"Perhaps none. Was it clothed?"

"A hat and overcoat. Both of which it abandoned."

"In that case, could you determine its sex?" Dupin asked.

"I suppose since no external male equipment was visible, it was most probably female."

"And it saw you?"

"Yes. It ran from me. I pursued. It climbed to the top of a warehouse with its bag, did so effortlessly, and disappeared on the other side of the building. Prior to that, it tried to hit me with a trash receptacle. A large and heavy one it lifted as easily as you lift your pipe."

"Obviously it failed in this endeavor," Dupin commented. "How long did it take you to get to the other side of the warehouse, as I am presuming you made careful examination there as well?"

"*Hasty* would be a better word. By then I had become concerned for my own safety. I suppose it took the creature less than five minutes to go over the roof."

"Did you arrive there quickly? The opposite side of the building, I mean?"

"Yes. You could say that."

"And the ape was no longer visible?"

"Correct."

"That is quite rapid, even for an animal, don't you think?"

"Indeed," I said, having caught the intent of Dupin's question.

"Which implies it did not necessarily run away, or even descend to the other side. I merely presumed."

"Now you see the error of your thinking."

"But you've made presumptions tonight," I said.

"Perhaps, but more reasonable presumptions than yours, I am certain. It is my impression that your simian is still in the vicinity, and did not scale the warehouse merely to climb down the other side and run down the street, when it could just as easily have taken the alley you used. And if the creature did climb down the other side, I believe it concealed itself. You might have walked right by it."

That gave me a shiver. "I admit that is logical, but I also admit that I didn't walk all that far for fear that it might be lurking about."

"That seems fair enough," Dupin said.

"There is something else," I said, and I told him about the basement and the body parts floating in water in the casement. I mentioned the red cloud that lay thick against the moon.

When I finished, he nodded, as if my presentation was the most normal event in the world. Thunder crashed then, lightning ripped across the sky, and rain began to hammer the street; a rain far more vigorous than earlier in the evening. For all his calm, when Dupin spoke, I thought I detected the faintest hint of concern.

"You say the moon was red?"

"A red cloud was over it. I have never seen such a thing before. At first I thought it a trick of the eye."

"It is not," Dupin said. "I should tell you about something I have researched while you were out chasing ape-women and observing the odd redness of the night's full moon, an event that suggests things are far more desperate than I first suspected."

I had seated myself by this time, had taken up my own pipe, and with nervous hand, found matches to light it.

Dupin broke open one of the books near the candle. "I thought I had read of that kind of electric blue lightning before, and the severed limbs also struck a chord of remembrance, as did the ape, which is why I was able to determine what you had seen, and that gives even further credence to my suspicions. Johann Conrad Dipple."

"Who?"

"Dipple. He was born in Germany in the late sixteen hundreds. He was a philosopher and something of a theologian. He was also considered a heretic, as his views on religion were certainly outside the lines of normal society."

"The same might be said of us," I remarked.

Dupin nodded. "True. But Dipple was thought to be an alchemist and a dabbler in the dark arts. He was in actuality a man of science. He was also an expert on all manner of ancient documents. He is known today for the creation of Dipple's oil, which is used in producing a dye we know as Prussian blue, but he also claimed to have invented an elixir of life. He lived for a time in Germany at a place known as Castle Frankenstein. This is where many of his experiments were performed, including one that led to such a tremendous explosion, it destroyed a tower of the castle, and led to a breaking of his lease. It was said by those who witnessed the explosion that a kind of lightning, a blue-white lightning, lifted up from the stones to the sky, followed by a burst of flame and an explosion that tore the turret apart and rained stones down on the countryside."

"So that is why you were so interested in the lightning, the story about it rising up from the warehouse instead of falling out of the sky?"

Dupin nodded, relit his pipe and continued. "It was rumored that he was attempting to transfer the souls of the living into freshly exhumed corpses. Exhumed clandestinely, by the way. He was said to use a funnel by which the souls of the living could be channeled into the bodies of the dead."

"Ridiculous," I said.

"Perhaps," Dupin replied. "It was also said his experiments caused the emergence of a blue-white lightning that he claimed to have pulled from a kind of borderland, and that he was able to open a path to this netherworld by means of certain mathematical formulas gleaned from what he called a renowned, rare, and accursed book. For this he was branded a devil worshiper, an interloper with demonic forces."

"Dupin," I said. "You have always ridiculed the supernatural."

"I did not say it was supernatural. I said he was a scientist that was branded as a demonologist. What intrigues me is his treatise titled *Maladies and Remedies of the Life of the Flesh*, as well as the mention of even rarer books and documents within it. One that was of special interest was called *The Necronomicon*, a book that was thought by many to be mythical."

"You have seen such a book?"

"I discovered it in the Paris library some years ago. It was pointed out to me by the historian M. No one at the library was aware of its significance, not even M. He knew only of its name and that it held some historical importance. He thought it may have something to do with witchcraft, which it does not. I was surprised to find it there. I considered it to be more than a little intriguing. It led me to further investigations into Dipple as not only the owner of such a book, but as a vivisectionist and a resurrectionist. He claimed to have discovered a formula that would allow him to live for 135 years, and later amended this to eternal life."

"Drivel," I said. "I am surprised you would concern yourself with such."

"It was his scientific method and deep understanding of mathematics that interested me. My dear friend, much of what has become acceptable science was first ridiculed as heresy. I need not point out to you the long list of scientists opposed by the Catholic Church and labeled heretics. The points of interest concerning Dipple have to do with what I have already told you about the similarity of the blue-white lightning, and the interesting connection with the found body parts, the ape, and the curious event of the blood-stained moon, which I will come back to shortly. Firstly however, was Dipple's mention of the rare book. *The Necronomicon*, written by Abdul Alhazred in AD 950, partially in math equations and partly in verse. He was sometimes referred to as 'the Mad Arab' by his detractors, though he was also given the moniker of 'Arab Poet of Yemen' by those less vicious. Of course, knowing my penchant for poetry, you might readily surmise that this is what first drew my attention to him. The other aspect of his personality, as mathematician and conjuror, was merely, at that time, of side interest, although I must say that later in life he certainly did go mad. He claimed to have discovered mathematical equations that could be used to open our world into another where powerful forces and beings existed. Not gods or demons, mind you, but different and true life forms that he called 'the Old Ones.' It was in this book that Dipple believed he found the key to eternal life."

"What became of Dipple?"

"He died," Dupin said, and smiled.

"So much for eternal life."

"Perhaps."

"Perhaps? You clearly said he died."

"His body died, but his assistant, who was imprisoned for a time, said his soul was passed on to another form. According to what little documentation there is on the matter, Dipple's experiments were concerned with removing a person's soul from a living form and transferring it to a corpse. It was successful, if his assistant, Hans Grimm can be believed. Grimm was a relative of Jacob Grimm, the future creator of Grimm's Fairy Tales. But of more immediate interest to us is something he reported, that a young lady Dipple was charmed by, and who he thought would be his companion, took a fall from a horse and was paralyzed. Grimm claimed they successfully transferred her soul from her ruined body into the corpse of a recently dead young lady, who had been procured by what one might call 'midnight gardening.' She was 'animated with life,' as Grimm described her, 'but was always of some strangeness.' That is a direct quote."

"Dupin, surely you don't take this nonsense seriously."

He didn't seem to hear me. "She was disgusted with her new form and was quoted by Grimm as saying 'she felt as if she was inside a house with empty rooms.' She leaped to her death from Castle Frankenstein. Lost to him, Dipple decided to concentrate on a greater love—himself. Being short of human volunteers who wanted to evacuate their soul and allow a visitor to inhabit their living form, he turned to animals for experimentation. The most important experiment was the night he died, or so says Grimm."

"The ancestor of the creator of Grimm's Fairy Tales seems an unlikely person to trust on matters of this sort."

"That could be. But during this time Dipple was having exotic animals shipped to him in Germany, and among these was a creature called a chimpanzee. Knowing himself sickly, and soon to die, he put his experiments to the ultimate test. He had his assistant, Grimm, by use of the formula and his funnel, transfer his soul from his disintegrating shell into the animal, which in turn eliminated the soul of the creature; the ape's body became the house of his soul. I should add that I have some doubts about the existence of a soul, so perhaps *essence* would be a more appropriate word. That said, *soul* has a nice sound to it, I think. The experiment, according to Grimm, resulted in an abundance of blue-white lightning that caused the explosion and left Grimm injured. In fact, later Grimm disappeared from the hospital where he was being held under observation, and arrest for alchemy. He was in a room with padded walls and a barred window. The bars were ripped out. It was determined the bars were pulled loose from the outside. Another curious matter was that the room in which he was contained was three floors up, a considerable drop. How did he get down without being injured? No rope or ladder was found. It was as if he had been carried away by something unknown."

"Come, Dupin, you cannot be serious? Are you suggesting this ape pulled out the bars and carried him down the side of the wall?"

"There are certainly more than a few points of similarity between the story of Dipple and the events of tonight, don't you think? Consider your description of how effortlessly the ape climbed the warehouse wall."

"But, if this is Dipple, and he is in Paris, my question is how? And his ape body would be old. Very old."

"If he managed eternal life by soul transference, then perhaps the ape body does not age as quickly as would be normal."

"If this were true, and I'm not saying I believe it, how would he go about his life? An ape certainly could not ride the train or stroll the street without being noticed."

"I am of the opinion that Grimm is still with him."

"But he would be very old as well."

"Considerably," Dupin agreed. "I believe that the body parts you saw are for Grimm. It is my theory that Grimm received a wound that put him near death when Castle Frankenstein blew up. Dipple saved him by transferring his soul to a corpse. Unlike Dipple's lady love, he managed to accept the transfer and survived."

"So why did Dipple go after the body parts himself? Wouldn't he have Grimm procure such things? It would be easier for the one with a human body to move about without drawing so much attention."

"It would. My take is that the human soul when transferred to the soul of a corpse has one considerable drawback. The body rots. The ape body was a living body. It does not; it may age, but not in the way it would otherwise due to this transformation. Grimm's body, on the other hand, has to be repaired from time to time with fresh parts. It may be that he was further damaged by the more recent explosion. Which indicates to me that they have not acquired the healthy ability to learn from their mistakes."

"After all this time, wouldn't Dipple have transferred Grimm's essence, or his own, into a living human being? Why would he maintain the body of an ape? And a female ape at that?"

"My thought on the matter is that Dipple may find the powerful body of an ape to his advantage. And to keep Grimm bent to his will, to maintain him as a servant, he only repairs him when he wears out a part, so to speak. Be it male or female parts, it is a matter of availability. If Grimm's soul were transferred into a living creature, and he could live for eternity, as male or female, then he might be willing to abandon Dipple. This way, with the ape's strength, and Dipple's knowledge of how to repair a corpse, and perhaps the constant promise of eventually giving Grimm a living human body, he keeps him at his side. Grimm knows full well if he leaves Dipple he will eventually rot. I think this is the Sword of Damocles that he holds over Grimm's head."

"That is outrageous," I said. "And wicked."

"Absolutely, but that does not make it untrue."

I felt cold. My pipe had died, as I had forgotten to smoke it. I relit it. "It's just too extraordinary," I said.

"Yet *The Necronomicon* suggests it is possible." With that, Dupin dug into the pile of books and produced a large volume, thrusting it into my hands. Looking at it, I saw that it was covered in leather, and that in the dead center was an eye-slit. I knew immediately that what I was looking at was the tanned skin of a human face. Worse, holding the book I felt nauseated. It was as if its very substance was made of bile. I managed to open the book. There was writing in Arabic, as well as a number of mathematical formulas; the words and numbers appeared to crawl. I slammed the book shut again. "Take it back," I said, and practically tossed it at him.

"I see you are bewildered, old friend," Dupin said, "but do keep in mind, as amazing as this sounds, it's science we are talking about, not the supernatural."

"It's a revolting book," I said.

"When I first found it in the library, I could only look at it for short periods of time. I had to become accustomed to it, like becoming acclimated to sailing at sea, and no longer suffering sea sickness. I am ashamed to admit that after a short time I stole the book. I felt somehow justified in doing this, it being rarely touched by anyone—for good reason, as you have experienced—and in one way I thought I might be doing the world a justice, hiding it away from the wrong eyes and hands. That was several years ago. I have studied Arabic, read the volume repeatedly, and already being reasonably versed in mathematics, rapidly began to understand the intent of it. Though, until reading the newspaper account, I had been skeptical. And then there is Dipple's history, the words of his companion, Grimm. I believe there is logic behind these calculations and ruminations, even if at first they seem to defy human comprehension. The reason for this is simple; it is not the logic of humans, but that of powerful beings who exist in the borderland. I have come to uncomfortably understand some of that logic, as much as is humanly possible to grasp. To carry this even farther, I say that Dipple is no longer himself, in not only body, but in thought. His constant tampering with the powers of the borderland have given the beings on the other side an entry into his mind, and they are learning to control him, to assist him in his desires, until their own plans come to fruition. It has taken time, but soon, he will not only be able to replace body parts, he will be capable of opening the gate to this borderland. We are fortunate he has not managed it already. These monsters are powerful, as powerful as any god man can create, and malicious without measure. When the situation is right, when Dipple's mind completely succumbs to theirs, and he is willing to use the formulas and spells to clear the path for their entry, they will cross over and claim this world. That will be the end of humankind, my friend. And let me tell you the thing I have been holding back. The redness of the moon is an indication that there is a rip in the fabric of that which protects us from these horrid things lying in wait. Having wasted their world to nothing, they lust after ours, and Dipple is opening the gate so they might enter."

"But how would Dipple profit from that? Allowing such things into our world?"

"Perhaps he has been made promises of power, whispers in his head that make him outrageous offers. Perhaps he is little more than a tool by now. All that matters, good friend, is that we cannot allow him to continue his work."

"If the red cloud over the moon is a sign, how much time do we have?"

"Let me put it this way: We will not wait until morning, and we will not need to question either the boy or the man who saw the lightning. By that time, I believe it will be too late."

There was a part of me that wondered if Dupin's studies had affected his mind. It wasn't an idea that held, however. I had seen what I had seen, and what Dupin had told me seemed to validate it. We immediately set out on our escapade, Dupin carrying a small bag slung over one shoulder by a strap.

The rain had blown itself out and the streets were washed clean. The air smelled as fresh as the first breath of life. We went along the streets briskly, swinging our canes, pausing only to look up at the moon. The red cloud was no longer visible, but there was still a scarlet tint to the moon that seemed unnatural. Sight of that gave even more spring to my step. When we arrived at our destination, there was no one about, and the ashes had been settled by the rain.

"Keep yourself alert," Dupin said, "in case our simian friend has returned and is in the basement collecting body parts."

We crossed the wet soot, stood at the mouth of the basement, and after a glance around to verify no one was in sight, we descended.

Red-tinged moonlight slipped down the stairs and brightened the basement. Everything was as it was the night before. Dupin looked about, used his cane to tap gently at a few of the empty beakers and tubes. He then made his way to the container where I had seen the amputated limbs and decapitated heads. They were still inside, more than a bit of rainwater having flooded into the casement, and there was a ripe stench of decaying flesh.

"These would no longer be of use to Dipple," Dupin said. "So we need not worry about him coming back for them."

I showed him where I had last seen the ape, then we walked to the other side. Dupin looked up and down the wall of the warehouse. We walked along its length. Nothing was found.

"Perhaps we should find a way to climb to the top," I said.

Dupin was staring at a puff of steam rising from the street. "No, I don't think so," he said.

He hastened to where the steam was thickest. It was rising up from a grate. He used his cane to pry at it, and I used mine to assist him. We lifted it and looked down at the dark, mist-coated water of the sewer rushing below. The stench was, to put it mildly, outstanding.

"This would make sense," Dupin said. "You were correct, he did indeed climb down on this side, but he disappeared quickly because he had an underground path."

"We're going down there?" I asked.

"You do wish to save the world and our cosmos, do you not?"

"When you put it that way, I suppose we must," I said. I was trying to add a joking atmosphere to the events, but it came out as serious as a diagnosis of leprosy.

We descended into the dark, resting our feet upon the brick ledge of the sewer. There was light from above to assist us, but if we were to move forward, we would be walking along the slick, brick runway into utter darkness. Or so I thought.

It was then that Dupin produced twists of paper, heavily oiled and waxed, from the pack he was carrying. As he removed them, I saw *The Necronomicon* was in the bag as well. It lay next to two dueling pistols. I had been frightened before, but somehow, seeing that dreadful book and those weapons, I was almost overwhelmed with terror, a sensation I would experience more than once that night. It was all I could do to take one of the twists and wait for Dupin to light it, for my mind was telling me to climb out of that dank hole and run. But if Dipple succeeded in letting the beings from the borderland through, run to where?

"Here," Dupin said, holding the flaming twist close to the damp brick wall. "It went this way."

I looked. A few coarse hairs were caught in the bricks.

With that as our guide, we proceeded. Even with the lit twists of wax and oil, the light was dim and there was a steam, or mist, rising from the sewer. We had to proceed slowly and carefully. The sewer rumbled along near us, heightened to near flood level by the tremendous rain. It was ever to our right, threatening to wash up over the walk. There were drips from the brick walls and the overhead streets. Each time a cold drop fell down my collar I started, as if icy fingertips had touched my neck.

We had gone a good distance when Dupin said, "Look. Ahead."

There was a pumpkin-colored glow from around a bend in the sewer, and we immediately tossed our twists into the water. Dupin produced the pistols from his bag, and gave me one.

"I presume they are powder-charged and loaded," I said.

"Of course," Dupin replied, "did you think I might want to beat an ape to death with the grips?"

Thus armed, we continued onward toward the light.

There was a widening of the sewer, and there was in fact a great space made of brick that I presumed might be for workmen, or might even have been a forgotten portion of the sewer that had once been part of the upper streets of Paris. There were several lamps placed here and there, some hung on nails driven into the brick, others placed on the flooring, some on rickety tables and chairs. It was a makeshift laboratory, and had most likely been thrown together from the ruins of the warehouse explosion.

On a tilted board a nude woman—or a man, or a little of both, was strapped. Its head was male, but the rest of its body was female, except for the feet, which were absurdly masculine. This body breathed in a labored manner, its head was thrown back, and a funnel was stuck down its throat. A hose rose out of the funnel and stretched to another makeshift platform nearby. There was a thin, insect-like antenna attached to the middle of the hose, and it wiggled erratically at the air.

The other platform held a cadaverously thin and nude human with a head that looked shriveled, the hair appearing as if it were a handful of strings fastened there with paste. The arms and legs showed heavy scarring, and it was obvious that much sewing had been done to secure the limbs, much like the hurried repair of an old rag doll. The lifeless head was tilted back, and the opposite end of the hose was shoved into another wooden funnel that was jammed into the corpse's mouth. One arm of the cadaver was short, the other long, while the legs varied in thickness. The lower half of the face was totally incongruous with the upper half. The features were sharp-boned and stood up beneath the flesh like rough furniture under a sheet. They were masculine, while the forehead and hairline, ragged as it was, had obviously been that of a woman, one recently dead and elderly was my conjecture.

The center of the corpse was blocked by the body of the ape, which was sewing hastily with a large needle and dark thread, fastening on an ankle and foot in the way you might lace up a shoe. It was so absurd, so grotesque, it was almost comic, like a grisly play at the Theatre of the Grand Guignol. One thing was clear, the corpse being sewn together was soon to house the life force of the other living, but obviously ill body. It had been cobbled together in the past in much the same way that the other was now being prepared.

Dupin pushed me gently into a darkened corner protected by a partial brick wall. We spoke in whispers.

"What are we waiting for?" I said.

"The borderland to be opened."

Of course I knew to what he referred, but it seemed to me that waiting for it to be opened, if indeed that was to happen, seemed like the height of folly. But it was Dupin, and now, arriving here, seeing what I was seeing, it all fit securely with the theory he had expounded; I decided to continue believing he knew of what he spoke. Dupin withdrew *The Necronomicon* from the bag, propped it against the wall.

"When I tell you," he said, "light up a twist and hold it so that I might read."

"From that loathsome book?" I gasped.

"It has the power to do evil, but also to restrain it."

I nodded, took one of the twists from the bag and a few matches and tucked them into my coat pocket. It was then I heard the chanting, and peeked carefully around the barrier.

The ape, or Dipple, I suppose, held a copy of a book that looked to be a twin of the one Dupin held. It was open and propped on a make-shift pedestal of two stacked chairs. Dipple was reading from it by dim lamplight. It was disconcerting to hear those chants coming from the mouth of an ape, sounding human-like, yet touched with the vocalizations of an animal. Though he spoke the words quickly and carefully, it was clear to me that he was more than casually familiar with them.

That was when the air above the quivering antenna opened in a swirl of light and dark floundering shapes. I can think of no other way to describe it. The opening widened. Tentacles whipped in and out of the gap. Blue-white lightning flashed from it and nearly struck the ape, but still he read. The corpse on the platform began to writhe and wiggle and the blue-white lightning leaped from the swirling mass and struck the corpse repeatedly and vibrated the antenna. The dead body glowed and heaved and tugged at its bonds, and then I saw its eyes flash wide. Across the way, the formerly living body had grown limp and gray as ash.

I looked at Dupin, who had come to my shoulder to observe what was happening.

"He is not bringing him back, as in the past," Dupin said. "He is offering Grimm's soul for sacrifice. After all this time, their partnership has ended. It is the beginning; the door has been opened a crack."

My body felt chilled. The hair on my head, as on Dupin's, stood up due to the electrical charge in the air. There was an obnoxious smell, reminiscent of the stink of decaying fish, rotting garbage, and foul disease.

"Yes, we have chosen the right moment," Dupin said, looking at the growing gap that had appeared in mid-air. "Take both pistols, and light the twist."

He handed me his weapon. I stuck both pistols in the waistband of my trousers, and lit the twist. Dupin took it from me, and stuck it in a gap in the bricks. He opened *The Necronomicon* to where he had marked it with a torn piece of paper, and began to read from it. The words poured from his mouth like living beings, taking on the form of dark shadows and lightning-bright color. His voice was loud and sonorous, as we were no longer attempting to conceal ourselves. I stepped out of the shadows and into the open. Dipple, alerted by Dupin's reading, turned and glared at me with his dark, simian eyes.

It was hard for me to concentrate on anything. Hearing the words from *The Necronomicon* made my skin feel as if it were crawling up from my heels, across my legs and back, and slithering underneath my scalp. The swirling gap of blue-white lightning revealed lashing tentacles, a massive squid-like eye, then a beak. It was all I could do not to fall to my knees in dread, or bolt and run like an asylum escapee.

That said, I was given courage when I realized that whatever Dupin was doing was having some effect, for the gash in the air began to shimmer and wrinkle and blink like an eye. The ape howled at this development, for it had glanced back at the rip in the air, then turned again to look at me, twisted its face into what could almost pass as a dark knot. It dropped the book on the chair and rushed for me. First it charged upright, like a human, then it was on all fours, its knuckles pounding against the bricks.

I drew my sword from the cane, held the cane itself in my left hand, the blade in my right, and awaited Dipple's dynamic charge.

It bounded towards me. I thrust at it with my sword. The strike was good, hitting no bone, and went directly through the ape's chest, but the beast's momentum drove me backwards. I lost the cane itself, and used both hands to hold the sword in place. I glanced at Dupin for help. None was forthcoming. He was reading from the book and utterly ignoring my plight.

Blue, white, red, and green fire danced around Dipple's head and poured from his mouth. I was able to hold the monster back with the sword, for it was a good thrust, and had brought about a horrible wound, yet its long arms thrashed out and hit my jaw, nearly knocking me senseless. I struggled to maintain consciousness, pushed back the sword with both hands, coiled my legs, and kicked out at the ape. I managed to knock him off me, but only for a moment.

I sat up and drew both pistols. It was loping towards me, pounding its fists against the bricks as it barreled along on all fours, letting forth an indescribable and ear-shattering sound that was neither human nor animal. I let loose an involuntary yell, and fired both pistols. The shots rang out as one. The ape threw up its hands, wheeled about and staggered back toward the stacked chairs, the book. It grabbed at the book for support, pulled that and the chairs down on top of it. Its chest heaved as though pumped with a bellows.

And then the freshly animated thing on the platform spat out the funnel as if it were light as air. Spat it out and yelled. It was a sound that came all the way from the primeval; a savage cry of creation. The body on the platform squirmed and writhed and snapped its bonds. It slid from the board, staggered forward, looked in my direction. Both pistols had been fired; the sword was still in Dipple. I grabbed up the hollow cane that had housed the sword, to use as a weapon.

This thing, this patchwork creation I assumed was Grimm, its private parts wrapped in a kind of swaddling, took one step in my direction, the blue-white fire crackling in its eyes, and then the patchwork creature turned to see the blinking eye staring out of the open door to the borderlands.

Grimm yanked the chairs off Dipple, lifted the ape-body up as easily as if it had been a feather pillow. It spread its legs wide for position, cocked its arms, and flung the ape upwards. The whirlpool from beyond sucked at Dipple, turning the old man in the old ape's body into a streak of dark fur, dragging it upwards. In that moment, Dipple was taken by those from beyond the borderland, pulled into their world like a hungry mouth taking in a tasty treat. Grimm, stumbling about on unfamiliar legs, grabbed *The Necronomicon* and tossed it at the wound in the air.

All this activity had not distracted Dupin from his reading. Still he chanted. There was a weak glow from behind the brick wall. I stumbled over there, putting a hand against the wall to hold myself up. When Dupin read the last passage with an oratory flourish, the air was sucked out of the room and out of my lungs. I gasped for breath, fell to the floor, momentarily unconscious. Within a heartbeat the air came back, and with it, that horrid rotting smell, then as instantly as it arrived, it was gone.

The air smelled only of foul sewer, which, considering the stench of what had gone before, was in that moment as pleasant and welcome as a young Parisian lady's perfume.

There was a flare of a match as Dupin rose from the floor where he, like me, had fallen. He lit a twist from the bag and held it up. There was little that we could see. Pulling the sword from his cane, he trudged forward with the light, and I followed. In its illumination we saw Grimm.

Or what was left of him. The creatures of the borderlands had not only taken Dipple and his *Necronomicon*, they had ripped Grimm into a dozen pieces and plastered him across the ceiling and along the wall like an exploded dumpling.

"Dipple failed," Dupin said. "And Grimm finished him off. And the Old Ones took him before they were forced to retreat."

"At least one of those terrible books has been destroyed," I said.

"I think we should make it two," Dupin said.

We broke up the chairs and used the greasy twists of paper we still had, along with the bag itself, and started a fire. The chair wood was old and rotten and caught fast, crackling and snapping as it burned. On top of this Dupin placed the remaining copy of *The Necronomicon*. The book was slow to catch, but when it did, the cover blew open and the pages flared. The eye hole in the cover filled with a gold pupil, a long black slit for an iris. It blinked once, then the fire claimed it. The pages flapped like a bird, lifted upward with a howling noise, before collapsing into a burst of black ash.

Standing there, we watched as the ash dissolved into the bricks like black snow on a warm windowpane.

I took a deep breath. "No regrets about the book?"

"Not after glimpsing what lay beyond," Dupin said. "I understand Dipple's curiosity, and though mine is considerable, it is not that strong."

"I don't even know what I saw," I said, "but whatever it was, whatever world the Old Ones live in, I could sense in that void every kind of evil I have ever known or suspected, and then some. I know you don't believe in fate, Dupin, but it's as if we were placed here to stop Dipple, to be present when Grimm had had enough of Dipple's plans."

"Nonsense," Dupin said. "Coincidence. As I said before. More common than you think. And had I not been acquainted with that horrid book, and Dipple's writings, we would have gone to bed to awake to a world we could not understand, and one in which we would not long survive. I should add that this is one adventure of ours that you might want to call fiction, and confine it to a magazine of melodrama; if you should write of it at all."

We went along the brick pathway then, with one last lit paper twist we had saved for light. It burned out before we made it back, but we were able to find our way by keeping in touch with the wall, finally arriving where moonlight spilled through the grating we had replaced upon entering the sewer. When we were on the street, the world looked strange, as if bathed in a bloody light, and that gave me pause. Looking up, we saw that a scarlet cloud was flowing in front of the sinking moon. The cloud was thick, and for a moment it covered the face of the moon completely. Then the cloud passed and faded and the sky was clear and tinted silver with the common light of stars and moon.

I looked at Dupin.

"It's quite all right," he said. "A last remnant of the borderland. Its calling card has been taken away."

"You're sure?"

"As sure as I can be," he said.

With that, we strolled homeward, the moon and the stars falling down behind the city of Paris. As we went, the sun rose, bloomed red, but a different kind of red to the cloud that had covered the moon; warm and inspiring, a bright badge of normalcy, that from here on out I knew was a lie.

This one hopped out of my head like an evil kangaroo. I was asked to write a story for an anthology about a lost world, or a lost place as the background, and this story came to me immediately. Some time later it became an animated episode in the second season of Love, Death, and Robots. *The first season used two other stories of mine, "The Dump" and "Fish Night." "The Tall Grass" is similar to a title Stephen King and Joe Hill used for a story, but mine came first and is nothing like theirs.*

THE TALL GRASS

I CAN'T REALLY EXPLAIN this properly, but I'll tell it to you, and you can make the best of it. It starts with a train. People don't travel as readily by train these days as they once did, but in my youthful days they did, and I have to admit that day was some time ago, considering my current, doddering age. It's hard to believe the century has turned, and I have turned with it, as worn out and rusty as those old coal-powered trains.

I am soon to fall off the edge of the cliff into the great darkness, but there was a time when I was young and the world was light. Then there was something that happened to me on a rail line that showed me something I didn't know was there, and since that time, I've never seen the world in exactly the same way.

What I can tell you is this. I was traveling across country by night in a very nice railcar. I had not just a seat on a train but a compartment to myself. A quite comfortable compartment, I might add. I was early into my business career then, having just started with a firm that I ended up working at for twenty-five years. To simplify, I had completed a cross-country business trip, and was on my way home. I wasn't married then, but one of the reasons I was eager to make it back to my hometown was a young woman named Ellen. We were quite close, and her company meant everything to me. It was our plan to marry.

I won't bore you with details, but that particular plan didn't work out.

And though I still think of that with some disappointment, for she was very beautiful, it has absolutely nothing to do with my story.

Thing is, the train was crossing the western country, in a barren stretch without towns, beneath a wide-open night sky with a high moon and a few crawling clouds. Back then, those kinds of places were far more common than lights and streets and motorcars are now. I had made the same ride several times on business, yet I always enjoyed looking out the window, even at night. This night, however, for whatever reason, I was up very late, unable to sleep. I had chosen not to eat dinner, and now that it was well past, I was a bit hungry, but there was nothing to be had.

The lamps inside the train had been extinguished, and out the window there was a moonlit sea of rocks and sand and in the distance beyond, shadowy blue-black mountains.

The train came to an odd stretch that I had somehow missed before on my journeys, as I was probably sleeping at the time. It was a great expanse of prairie grass, and it shifted in the moonlight like waves of gold-green seawater pulled by the tide making forces of the moon.

I was watching all of this, trying to figure it, determining how odd it looked and how often I had to have passed it and had never seen it. Oh, I had seen lots of tall grass, but nothing like this. The grass was not only head high, or higher, it was thick and it had what I can only describe as an unusual look about it, as if I were seeing it with eyes that belonged to someone else. I know how peculiar that sounds, but it's the only way I know how to explain it.

Then the train jerked, as if some great hand had grabbed it. It screeched on the rails and there was a cacophony of sounds before the engine came to a hard stop.

I had no idea what had occurred. I opened the compartment door, though at first the door seemed locked and only gave way with considerable effort. I stepped out in the hallway. No one was there.

Edging along the hallway, I came to the smoking car, but there was no one there either. It seemed the other passengers were in a tight sleep and unaware of our stopping. I walked through the car, sniffing at the remains of tobacco smoke, and opened a door that went out on a connecting platform that was positioned between the smoking car and another passenger car. I looked in the passenger car through the little window at the door. There was no one there. This didn't entirely surprise me, as the train had taken on a very small load of passengers, and many of them, like me, had purchased personal cabins.

I looked out at the countryside and saw there were lights in the distance, beyond the grass, or to be more exact, positioned out in it. It shocked me, because we were in the middle of absolutely nowhere, and the fact that there was a town nearby was a total surprise to me.

I walked to the edge of the platform. There was a folded and hinged metal stair there, and with the toe of my shoe I kicked it, causing it to flip out and extend to the ground.

I climbed down the steps and looked along the rail. There was no one at first, and then there was a light swinging its way toward me, and finally a shadowy shape behind the light. In a moment I saw that it was a rail man, dressed in cap and coat and company trousers.

"You best stay on board, sir," he said.

I could see him clearly now. He was an average-looking man, small in size with an odd walk about him; the sort people who practically live on trains acquire, as do sailors on ships at sea.

"I was just curious," I said. "What has happened?"

"A brief stop," he said. "I suggest you go back inside."

"Is no one else awake?" I said.

"You seem to be it, sir," he said. "I find those that go to sleep before twelve stay that way when this happens."

I thought that a curious answer. I said, "Does it happen often?"

"No. Not really."

"What's wrong? Are there repairs going on?"

"We are building up another head of steam," he said.

"Then surely I have time to step out here and have a smoke in the open air," I said.

"I suppose that's true, sir," he said. "But I wouldn't wander far. Once we're ready to go, we'll go. I'll call for you to get on board, but only a few times, and then we'll go, no matter what. We won't tarry, not here. Not between midnight and two."

And then he went on by me, swinging the light.

I was intrigued by what he had said, about not tarrying. I looked out at the waving grass and the lights, which I now realized were not that far away. I took out my makings and rolled a cigarette and put a match to it and puffed.

I can't really explain what possessed me. The oddness of the moment, I suppose. But I decided it would be interesting to walk out in the tall grass, just to measure its height, and to maybe get a closer look at those lights. I strolled out a ways, and within moments I was deep in the grass. As I walked, the earth sloped downwards and the grass whispered in the wind. When I stopped walking, the grass was over my head, and behind me where the ground was higher, the grass stood tall against the moonlight, like rows of spearheads held high by an army of warriors.

I stood there in the midst of the grass and smoked and listened for activity back at the train, but neither heard the lantern man or the sound of the train getting ready to leave. I relaxed a bit, enjoying the cool night wind and the way it moved through the prairie. I decided to stroll about while I smoked, parting the grass as I went. I could see the lights still, but they always seemed to be farther away than I thought, and my moving in their direction didn't seem to bring me closer; they receded like the horizon.

When I finished my cigarette, I dropped it and put my heel to it, grinding it into the ground, and turned to go back to the train.

I was a bit startled to discover I couldn't find the path I had taken. Surely, the grass had been bent or pushed aside by my passing, but there was no sign of it. It had quickly sprung back into shape. I couldn't find the rise I had come down. The position of the moon was impossible to locate, even though there was plenty of moonlight; the moon had gone away and left its light there.

Gradually I became concerned. I had somehow gotten turned about, and the train would soon be leaving, and I had been warned that no one would wait for me. I thought perhaps it was best if I ceased thrashing about through the grass, and just stopped, lest I become more confused. I concluded that I couldn't have gone too far from the railway, and that I should be able to hear the train man should he call out for "all aboard."

So, there I was, standing in tall grass like a fool. Lost from the train and listening intently for the man to call out. I kept glancing about to try and see if I could find a path back the way I came. As I said before, it stood to reason that I had tromped down some grass, and that I couldn't be that far away. It was also, as I said, a very well-lit night, plenty of moonlight. It rested like swipes of cream cheese on the tall grass, so it was inconceivable to me that I had gotten lost in such a short time and walking such a short distance. I also considered those lights as bearings, but they had moved, fluttering about like will-o'-the-wisps, so using them as markers was impossible.

I was lost, and I began to entertain the disturbing thought that I might miss the train and be left where I was. It would be bad enough to miss the train, but here, out in the emptiness of nowhere, if I wasn't missed, or no one came back this way for a time, I might actually starve, or be devoured by wild animals, or die of exposure.

That's when I heard someone coming through the grass. They weren't right on top of me, but they were close, and of course, my first thought was it was the man from the train come to look for me. I started to call out, but hesitated.

I can't entirely explain the hesitation, but there was a part of me that felt reluctant, and so instead of calling out, I waited. The noise grew louder.

I cautiously parted the grass with my fingers, and looked in the direction of the sound, and coming through the grass were a number of men, all of them peculiarly bald, the moonlight reflecting off their heads like mirrors. The grass whipped open as they came and closed back behind them. For a brief moment I felt relieved, as they must be other passengers or train employees sent to look for me, and would direct me to back to the train. It would be an embarrassing moment, but in the end, all would be well.

And then I realized something. I hadn't been actually absorbing what I was seeing. They were human-shaped alright, but . . . they had no faces. There was a head, and there were spots where the usual items should be, nose, eyes, mouth, but those spots were indentions. The moonlight gathered on those shiny white faces, and reflected back out. They were the lights in the grass and they were why the lights moved, because they moved. There were other lights beyond them, way out, and I drew the conclusion that there were many of these human-shaped things, out in the grass, close and far away, moving toward me, and moving away, thick as aphids. They had a jerky movement about them, as if they were squirming on a griddle. They pushed through the grass and fanned out wide, and some of them had sticks, and they began to beat the grass before them. I might add that as they did, the grass, like a living thing, whipped away from their strikes and opened wide and closed up behind them. They were coming ever nearer to where I was. I could see they were of all different shapes and sizes and attire. Some of them wore very old clothes, and there were others who were dressed in rags, and even a couple who were completely devoid of clothes, and sexless, smooth all over, as if anything that distinguished their sex or their humanity had been ironed out. Still, I could tell now, by the general shape of the bodies, that some of them may have been women, and certainly some of the smaller ones were children. I even saw moving among them a shiny white body in the shape of a dog.

In the same way I had felt it unwise to call out to them, I now felt it unwise to wait where I was. I knew they knew I was in the grass, and that they were looking for me.

I broke and ran. I was spotted, because behind me, from those faces without mouths, there somehow rose up a cry. A kind of squeal, like something being slowly ground down beneath a boot heel.

I heard them as they rushed through the grass after me. I could hear their feet thundering against the ground. It was as if a small heard of buffalo were in pursuit. I charged through the grass blindly. Once I glanced back over my shoulder and saw their numbers were larger than I first thought. Their shapes broke out of the grass, left and right and close and wide. The grass was full of them, and their faces glowed as if inside their thin flesh were lit lanterns.

Finally there was a place where the grass was missing and there was only earth. It was a relief from the cloying grass, but it was a relief that passed swiftly, for now I was fully exposed. Moving rapidly toward me from the front were more of those moonlit things. I turned, and saw behind me the others were very near. They began to run all out toward me; they were also closing in from my right.

There was but one way for me to go, to the left and wide, back into the grass. I did just that. I ran as hard as I could run. The grass sloped up slightly, and I fought to climb the hill; the hill that I had lost such a short time ago. It had reappeared, or rather I had stumbled upon it.

My feet kept slipping as I climbed up it. I glanced down, and there in that weird light I could see that my boots were sliding in what looked to be rotting piles of fat-glazed bones; the earth was slick with them.

I could hear the things closing behind me, making that sound that a face without a mouth should be unable to make; that horrid screech. It was deafening.

I was almost at the peak of the hill. I could see the grass swaying up there. I could hear it whispering in the wind between the screeches of those pursuing me, and just as I made the top of the hill and poked my head through the grass and saw the train, I was grabbed.

Here is a peculiar thing that from time to time I remember, and shiver when I do, but those hands that had hold of my legs were cold as arctic air. I could feel them through my clothes, they were so cold. I tried to kick loose, but wasn't having any luck. I had fallen when they grabbed me, and I was clutching at the grass at the top of the hill. It was pulling through my hands and fingers, and the edges were sharp; they cut into me like razors. I could feel the warm blood running through my fingers, but still I hung to that grass.

Glancing back I saw that I was seized by several of the things, and the dog-like shape had clamped its jaws on the heel of my boot. I saw too that the things were not entirely without features after all; or at least now they had acquired one all-encompassing feature. A split appeared in their faces where a mouth should be, but it was impossibly wide and festooned with more teeth than a shark, long and sharp, many of them crooked as poorly driven nails, stained in spots the color of very old cheese. Their breath rose up like methane from a privy and burned my eyes. There was no doubt in my mind that they meant to bite me; and I somehow knew that if I was bitten, I would not be chewed and eaten, but that the bite would make me like them. That my bones would come free of me along with my features and everything that made me human, and I knew too that these things were originally from train stops, and from frontier scouting parties, adventurers and surveyors, and all manner of folks who had at one time had been crossing these desolate lands and found themselves here, a place not only unknown to the map, but unknown to human understanding. All of this came to me and instantly filled me up with dread. It was as if their very touch had revealed it to me.

I kicked wildly, wrenching my boot heel from the dog-shape's toothy grasp. I struggled. I heard teeth snap on empty air as I kicked loose. And then there was warmth and a glow over my head. I looked up to see the train man with a great flaming torch, and he was waving it about, sticking it into the teeth-packed faces of those poor lost souls.

They screeched and they bellowed, they hissed and they moaned. But the fire did the trick. They let go of me and receded back into the waves of grass, and the grass folded back around them, like the ocean swallowing sailors. I saw last the dog-shape dive into the grass like a porpoise, and then it and them were gone, and so were the lights, and the moonlight lost its slick glaze and it was just a light. The torch flickered over my head, and I could feel its heat.

The next thing I knew the train man was pulling me to the top of the hill, and I collapsed and trembled like a mass of gelatin spilled on a floor.

"They don't like it up here, sir," the train man said, pushing the blazing end of his torch against the ground, rubbing it in the dirt, snuffing it out. The smell of pitch tingled my nostrils. "No, they don't like it at all."

"What are they?" I said.

"I think you know, sir. I do. Somewhere deep inside me I know. There aren't any words for it, but I know, and you know. They touched me once, but thank goodness I was only near the grass, not in it. Not like you were, sir."

He led me back to the train. He said, "I should have been more emphatic, but you looked like a reasonable chap to me. Not someone to wander off."

"I wish I had been reasonable."

"It's like looking to the other side, isn't it, sir?" he said. "Or rather, it is a look to one of many sides, I suspect. Little lost worlds inside our own. The train breaks down here often. There have been others who have left the train. I suspect you met some of them tonight. You saw what they have become, or so I think, I can't explain all the others. Wanderers, I suspect. It's always here the train stops, or breaks down. Usually it just sort of loses steam. It can have plenty and still lose it, and we have to build it all up again. Always this time of night. Rarely a problem, really. Another thing, I lock all the doors at night to keep folks in, should they come awake. I lock the general passenger cars on both ends. Most don't wake up anyway, not this time of night, not after midnight, not if they've gone to sleep before that time, and are good solid in. Midnight between two A.M., that's when it always happens, the train losing steam here near the crawling grass. I guess those of us awake at that time can see some things that others can't. In this spot anyway. That's what I suppose. It's like a door opens out there during that time. They got their spot, their limitations, but you don't want to be out there, no sir. You're quite lucky."

"Thank you," I said.

"Guess I missed your lock, sir. Or it works poorly. I apologize for that. Had I done right, you wouldn't have been able to get out. If someone should stay awake and find the room locked, we pretend it's a stuck doorway. Talk to them through the door, and tell them we can't get it fixed until morning. A few people have been quite put out by that. The ones who were awake when we stopped here. But it's best that way. I'm sure you'll agree, sir."

"I do," I said. "Thank you again. I can't say it enough."

"Oh, no problem. You had almost made it out of the grass, and you were near the top of the hill, so it was easy for me help you. I always keep a torch nearby that can easily be lit. They don't like fire, and they don't come up close to the train. They don't get out of the grass, as far as I can determine. But I will tell you true, had I heard your scream too far beyond the hill, well, I wouldn't have come after you. And they would have had you."

"I screamed?"

"Loudly."

I got on the train and walked back to my compartment, still trembling. I checked my door and saw that my lock had been thrown from the outside, but it was faulty, and all it took was a little shaking to have it come free of the door frame. That's how I had got out of my room.

The train man brought me a nip of whisky, and I told him about the lock, and drank the whisky. "I'll have the lock fixed right away, sir. Best not to mention all this," he said. "No one will believe it, and it could cause problems with the cross-country line. People have to get places, you know."

I nodded.

"Goodnight, sir. Pleasant dreams."

This was such an odd invocation to all that had happened, I almost laughed.

He went away, closing up my compartment, and I looked out the window. All there was to see was the grass, waving in the wind, tipped with moonlight.

The train started to move, and pretty soon we were on our way. And that was the end of the matter, and this is the first time I have mentioned it since it happened so long ago. But, I assure you. It happened just the way I told you, crossing the Western void, in the year of 1901.

"Case of the Stalking Shadow" is one of the early Dana Roberts stories, written before my daughter, Kasey, and I blended characters so that her character Jana and my character Dana became a team. As Kasey has said, had we known we were going to do that, we would have named them differently, as their names sound too much alike. But, there you have it.

Kasey and I have written about the characters and the series before, and I have written about this story. This is Dana Roberts's early discovery that what we think of as magic is actually interdimensional, science fictional. It sets the course for her career as a Supernormal Investigator, as she calls herself, not a Supernatural Detective.

Dana believes that what we call supernatural is the science of other dimensions that slips into ours and, along with them, some pretty nasty culprits that just happen to be cousins to Lovecraft's Old Ones.

The Dana stories before Kasey were a bit stiff, on purpose. They are modeled on the classic told-in-a-bar-or-at-a-club stories of old, although those detectives are nearly always male. I think Kasey joining me let me let loose my normal humor in the stories, and certainly Kasey added more humor to the series and gave the later stories their shape. Enough that I feel after she came to write with me that her influence is dominant. We both write about the same amount, but the tonality for the later stories is hers. I hope this story will whet your appetite to read others in the series, collected in Terror Is Our Business.

THE CASE OF THE STALKING SHADOW

For Kasey Lansdale

I'VE MENTIONED DANA Roberts before, though with less kindness than I do now, and if anyone would have told me that I would be defending, even supporting, someone who in layman's terms might be known as a ghost breaker, or a dealer in the supernatural, I would have laughed them out of the room.

It should also be noted that Dana does not consider what she does as dealing with the supernatural, which she believes is a term that often assigns some sort of religious aspect to her work. She believes what others call the supernatural is an unknown reality of this world, or some dimensional crossover that has yet to be explained and, if truly understood, would be designated as science.

But, here I go trying to explain her books, which after her first visit to our club I have read extensively. That said, I should also note that my conclusions about her observations, her work, might be erroneous. I'm a reader, not a scholar, and above all, I love a good story.

The first time she was with us, she told us of an adventure she called "The Case of the Lighthouse Shambler." At the end of her tale, or her report, if you take it as fact—and I do—she showed us something trapped in a mirror's reflection that was, in my view, impossible to explain away. She was also missing the tip of her right index finger, which went along nicely with the story she had just finished.

Her visit to our club was, without a doubt, a highlight.

Though I suppose I've gotten a little out of order, I should pause and tell you something of our group. It now stands at twelve—three women and nine men. Most of us are middle age, or better. I should also mention that during our last meeting, I recorded Dana's first story for our gathering, unbeknownst to her. My intent was to do so, and then replay parts of it to our treasurer, Kevin, with the intent of obvious ridicule and a declaration that money spent on spook hunters as guests were wasted dues.

Instead, I was so captivated with Dana's story that I went home forgetting I had recorded her, and, of course, Kevin had heard it all firsthand and had been as captivated with her adventure as I was.

A few weeks later I was finally brave enough to call Dana's business, which is registered simply as DANA ROBERTS, SUPERNORMAL INVESTIGATIONS, and tell her what I had done. There was no need for it, as she would never know, but I harbored a certain amount of guilt, and liked the idea of having contact with her, and encouraged her to come to the club again.

To my relief, she found my original skepticism more than acceptable, and asked if I might like to transcribe my recording for publication in her monthly newsletter. I not only agreed, but it appeared in the April online magazine *Dana Roberts Reports*.

And so, here is another story, recorded and transcribed with her enthusiastic permission.

The night she came to us again as a speaker, she was elegantly dressed, and looked fine in dark slacks and an ivory blouse. Her blond hair was combed back and tied loosely at her neck, and she wore her usual disarming smile.

She took her place in the large and comfortable guest chair, and with a tall drink in her hand and the lights dimmed, a fire crackling in the fireplace, she began to tell a story she called "The Case of the Stalking Shadow."

It follows.

Since most of the events of the last few months have turned out to be hoaxes, or of little interest, and because I am your invited guest, I decided tonight to fall back on one of my earlier cases—my first, in fact—and the one that led me into this profession. Though at the time, I didn't know I was going to become a serious investigator of this sort of thing, or that it would require so much work, as well as putting myself continually in the face of danger. I've done more research for my current job than I ever did gaining my PhD in anthropology. Mistakes in what I do can have dire consequences, so it's best to know what one is doing, at least where it can be known.

I was not paid for this investigation. It was done for myself, with the aid of a friend, and it happened when I was in my late teens. In the process of my discovering my lifelong occupation, I nearly lost my life on more than one occasion, for there were several touchy moments.

Had this particular case gone wrong, then I would not be here today to entertain you with my adventures, nor would my friend and cousin Jane be alive, where she may be right now.

Simply put, I come from what must be defined as a wealthy family.

There were times when there was less wealth, but there was always money. This was also true of my close relatives, and so it was that my Aunt Elizabeth, on my father's side, invited us each year to her home for the summer. It was a kid event, and children of both my mother's and father's siblings were gathered each year when school let out to spend a week with Aunt Elizabeth, whose husband was in oil and often gone for months at a time. I suppose, having no children of her own, she liked the company, and in later years when her husband, my then Uncle Chester, ran off with a woman from Brazil, it became more clear to me why she looked forward each year to a family gathering, and why she surrounded herself with so many other activities, and spent Uncle Chester's money with a kind of abandon that could only speak to the idea of getting hers while there was something to be got.

But, that is all sour family business, and I will pass over it. I'm sure I've told too much already.

The year I'm talking about, when I was thirteen, my aunt and uncle had moved from their smaller property upstate, and had bought what could only be described as a classic estate, made to look very much like those huge British properties we see frequently in older movies and television programs. It was in America, in the deep South, but it certainly had the looks of a traditional upper-level British residence, with enormous acreage to match. In the latter respect, it was more common to America's vast spaces. One hundred acres, the largest portion of it wooded, with a house with no less than forty-five rooms, and a surrounding area dotted with gardens and shrubs trimmed in the shape of animals: lions and tigers and bears.

It was overdone and overblown. For a child, those vast rooms and that enormous acreage was a kind of paradise. Or, so it seemed at the time of that initial gathering of myself and my cousins.

To get more directly to the point, after arrival, and a few days of getting to know one another—for in some cases, our lives were so different, and things had changed so dramatically for each of us in such a short period of time—it was necessary to reacquaint. We were on the verge of leaving childhood, or most of us were, though there were some younger. For me, this year was to be particularly important, and in many ways I feel it was the last year of what I think of as true childhood. Certainly, I was not grown after this year passed, but my interests began to move in other directions. Boys and cars and dating, the whole nine yards. And, of course, what happened changed me forever.

But this summer I'm talking about, we spent a vast amount of time playing the old childhood games. It was a wonderful and leisurely existence that consisted of swimming in the pool, croquet, badminton, and the like. At night, since my aunt would not allow a television, we played board games of all varieties, and as there were a huge number of us cousins, we were often pitted against one another in different parts of the house with different games.

One night, perhaps three days into my visit, my cousin Jane and I found ourselves in a large room, alone, where we were playing chess, and between moves she suddenly said, without really waiting for a reply: "Have you been in the woods behind the estate? I find it quite queer."

"Queer?" I said.

"Strange. I suppose it's my imagination, and being a city girl. I'm not used to the proximity of so many trees."

I didn't know it at the time, and would probably not have appreciated it, but those trees had been there for hundreds of years, and though other areas had been logged out and replaced with "crops" of pines in long rows, this was the remains of aboriginal forests. Jumping ahead slightly, the trees were not only of a younger time, but they were huge and grew in such a way the limbs had grown together and formed a kind of canopy that didn't allow brush and vines to grow beneath them. So when someone says there are as many trees now as there once were, you can be certain they are describing crop trees, grown close together, without the variance of nature. These trees were from a time when forests were forests, so to speak.

Anyway, she said perhaps a few more words about the trees, and how she thought the whole place odd, but I didn't pay any real attention to her, and there was nothing in her manner that I determined to be dread or worry of any kind. So, her comments didn't really have impact on me, and it wasn't until later that I thought back on our conversation and realized how accurately impressionable Jane had been.

There was something strange about those woods.

After another day or so, the pool and the nighttime games lost some of their appeal. We did some night swimming, lounging around the pool, but one moonlit night, one of the younger children amongst us—Billy, who was ten—suggested that it might be fun to play a game of tag in the woods.

Now, from an adult standpoint, this seems like a bad choice, mucking about in the woods at night, but we were young, and it was a very bright night, and though deeper into the acreage the trees were, as I formerly described them, up close to the house they were spread about more. There were adequate shadows for hiding, but they were less thick there, and grew in an odd manner, as if the soil were bad. There was no canopy overhead, but instead there was plenty of openness to let in the moonlight, which made the area more appealing for the sort of game we planned. But what I'm trying to point out here is how distinctly different these trees were from the ones I told you about before. That said, I now realize these trees were even older, far older, but were of a totally different nature.

We decided a game would be delicious. We chose up teams.

One team constituted eight cousins, the other seven. The game was somewhere between hide-and-go-seek and tag. One team would hide, the other would seek. If an adversary, for want of a better name, were discovered, they could run and hide again. The trick was to chase them down, tag them, making them a member of the hunting team. In time, the idea was to tag everyone into the Number Two Team, and then the game would switch out.

How we started was Number Two Team was to stay at the swimming pool, while Number One Team had a fifteen-minute head start into the woods. It was suggested that the more open part of the woods was to be our area, but that no one should go into the thicker and darker part, because that was a lot of acreage and more difficult.

Oddly enough, we would have been better off to have played there, instead of where we ended up.

At the signal, we shot off like quail, splitting up in the woods to hide, each of us going our own route. It was every cousin for themselves.

I went through the trees, and proceeded immediately to the back of the sparser woods, and came to the edge where it thickened. The trees in the sparser area were of common variety, but of uneven shape. They didn't grow high, but were thickly festooned with sickly widespread branches, and beneath them were plenty of shadows.

As if it were yesterday, I remember that as soon as I came to that section of trees, I was besieged by an unreasonable sensation of discomfort. The discomfort, at this point, wasn't fear, it was more a malaise that had descended on me heavy as a wool blanket. I thought it had to do with my overextending of myself while on vacation, because even though young, I was used to a much more controlled environment and an earlier bedtime.

The trees seemed far more shadowy than they had appeared from a distance, and there was also an impression of being watched. No, that isn't quite right. Not of being watched so much as of a presence in the general locale. Something so close that I should be able to see it, but couldn't. Something I should be able to see, but instinctively felt I didn't want to.

I marked this down to exhaustion, and went about finding a good place to hide. I could hear the seekers beginning to run toward the woods, and then I heard someone scream, having been tagged immediately. I chose a place between two trees that had grown together high and low in such a way as to appear to be a huge letter H placed on a pedestal; the trees met in such tight formation, they provided a near singular trunk, and the bar of the H was an intermingled branch of both trees. I darted behind them, scooted down, and put my back against the trunk.

No sooner had I chosen my spot than it occurred to me that its unusual nature might, in fact, attract one of the seekers, but by then, I felt it was too late and pressed my back against the tree, awaiting whatever fate might come.

From where I sat, I could see the deeper woods, and I had an urge to run into it, away from the grove of trees where I now hid. I also disliked the idea of having my back against the tree and being discovered suddenly and frightened by the hunters. I didn't want that surprise to cause me to squeal the way I had heard someone squeal earlier. I liked to think of myself as more mature than a child's game to begin with, and was beginning to regret my involvement in the matter.

I sat and listened for footfalls, but the game went on behind me. I could hear yelling and some words, and I was bewildered that no one had come to look for me, as my hiding place wasn't exactly profound.

After a while, I ceased to hear the children, and noticed that the moonlight in the grove, where the limbs were less overbearing, had grown thinner.

I stood up and turned and looked through the split in the H tree. It was very quiet now, so much, in fact, I could almost hear the worms crawling inside the earth. I stood there peeking between the bars of the H, and then I saw one of the children coming toward me. I couldn't make out who it was, as they were drenched in shadow, but they were coming up the slight rise into the ragged run of trees. At first, I felt glad to see them, as I was ready for my part in this silly game to be over, and was planning on begging off being a seeker. I felt I could do this quite happily and conveniently, and the teams would then be Even Steven, as my father used to say.

However, as the shape came closer, I began to have a greater feeling of unease than before. The shape came along with an unusual step that seemed somewhere between a glide and a skip. There was something disconcerting about its manner. It was turning its shadowed head left and right, as I would have expected a seeker to do, but there was a deeply ingrained part of me that rejected this as its purpose.

Closer it came, the more my nervousness was compounded, for the light didn't delineate its features in any way. In fact, the shape seemed not to be a shadow at all, but the dark caricature of a human being. I eased behind the trunk and hid.

A feeling of dread turned to a feeling of fear. I was assailed with the notion that I ought to run away quickly, but to do that, I would have to step out and reveal myself, and that idea was even more frightening and oppressive. So, I stayed in my place, actually shivering. Without seeing it, I could sense that it was coming closer. There was a noise associated with its approach, but to this day, I can't identify that noise. It was not footfalls on leaves or ground, but a strange sound that made me both fearful, and at the same time, sad. It was the kind of sound that reached down into the brain and bones and gave you an influx of information that spoke not to the logical part of your being, but to some place more primal. I know that is inadequate, but I can't explain it any better. I wish that I could, because if I could imitate that sound, most of this story would be unnecessary to tell. You would understand much of it immediately.

I spoke of shivering with fear, but until that day, I didn't know a person's knees could actually knock together during the process, or that the sound of one's heart could be so loud. I was certain both sounds would be evident to the shadow, but I held my ground. It was fear that held me there, as surely as if my body had been coated in an amazingly powerful glue and I had been fastened and dried to that tree with it.

Eventually, I steeled my courage, turned, and peeked between the trunks of the H tree. Looking right at me was the shadow. Not more than a foot away. There wasn't a face, just the shape of a head and utter blackness. The surprise caused me to let out with a shriek— just the sort I'd tried to avoid—and I leapt back, and without really considering it, I broke around the tree and tore through the woods toward the house as if my rear end were on fire.

I looked back over my shoulder, and there came the thing, flapping its arms, its legs flailing like a wind-blown scarecrow.

I tripped once, rising just as the thing touched my shoulder, only for a moment. A cold went through me as it did. It was the sort of cold I imagined would be in the arctic, the sensation akin to stepping out of a warm tent, soaking wet, into an icy wind. I charged along with all my might, trying to outrun the thing I knew was right behind me. It was breathing, and its breath was as cold as its touch on the back of my neck. As it ran, the sound of its feet brought to mind the terrors I had felt earlier when I first saw it making its way through the woods: that indescribable sound that held within it all the terrors of this world, and any world imagined.

I reached the edge of the woods, and then I was into the clearing. I tried not to look back, tried not to do anything that might break my stride, but there was no stopping me. I couldn't help myself. When I looked back, there at the line of the woods, full in the moonlight, stood the thing waving its arms about in a frustrated manner, but no longer running after me.

I thundered down a slight rise and broke into the yard where the topiary animals stood, then clattered along the cobblestone path and into the house.

When I was in the hallway, I stopped to get my breath. I thought of the others, and though I was concerned, at that moment I was physically unable to return to those woods, or even the yard, to yell for the others.

Then I heard them, upstairs. I went up and saw they were all in the Evening Room. When Jane saw me, her eyes narrowed, but she didn't speak. The others went about joshing me immediately, and it was just enough to keep me from blurting out what I had seen. It seemed that everyone in the game had been caught but me, and that I had been given up on, and that switching the game about so that the other side might be the pursuer had been forgotten. Hot chocolate was being served, and everything seemed astonishingly normal.

I considered explaining all that had occurred to me, but was struck with the absurdity of it. Instead, I went to the window and looked out toward the forest. There was nothing there.

Jane and I shared a room, as we were the closest of the cousins. As it came time for bed, I found myself unwilling to turn out the light. I sat by the window and looked out at the night.

Jane sat on her bed in her pajamas, looking at me. She said, "You saw it, didn't you?"

She might as well have hit me with a brick.

"Saw what?" I said.

"It," she said. "The shadow."

"You've seen it too?"

She nodded. "I told you the woods were strange. But, I had no idea until tonight how strange. After the game ended, the others thought it quite funny that you might still be hiding in the woods, not knowing we were done. I was worried, though. . . ."

How so? I thought, but I didn't want to interrupt her train of thought.

"I actually allowed myself to be caught early," Jane said. "I wanted out of the game, and I planned to feign some problem or another, and come back to the house. It was all over pretty quick, however, and this wasn't necessary. Everyone was tagged out. Except you. But no one wanted to stay in the woods or go back into them, so they came back to the house. I think they were frightened. I know I was. And I couldn't put my finger on it. But being in that woods, and especially the nearer I came to that section where it thinned and the trees grew strange, I was so discomforted, it was all I could do to hold back tears. Then, from the window, I saw you running. And I saw it. The shadow that was shaped like a man. It stopped just beyond the line of trees."

I nodded. "I thought I imagined it."

"Not unless I imagined it too."

"But what is it?" I asked.

Jane walked to where I stood and looked out the window. The man-shaped shadow did not appear, and the woods were much darker now, as the moon was beginning to drop low.

"I don't know," she said. "But I've heard that some spots on Earth are the homes of evil spirits. Sections where the world opens up into a place that is not of here."

"Not of here?"

"Some slice in our world or their world that lets one of us, or one of them, slip in."

"Where would you hear such a thing?" I asked.

"Back home, in Lansdale, Pennsylvania. They say there was an H tree there. Like the one in these woods. I've seen it in the daytime, and it makes me nervous. I know it's there."

"I hid behind it," I said. "That's where the shadow found me."

"Lansdale was home to one of the three known H trees, as they were called."

This, of course, was exactly what I had called the tree upon seeing it.

"It was said to be a portal to another world," Jane said. "Some said hell. Eventually, it was bulldozed down, and a housing project was built over the site."

"Did anything happen after it was torn down?" I asked.

Jane shrugged. "I can't say. I just know the legend. But I've seen pictures of the tree, and it looks like the one in the woods here. I think it could be the same sort of thing."

"Seems to me, pushing it over wouldn't do anything," I said.

"I don't know. But the housing division is still there, and I've never heard of anything happening."

"Maybe because it was never a portal to hell, or anywhere else," I said. "It was just a tree."

"Could be," Jane said. "And that could be just an odd tree in the woods out there." She pointed out the window. "Or, it could be what the one in Lansdale was supposed to be. A doorway."

"It doesn't make any sense," I said.

"Neither does a shadow chasing you out of the woods."

"There has to be a logical explanation."

"When you figure it out," Jane said, "let me know."

"We should tell the others," I said.

"They won't believe us," Jane said, "but they're scared of the woods. I can tell. They sense something is out there. That's why the game ended early. I believe our best course of action is to not suggest anything that might involve those woods, and ride out the week."

I agreed, and that's exactly what we did.

The week passed on, and no one went back in the woods. But I did watch for the shadow from the backyard, and at night, from the window. Jane watched with me. Sometimes, we brought hot chocolate up to the window and sat there in the dark and drank it and kept what we called The Shadow Watch.

The moon wasn't as bright the following nights, and before long, if we were to see it, it would have had to stand underneath the backyard lights. It didn't.

The week came to an end, and all of us cousins went home.

There was an invitation the next summer to go back, but I didn't go. I had tried to dismiss the whole event as a kind of waking nightmare, but there were nights when I would awaken feeling certain that I was running too slow and the shadow was about to overtake me.

It was on those nights that I would go to the window in my room, which looked out over a well-lit city street with no woods beyond. It made me feel less stressed and worried to see those streets and cars and people walking about well past midnight. And none of them were shadows.

Jane wrote me now and again, and she mentioned the shadow once, but the next letter did not, and pretty soon there were no letters. We kept in touch by email, and I saw her at a couple of family functions, and then three years or so passed without us being in communication at all.

I was in college by then, and the whole matter of the shadow was seldom thought of, though there were occasions when it came to me out of my subconscious like a great black tide. There were times when I really thought I would like to talk to Jane about the matter, but there was another part of me that felt talking to her would make it real again. I had almost convinced myself it had all been part of my imagination, and that Jane hadn't really seen anything, and that I misremembered what she had told me.

That's how the mind operates when it doesn't want to face something. I began my studies, with anthropology as my major, and in the process, somewhere, I came across a theory that sometimes, instead of the eye sending a message to the brain, the brain sends a message to the eye. It is a rare occurrence, but some scientists believe this explains sincere ghostly sightings. To the viewer, it would be as real as you are to me as I sit here telling you this story. But, the problem with this view was, Jane had seen it as well, so it was a nice theory, but not entirely comforting.

And then out of the blue, I received a letter from Jane. Not an email. Not a phone call. But an old-fashioned letter, thin in the envelope, and short on message.

It read: *I'm going back on Christmas Eve. I have to know.*

I knew exactly what she meant. I knew I had to go back too. I had to have an answer.

Now, let me give you a bit of background on my aunt's place. She and her husband separated, and the house and property were put up for sale. I knew this from my mother and father. They had been offered an opportunity to buy the house, but had passed due to the expense of it all.

Interestingly enough, I learned that Jane's family, who had later been offered the opportunity, could afford it, and plans were made. Jane's father had died the year before, and a large inheritance was left to Jane's mother. No sooner had the house been bought than her mother died, leaving Jane with the property.

Perhaps this was the catalyst that convinced Jane to go back.

I acquired Jane's phone number and called her. We talked briefly, and did not mention the shadow. It's like our conversation was in code. We made plans: a time to arrive and how to meet, that sort of thing.

Before I left, I did a bit of research.

I didn't know what it was I was looking for, but if Jane was right, her hometown of Lansdale, Pennsylvania, was supposedly a former home to an H tree. I looked it up on the Internet and read pretty much what Jane had told me. As far back as the Native Americans, there had been stories of Things coming through the gap in the H tree. Spirits. Monsters. Demons. Shadows.

As Jane had said, the H had been destroyed by builders, and a sub-division of homes was built over it. I looked for any indication that there had been abnormal activity in that spot, but except for a few burglaries, and one murder of a husband by a wife, there was nothing out of the average.

Upon arrival, at the airport, I picked up my rental car and drove to a Walmart and bought a gas can, two cheap cigarette lighters, and a laser pointer. Keep in mind, now, that I was doing all of this out of assumption, not out of any real knowledge of the situation. There was no real knowledge to be had, only experience. Experience that might lead to disappointment, and the kind of disappointment that could result in a lack of further experience in all matters. I had that in mind as I drove, watching the sun drop in the west.

When I arrived at the property and the house, it had changed. The house was still large and regal, but the yards had grown up, and the swimming pool was an empty pit lined at the bottom with broken seams and invading weeds. The topiary shrubs had become masses of green twists and turns without any identifying structure.

I parked and got out. Jane greeted me at the door. Like me, she was dressed simply, in jeans, a T-shirt, and tennis shoes. She led me inside.

She had bought a few sandwich goods, and we made a hasty meal of cheese and meat and coffee, and then she showed me the things she had brought for "protection," as she put it.

There were crosses and holy water and wafers and a prayer book. Though I don't believe that religion itself holds power, the objects and the prayers, when delivered with conviction, do. Symbols like crosses and holy water and wafers that have been blessed by a priest who is a true believer contain authority. Objects from other religions are the same. It's not the gods that give them power, it is the dedication given them by the believer. In my case, even though I was not a believer, the idea that a believer had blessed the items was something I hoped endowed them with abilities.

On the other hand, I bore great faith in the simple things—like gasoline and fire starters.

Shortly after our meal, we took a few moments to discuss what we had seen those years ago, and were soon in agreement. This agreement extended to the point that we admitted that we had been, at least to some degree, in denial since that time.

Out back, we stood and looked at the woods for a long moment. The moon was rising. It was going to be nearly full. Not as full as that night when I had first seen the shadow, but bright enough.

Jane had her crosses and the like in a small satchel with a strap. She slung it over her shoulder. I carried the gas can, and had the lighters and laser pointer in my pants pocket. By the time we reached the bleak section of woods and the H tree was visible, it was as if my feet had anvils fastened to them. I could hardly lift them. I began to feel more and more miserable. I eyed Jane, saw there were tears in her eyes. When we were at the H tree, I began to shake.

We circled the tree, seeing it from all angles. Stopping, I began to pour gasoline onto its base, splashing some on the trunk from all sides. Jane pulled her wafers and holy water and crucifixes from her bag, and proceeded to place them on the ground around the tree. She took out the prayer book and began to read. Then, out of the gap between the trees, a shadow leaned toward her.

I tried to yell, to warn her, but the words were frozen in my mouth like dead seals in an iceberg. The shadow grabbed her by the throat, causing her to let out with a grunt, and then she was pulled through the portal and out of sight.

I suspected there would be danger, but on some level, I thought we would approach the tree, read a prayer, stick a cross in the ground, set the tree on fire, and flee, hoping the entire forest, the house, and surrounding property wouldn't burn down with it.

I had also hoped, for reasons previously stated, that the religious symbols would carry weight against whatever it was that lay inside that gateway, but either the materials had not been properly blessed or we were dealing with something immune to those kinds of artifacts.

Now, here comes the hard part. This is very hard for me to admit, even to this day. But the moment Jane was snatched through that portal, I broke and ran. I offer as excuse only two things: I was young, and I was terrified.

I ran all the way to the back door of the house. No sooner had I arrived there than I was overcome with grief. It took me a moment to fortify myself, but when that was done, I turned, and started back with renewed determination.

I came to the H, and with a stick, I probed the gap between the trees. Nothing happened, though at any instant, I expected the shadow to lean forward and grab me. I picked up the bottle of holy water that Jane had left, hoping it might be better than a prayer book, climbed over the communal trunk, ducked beneath the limb that made the bar on the H, and boldly stepped through the portal.

It was gray inside, like the sun seen through a heavy curtain, but there was no sunlight. The air seemed to be fused with light, dim as it was. There were boulderlike shapes visible. They were tall and big around. All of them leaned, and not all in the same direction. Each was fog-shrouded. There were shadows flickering all about, moving from one structure to another, being absorbed by them, like ink running through the cracks in floorboards.

Baffled, I stood there with the bottle of holy water clutched in my fist, trying to decide what to do. Eventually, the only thing that came to me was to start forward in search of Jane. As I neared the boulders, I gasped for breath. They were not boulders at all but structures made of bones and withering flesh. The shadows were tucked tight between the bone and skin like viscera. I stood there staring, and then one of the bones—an arm bone—moved and flexed the skeletal fingers, snatched at the air, and reached for me.

Startled, I let out a sharp cry and stepped back.

The structure pivoted, and a thousand eyes opened in the worn skin. It was a living thing made of bone and skin and shadow, and it slid along, a gray slime oozing out from beneath it like the trail of a slug.

I bolted in what I hoped was the general direction I had come, but directions were confused. I wheeled and flung the holy water violently against the thing, but the only reaction I got was a broken bottle and water leaking ineffectually down its side. As it pivoted, I saw sticking out from it a shape that had yet to become bone and dried skin. It writhed like a worm in tar. Then, it screamed and called out.

It was Jane, attached to the departing thing like a fly stuck to fly paper.

Other mounds of bone and shadow and flesh were starting to move now, and they were akin to hills sliding in my direction. They were seeking me, mewing as they went, their sliding giving forth that horrid shuffling sound I had heard years before from the running shadow.

The sound made me ill. My head jumped full of all manner of horrid things.

I realized escape was impossible. That no matter which way I turned, they were there.

Now the shadows, as if greased, slipped out of gaps in the bones and skin, moved toward me, their dark feet sliding, their arms waving, their odd, empty, dark faces turning from side to side.

I knew for certain that it was over for Jane and myself.

And then I remembered the laser pointer in my pocket. I had brought it because shadows are an absence of light, and if there is one thing that is the enemy of darkness, it is the sharp beam of a laser.

That said, I was unprepared for the reaction I received when I snapped it on. The light went right through one of the shadows, making entry into it like the thrust of a rapier. The shadow stopped moving, one hand flying to the wound. The beam, still directed to that spot, clipped off its hand at the wrist. It was far more than I expected; my best-case plan had been that the light would be annoying.

I knew then that I had a modern weapon to combat an ancient evil. I swung the light like a sword, and as I did, the shadows came apart and fell in splashes of inky liquid and were absorbed by the gray ground. Within moments, the shadows were attempting to leap back inside the structures, but I followed them with my beam, discovering I could cut flesh and bone with it as well, for what had once been human had been sucked dry of its essence and was now a fabric of this world.

As I cut through them, the bones were dark inside, full of shadow, and the skin bled shadows; the ground was sucking them up like a sponge soaking up water.

I darted to the beast that held Jane. It was sliding along at a brisk pace. I grabbed one of Jane's outreaching hands and tugged. I was pulled to my knees as the thing flowed away. I didn't let go. I went dragging along, clinging to Jane with one hand, the laser with the other.

Eventually, I lost my grip, stumbled to my feet, and pursued the monster as it moved into a gray mist that nearly disguised it. A shadow came out of the mist and grabbed me. When it did, an intense coldness went over my body it. It was so cold, I almost passed out.

I cut with the laser. The shadow let go and fell apart. I had split it from the top of its head to the area that on a human would have been the groin.

I ran after Jane. The mist had become so thick, I almost lost her. I ran up on the creature without realizing it, and when I did, its stickiness clung to me and sucked at me. I was almost lifted off my feet, but again, I utilized the laser, and it let me go.

Aware of my determination, it let go of Jane too. She fell at my feet. My last sight of the thing was of it moving into the mist, and of bony arms waving and eyes blinking and shadows twisting down deep inside of it.

I pulled Jane upright, and it was purely by coincidence that I saw a bit of true light—a kind of glow poking through the mist.

Yanking her along, we ran for it. As we neared, it became brighter yet, like a large goal post. We darted through it and fell to the ground in a tumble. Making sure Jane was all right, I cautioned her away, and stuck the laser in my pocket.

I pulled out one of the cigarette lighters I had bought. Shadowy arms reached through the gap in the trees, into the light. The fingers snapped at me like the fangs of a snake. I avoided them with an agility I didn't know I possessed.

The shadow came through in all its dark glory. I bent low and clicked the lighter and put the flame to the spot where I had poured gasoline. A blaze leaped up and engulfed the shadow and rolled it up into a ball of fire.

With a shaking hand, I went around to the other side of the H tree, put a lick of flame to it. Coated in gasoline, it lit, but weakly.

I flicked off the lighter and grabbed up the can with its remaining gas and tossed it toward the fire. The flames fanned up the gas stream and almost reached the can before I dropped it and the blaze ran into it and the can exploded.

My ears rang. The next thing I knew, I was on the ground and Jane was beating out tufts of fire that had landed on my pants and the front of my shirt. It was pure luck that kept me from catching ablaze.

We watched as the tree burned. Shadow shapes were visible inside the H, looking out of the gray, as if to note us one last time before the fire closed the gateway forever.

The tree burned all night and into the next morning. We watched it from where we sat on the ground. The air was no longer heavy with foreboding. It seemed . . . how shall I say it . . . well, empty.

I feared the flames might jump to the rest of the trees, but they didn't. The H tree burned flat to the ground, not even leaving a stump.

All that was left was a burned spot, dark as a hole through the center of the earth.

Jane and I parted the next morning, and for some reason we have never spoken again. At all. Maybe the connection at that time of our young life, that shared memory, was too much to bear.

But I did hear from her lawyer. I was offered an opportunity to buy the house and property where the H tree had been. Cheap.

It was more than I could manage actually—cheap as it was—but I acquired a loan and bought the place. I felt I had conquered it, and buying it was the final indicator.

I still own it. No more shadows creep. And that spot of woods where the tree grew, I had removed by bulldozer. I put down a stretch of concrete and built a tennis court, and to this day there has not been one inkling of unusual activity, except for the fact that my tennis game has improved far beyond my expectations.

Finished, Dana leaned back in her chair and sipped from her drink.

"So, that's how I got my start as an investigator of the unusual. Beyond that revelation, I suppose you might want me to explain exactly what happened there inside that strange world, but I cannot. It is beyond my full knowledge. I can only surmise that our ideas of hell and demonic regions have arisen from this and other dimensional gaps in the fabric of time and space. What the things did with this stolen flesh and bone is most likely nothing that would make sense to our intellect.

"I can only say that the shadows appeared to need it, to absorb it, to live off of it. However, their true motivation is impossible to know."

With that, she downed her drink, smiled, stood up, shook hands with each of us, and left us there in the firelight, stunned, considering all she had told us.

I've been writing about my cursed Reverend for some time. He is more of a slave to God than a loving believer. I have written about him several times, and he has faced a number of supernatural and supernormal threats during his adventures. This is the most obviously Lovecraft-inspired tale of his collected adventures, but it also fits old folk tales I heard growing up about things that lived in abandoned water wells, or lurked in the dark woods. Ambrose Bierce was also an inspiration, though that may be less obvious. Robert E. Howard's Solomon Kane is at the back of it as well. Of course, it takes place in the Old West, and as I'm a fan of that era, that is a major part of its construction. If you ever see a sky that seems to crawl, then you might want to stay away from abandoned water wells and dark woods.

THE CRAWLING SKY

Chapter 1
Wood Tick

WOOD TICK WASN'T so much a town as it was a wide rip in the forest. The Reverend Jebidiah Mercer rode in on an ebony horse on a coolish autumn day beneath an overcast sky of humped-up, slow-blowing, gun-metal-gray clouds; they seemed to crawl. It was his experience nothing good ever took place under a crawling sky. It was an omen, and he didn't like omens, because, so far in his experience, none of them were good.

Before him, he saw a sad excuse for a town: a narrow clay road and a few buildings, not so much built up as tossed up, six altogether, three of them leaning south from northern winds that had pushed them. One of them had had a fireplace of stone, but it had toppled, and no one had bothered to rebuild it. The stones lay scattered about like discarded cartridges. Grass, yellowed by time, had grown up through the stones, and even a small tree had sprouted between them. Where the fall of the fireplace had left a gap was a stretch of fabric, probably a slice of tent; it had been nailed up tight and it had turned dark from years of weather.

In the middle of the town there was a wagon with wooden bars set into it and a flat heavy roof. No horses. Its axle rested on the ground, giving the wagon a tilt. Inside, leaning, the Reverend could see a man clutching at the bars, cursing as a half dozen young boys who looked likely to grow up to be ugly men were throwing rocks at him. An old man was sitting on the precarious porch of one of the leaning buildings, whittling on a stick. A few other folks moved about, crossing the street with the enthusiasm of the ill, giving no mind to the boys or the man in the barred wagon.

Reverend Mercer got off his horse and walked it to a hitching post in front of the sagging porch and looked at the man who was whittling. The man had a goiter on the side of his neck and he had tied it off in a dirty sack that fastened under his jaw and to the top of his head under his hat. The hat was wide and dropped a shadow on his face. The face needed concealment. He had the kind of features that made you wince; one thing God could do was he could sure make ugly.

"Sir, may I ask you something?" the Reverend said to the whittling man.

"I reckon."

"Why is that man in that cage?"

"That there is Wood Tick's jail. All we got. We been meaning to build one, but we don't have that much need for it. Folks do anything really wrong, we hang 'em."

"What did he do?"

"He's just half-witted."

"That's a crime?"

"If we want it to be. He's always talkin' this and that, and it gets old. He used to be all right, but he ain't now. We don't know what ails him.

He's got stories about haints and his wife done run off and he claims a haint got her."

"Haints?"

"That's right."

Reverend Mercer turned his head toward the cage and the boys tossing rocks. They were flinging them in good and hard, and pretty accurate.

"Having rocks thrown at him cannot be productive," the Reverend said.

"Well, if God didn't want him half-witted and the target of rocks, he'd have made him smarter and less directed to bullshit."

"I am a man of God and I have to agree with you. God's plan doesn't seem to have a lot of sympathy in it. But humanity can do better. We could at least save this poor man from children throwing rocks."

"Sheriff doesn't think so."

"And who is the sheriff?"

"That would be me. You ain't gonna give me trouble, are you?"

"I just think a man should not be put behind bars and have rocks thrown at him for being half-witted."

"Yeah, well, you can take him with you, long as you don't bring him back. Take him with you and I'll let him out."

The Reverend nodded. "I can do that. But I need something to eat first. Any place for that?"

"You can go over to Miss Mary's, which is a house about a mile down from the town, and you can hire her to fix you somethin'. But you better have a strong stomach."

"Not much of a recommendation."

"No, it's not. I reckon I could fry you up some meat for a bit of coin, you ready to let go of it."

"I have money."

"Good. I don't. I got some horse meat I can fix. It's just on this side of being good enough to eat. Another hour, you might get poisoned by it."

"Appetizing as that sounds, perhaps I should see Miss Mary."

"She fixes soups from roots and wild plants and such. No matter what she fixes, it all tastes the same and it gives you the squirts. She ain't much to look at neither, but she sells herself out, you want to buy some of that."

"No. I am good. I will take the horse meat, long as I can watch you fry it."

"All right. I'm just about through whittling."

"Are you making something?"

"No. Just whittlin'."

"So, what is there to get through with?"

"Why, my pleasure, of course. I enjoy my whittlin'."

The old man, who gave the Reverend his name as if he had given up a dark secret, was called Jud. Up close, Jud was even nastier-looking than from the distance of the hitching post and the porch. He had pores wide enough and deep enough in his skin to keep pooled water and his nose had been broken so many times, it moved from side to side when he talked. He was missing a lot of teeth, and what he had were brown from tobacco and rot. His hands were dirty and his fingers were dirtier yet, and the Reverend couldn't help but wonder what those fingers had poked into.

Inside, the place leaned and there were missing floorboards. A wooden stove was at the far end of the room, and a stovepipe wound out of it and went up through a gap in the roof that would let in rain, and had, because the stove was partially rusted. It rested heavy on the worn flooring. The floor sagged and it seemed to the Reverend that if it experienced one more rotted fiber, one more termite bite, the stove would crash through. Hanging on hooks on the wall were slabs of horsemeat covered in flies. Some of the meat looked a little green and there was a slick of mold over a lot of it.

"That the meat you're talkin' about?"

"Yep," Jud said, scratching at his filthy goiter sack.

"It looks pretty green."

"I said it was turnin'. Want it or not?"

"Might I cook it myself?"

"Still have to pay me."

"How much?"

"Two bits."

"Two bits for rancid meat I cook myself?"

"It's still two bits if I cook it."

"You drive quite the bargain, Jud."

"I pride myself on my dealin'."

"Best you do not pride yourself on hygiene."

"What's that? That some kind of remark?"

Reverend Mercer pushed back his long black coat and showed the butts of his twin revolvers. "Sometimes a man can learn to like things he does not on most days care to endure."

Jud checked out the revolvers. "You got a point there, Reverend. I was thinkin' you was just a blabbermouth for God, but you tote them pistols like a man who's seen the elephant."

"Seen the elephant I have. And all his children."

The Reverend brushed the flies away from the horsemeat and found a bit of it that looked better than the rest, used his pocketknife to cut it loose. He picked insects out of a greasy pan and put the meat in it. He put some wood in the stove and lit it and got a fire going. In a short time the meat was frying. He decided to cook it long and cook it through, burn it a bit. That way maybe he wouldn't die of stomach poisoning.

"You have anything else that might sweeten this deal?" the Reverend asked.

"It's the horse meat or nothin'."

"And in what commerce will you deal when it turns rancid, or runs out?"

"I've got a couple more old horses, and one old mule. Somebody will have to go."

"Have you considered a garden?"

"My hand wasn't meant to fit a hoe. It gets desperate, I'll shoot a squirrel or a possum or a coon or some such. Dog ain't bad, you cook 'em good."

"How many people reside in this town?"

"About forty, forty-one if you count Norville out there in the box. But, way things look, considerin' our deal, he'll be leavin'. 'Sides, he don't live here direct anyway."

"That number count the kids?"

"Yeah, they all belong to Mary. They're thirteen and on down to six years. Drops them like turds and don't know for sure who's the daddy, though there's one of them out there that looks a mite like me."

"Bless his heart," the Reverend said.

"Yeah, reckon that's the truth. Couple of 'em have died over the years. One got kicked in the head by a horse and the other one got caught up in the river and drowned. Stupid little bastard should have learned to swim. There was an older girl, but she took up with Norville out there, and now she's run off from him."

When the meat was as black as a pit and smoking like a rich man's cigar, Reverend Mercer discovered there were no plates, and he ate it from the frying pan, using his knife as a utensil. It was a rugged piece of meat to wrestle and it tasted like the ass end of a skunk. He ate just enough to knock the corners off his hunger, then gave it up.

Jud asked if he were through with it, and when the Reverend said he was, he came over, picked up the leavings with his hands and tore at it like a wolf.

"Hell, this is all right," Jud said. "I need you on as a cook."

"Not likely. How do people make a living around here?"

"Lumber. Cut it and mule it out. That's a thing about East Texas, plenty of lumber."

"Someday there will be a lot less, that is my reasoning."

"It all grows back."

"People grow back faster, and we could do with a lot less of them."

"On that matter, Reverend, I agree with you."

When the Reverend went outside with Jud to let Norville loose, the kids were still throwing rocks. The Reverend picked up a rock and winged it through the air and caught one of the kids on the side of the head hard enough to knock him down.

"Damn," Jud said. "That there was a kid."

"Now he's a kid with a knot on his head."

"You're a different kind of Reverend."

The kid got up and ran, holding his hand to his head, squealing.

"Keep going you horrible little bastard," Reverend Mercer said. When the kid was gone, the Reverend said, "Actually, I was aiming to hit him in the back, but that worked out quite well."

They walked over to the cage. There was a metal lock and a big padlock on the thick wooden bars. Reverend Mercer had wondered why the man didn't just kick them out, but then he saw the reason. He was chained to the floor of the wagon. The chain fit into a big metal loop there, and then went to his ankle where a bracelet of iron held him fast. Norville had a lot of lumps on his head and his bottom lip was swollen up and he was bleeding all over.

"This is no way to treat a man," Reverend Mercer said.

"He could have been a few rocks shy of a dozen knots, you hadn't stopped to cook and eat a steak."

"True enough," the Reverend said.

CHAPTER 2
Norville's Story: The House in the Pines

The sheriff unlocked the cage and went inside and unlocked the clamp around Norville's ankle. Norville, barefoot, came out of the cage and walked around and looked at the sky, stretching his back as he did. Jud sauntered over to the long porch and reached under it and pulled out some old boots. He gave them to Norville. Norville pulled them on, then came around the side of the cage and studied the Reverend.

"Thank you for lettin' me out," Norville said. "I ain't crazy, you know. I seen what I seen and they don't want to hear it none."

"'Cause you're crazy," Jud said.

"What did you see?" the Reverend asked.

"He starts talkin' that business again, I'll throw him back in the box," Jud said. "Our deal was he goes with you, and I figure you've worn out your welcome."

"What I've worn out is my stomach," Reverend Mercer said. "That meat is backing up on me."

"Take care of your stomach problems somewhere else, and take that crazy sonofabitch with you."

"Does he have a horse?"

"The back of yours," Jud said. "Best get him on it, and you two get out."

"Norville," the Reverend said, "come with me."

"I don't mind comin'," Norville said, walking briskly after the Reverend.

Reverend Mercer unhitched his horse and climbed into the saddle. He extended a hand for Norville, helped him slip up on the rear of the horse. Norville put his arms around Reverend Mercer's waist. The Reverend said, "Keep the hands high or they'll find you facedown outside of town in the pine straw."

"You stay gone, you hear?" Jud said, walking up on the porch.

"This place does not hold much charm for me, Sheriff Jud," Reverend Mercer said. "But, just in case you should overvalue your position, you do not concern me in the least. It is this town that concerns me. It stinks and it is worthless and should be burned to the ground."

"You go on now," Jud said.

"That I will, but at my own speed."

The Reverend rode off then, glancing back lest Jud decide to back shoot. But it was a needless concern. He saw Jud go inside the shack, perhaps to fry up some more rancid horsemeat.

They rode about three miles out of town, and Reverend Mercer stopped by a stream. They got down off the horse and let it drink. While the horse quenched its thirst, the Reverend removed the animal's saddle, then he pulled the horse away from the water lest it bloat. He took some grooming items out of a saddlebag and went to work, giving the horse a good brushing and rubdown.

Norville plucked a blade of grass and put it in his mouth and worked it around, found a tree to sit under, said, "I ain't no bowl of nuts. I seen what I seen. Why did you help me anyway? For all you know, I am a nut."

"I am on a mission from God. I do not like it, but it is my mission. I'm a hunter of the dark and a giver of the light. I'm the hammer and the anvil. The bone and the sinew. The sword and the gun. God's man who sets things right. Or at least right as God sees them. Me and him, we do not always agree. And let me tell you, he is not the God of Jesus, he is the God of David, and the angry city killers and man killers and animal killers of the Old Testament. He is constantly jealous and angry and if there is any plan to all this, I have yet to see it."

"Actually, I was just wantin' to know if you thought I was nuts."

"It is my lot in life to destroy evil. There is more evil than there is me, I might add."

"So . . . you think I'm a nut, or what?"

"Tell me your story."

"If you think I'm a nut, are you just gonna leave me?"

"No. I will shoot you first and leave your body. . . . Just joking. I do not joke much, so I'm poor at it."

The Reverend tied up the horse and they went over and sat together under the tree and drank water from the Reverend's canteen. Norville told his story.

"My daddy, after killin' my mother over turnip soup back in the Carolinas, hitched up the wagon and put me and my sister in it and come to Texas."

"He killed your mother over soup?"

"Deader than a rock. Hit her upside the head with a snatch of turnips."

"A snatch of turnips? What in the world is 'a snatch of turnips'?"

"Bunch of them. They was on the table where she'd cut up some for soup, still had the greens on 'em. He grabbed the greens and swung them turnips. Must have been seven or eight big ole knotty ones. Hit her upside the head and knocked her brain loose I reckon. She died that night, right there on the floor. Wouldn't let us help her any. He said God didn't want her to die from gettin' hit with turnips, he'd spare her."

"Frankly, God is not all that merciful. . . . You seen this? Your father hitting your mother with the turnips?"

"Yep. I was six or so. My sister four. Daddy didn't like turnips in any kind of way, let alone a soup. So he took us to Texas after he burned down the cabin with Mama in it, and I been in Texas ever since, but mostly over toward the middle of the state. About a year ago he died and my sister got a bad cough and couldn't get over it. Coughed herself to death. So I lit out on my own."

"I would think that is appropriate at your age, being on your own. How old are you. Thirty?"

"Twenty-six. I'm just tired. So I was riding through the country here, living off the land, squirrels and such, and I come to this shack in the woods and there weren't no one livin' there. I mean I found it by accident, 'cause it wasn't on a real trail. It was just down in the woods and it had a good roof on it, and there was a well. I yelled to see anyone was home, and they wasn't, and the door pushed open. I could see hadn't nobody been there in a long time. They had just gone off and left it. It was a nice house, and had real glass in the windows, and whoever had made it had done good on it, 'cause it was put together good and sound. They had trimmed away trees and had a yard of sorts.

"I started livin' there, and it wasn't bad. It had that well, but when I come up on it for a look, I seen that it had been filled in with rocks and such, and there wasn't no gettin' at the water. But there was a creek no more than a hundred feet from the place, and it was spring-fed, and I was right at the source. There was plenty of game, and I had a garden patch where I grew turnips and the like."

"I would have thought you would have had your fill of turnips in all shapes and forms."

"I liked that soup my mama made. I still remember it. Daddy didn't have no cause to do that over some soup."

"Now we are commanding the same line of thought."

"Anyway, the place was just perfect. I started to clean out the well. Spendin' a bit of time each day pullin' rocks out of it. In the meantime, I just used the spring down behind the house, but the well was closer, and it had a good stone curbin' around it, and I thought it would be nice if it was freed up for water. I wouldn't have to tote so far.

"Meanwhile, I discovered the town of Wood Tick. It isn't much, as you seen, but there was one thing nice about it, and every man in that town knew it and wanted that nice thing. Sissy. She was one of Mary's daughters. The only one she knew who her father was. A drummer who passed through and sold her six yards of wool and about five minutes in a back room.

"Thing is, there wasn't no real competition in Wood Tick for Sissy. That town has the ugliest men you ever seen, and about half of them have goiters and such. She was fifteen and I was just five years older, and I took to courtin' her."

"She was nothing but a child."

"Not in these parts. Ain't no unusual thing for men to marry younger girls, and Sissy was mature."

"In the chest or in the head?"

"Both. So we got married, or rather, we just decided we was married, and we moved out to that cabin."

"And you still had no idea who built it, who it belonged to?"

"Sissy knew, and she told me all about it. She said there had been an old woman who lived there, and that she wasn't the one who built the house in the first place, but she died there, and then a family ended up with the land, squatted on it, but after a month, they disappeared, all except for the younger daughter, who they found walkin' the road, talkin' to herself. She kept sayin' 'It sucked and it crawled' or some such. She stayed with Mary in town who did some doctorin', but wasn't nothing could be done for her. She died. They said she looked like she aged fifty years in a few days when they put her down.

"Folks went out to the house but there wasn't nothin' to be found, and the well was all rocked in. Then another family moved in, and they'd come into town from time to time, and then they didn't anymore. They just disappeared. In time, one of the townspeople moved in, a fellow who weaved ropes and sold hides and such, and then he too was gone. No sign as to where. Then there was this man come through town, a preacher like you, and he ended up out there, and he said the house was evil, and he stayed on for a long time, but finally he'd had enough and came into town and said the place ought to be set afire and the ground plowed up and salted so nothing would grow there and no one would want to be there."

"So he survived?"

"He did until he hung himself in a barn. He left a note said: 'I seen too much.'"

"Concise," the Reverend said.

"And then I come there and brought Sissy with me."

"After all that, you came here and brought a woman as well. Could it be, sir, that you are not too bright?"

"I didn't believe all them stories then."

"But you do now?"

"I do. And I want to go back and set something straight on account of Sissy. That's what I was tryin' to tell them in town, that somethin' had happened to her, but when I told them what, wouldn't nobody listen. They just figured I was two nuts shy a squirrel's lunch and throwed me in that damned old cage. I'd still have been there wasn't for you. Now, you done good by me, and I appreciate it, and I'd like you to ride me over close to the house, you don't have to come up on it, but I got some business I want to take care of."

"Actually, the business you refer to is exactly my business."

"Haints and such?"

"I suppose you could put it that way. But please, tell me about Sissy. About what happened."

Norville nodded and swigged some water from the canteen and screwed the cap on. He took a deep breath and leaned loosely against the tree.

"Me and Sissy, we was doin' all right at first, makin' a life for ourselves. I took to cleanin' out that old well. I had to climb down in it and haul the rocks up by the bucket, and some of them was so big I had to wrap a rope around them and hook my mule up and haul them out. I got down real deep, and still didn't reach water. I come to where it was just nothin' but mud, and I stuck a stick down in the mud, and it was deep, and there really wasn't any more I could do, so I gave it up and kept carrying water from the spring. I took to fixin' up some rotten spots on the house, nailin' new shingles on the roof. Sissy planted flowers and it all looked nice. Then, of a sudden, it got so she couldn't sleep nights. She kept sayin' she was sure there was somethin' outside, and that she'd seen a face at the window, but when I got my gun and went out, wasn't nothin' there but the yard and that pile of rocks I'd pulled out of the well. But the second time I went out there, I had the feelin' someone was watching, maybe from the woods, and my skin started to crawl. I ain't never felt that uncomfortable. I started back to the house, and then I got this idea that I was bein' followed. I stopped and started to look back, but I couldn't bring myself to do it. Just couldn't. I felt if I looked back I'd see somethin' I didn't want to see. I'm ashamed to say I broke and ran and I closed the door quickly and locked it, and outside the door I could hear somethin' breathin'.

"From then on, by the time it was dark, we was inside. I boarded up most of the windows. In the day, it seemed silly, but when night come around, it got so we both felt as if something was moving around and around the house, and I even fancied once that it was on the roof, and at the chimney. I built a fire in the chimney quick-like, and kept one going at night, even when it was hot, and finally I rocked it up and we cooked outside durin' the day and had cold suppers at night. Got so we dreaded the night. We were frightened out of our gourds. We took to sleepin' a few hours in the day, and I did what I could to tend the garden and hunt for food, but I didn't like being too far from the house or Sissy.

"Now, the thing to do would have been to just pack up and leave. We talked about it. But the house and that land was what we had, even if it was just by squatter's rights, and we thought maybe we were being silly, except we got so it wasn't just a feelin' we had, or sounds—we could smell it. It smelled like old meat and stagnant water, all at once. It floated around the house at night, through them boarded windows and under the front door. It was like it was gettin' stronger and bolder.

"One mornin' we came out and all the flowers Sissy had planted had been jerked out of the ground, and there was a dead coon on the doorstep, its head yanked off."

"Yanked off?"

"You could tell from the way there was strings of meat comin' out of the neck. It had been twisted and pulled plumb off, like a wrung chicken neck, and from the looks of it, it appeared someone, or something, had sucked on its neck. Curious, I cut that coon open. Hardly had a drop of blood in it. Ain't that somethin'?"

"That's something all right."

"Our mule disappeared next. No sign of it. We thought it over and decided we needed to get out, but we didn't know where to go and we didn't have any real money. Then one mornin' I come out, and on the stones I'd set in front of the house for steps, there was a muddy print on them. It was a big print and it didn't have no kind of shape I could recognize, no kind of animal, but it had toes and a heel. Mud trailed off into the weeds. I got my pistol and went out there, but didn't find nothin'. No more prints. Nothin'.

"That night I heard a board crack at the bedroom window, and I got up with a gun in my hand. I seen that one of the boards I'd nailed over the window outside had been pulled loose, and a face was pressed up against the glass. It was dark, but I could see enough 'cause of the moonlight, and it wasn't like a man's face. It was the eyes and mouth that made it so different, like it had come out of a human mold of some sort, but the mold had been twisted or dropped or both, and what was made from it was this . . . this thing. The face was as pale as a whore's butt, and twisted up, and its eyes were blood red and shone at the window as clear as if the thing was standin' in front of me. I shot at it, shatterin' an expensive pane of glass, and then it was gone in the wink of that pistol's flare.

"I decided it had to end, and I told Sissy to stick, and I gave her the pistol, and I took the firewood axe and went outside and she bolted the door behind me. I went on around to the side of the house, and I thought I caught sight of it, a nude body, maybe, but with strange feet. Wasn't nothin' more than a glimpse of it as it went around the edge of the house and I ran after it. I must have run around that damn house three times. It acted like it was a kid playin' a game with me. Then I saw somethin' white that at first I couldn't imagine was it, because it seemed like a sheet being pulled through the bedroom window I'd shot out."

"You mean it was wraith-like . . . a haint, as you said before?"

Norville nodded. "I ran to the door, but it was bolted, of course, the way I told Sissy to do. I ran back to the window and started using the axe to chop out the rest of it, knocked the panes and the frame out, and I crawled through, pieces of glass stickin' and cuttin' me.

"Sissy wasn't there. But the pistol was on the floor. I dropped the axe and snatched it up, and then I heard her scream real loud and rushed out into the main room, and there I seen it. It was chewin'. . . . You got to believe me, preacher. It had spread its mouth wide, like a snake, and it had more teeth in its face than a dozen folk, and teeth more like an animal, and it was bitin' her head off. It jerked its jaws from side to side, and blood went everywhere. I shot at it. I shot at it five times and I hit it five times.

"It didn't so much as make the thing move. I might as well have been rubbin' its belly. It lifted its eyes and looked at me, and . . . as God is my witness, it spat out what was left of poor Sissy's head, and slapped its mouth over her blood-pumpin' neck, and went to suckin' on it like a kid with a sucker.

"I ain't ashamed to admit it, my knees went weak. I dropped the pistol and ran and got the axe. When I turned, it was on me. I swung that axe, and hit it. The blade went in, went in deep . . . and there wasn't no blood, didn't spurt a drop. Thing grabbed me up and flung me at the window, and damned if I didn't go straight through it and land out on my back, on top of some of them rocks I'd pulled out of the well. It flowed through that window like it was water, and it come at me. I rolled over and grabbed one of the rocks and flung it and hit that thing square in its bony chest. What five shots from a pistol and a hack from an axe couldn't do, the rock did.

"Monster yelled like the fire of hell had been shoved down its throat, and it ran straightaway for the well faster than I've ever seen anything move, its body twistin' in all directions, like it was going to come apart, or like the bones was shiftin' inside of it. It ran and dove into the well and I heard it hit the mud below.

"I climbed back through the window, rushed into the main room, tryin' not to look at poor Sissy's body, and I got the double barrel off the mantle and lit the lantern and went back outside through the front door with the lantern in one hand, the shotgun in the other.

"First I held the lantern over the well, got me a look, but didn't see nothin' but darkness. I bent over the curbin' and lowered the lantern in some, fearin' that thing might grab me. The sides of the well were covered with a kind of slime, and I could see the mud down below, and if the thing had gone into it, there wasn't no sign now except a bit of a ripple.

"I hid out in the woods. I went back the next mornin' and got Sissy's body and buried it out back of the place, and then before it was dark, I boarded up all the windows good and locked the door and I got the shotgun and sat with it all night in the middle of the big room. I knew it wouldn't do me no good, but that was all I had. Me and that shotgun.

"But didn't nothin' bother me, though I could hear it and smell it movin' around outside the house. Come morning, I was brave enough to go out, and Sissy's body had been pulled from the grave and gnawed on. I reckon animals could have done it in the night, but I didn't think so. I buried her again, this time deep, and mounded up dirt and packed it down. I cut some sticks and tied a cross together and stuck that up, then I walked into town and told my story. They didn't even think I was a murderer. They didn't question if I might have killed Sissy, which is what I thought they might do. They locked me up for bein' a crazy, and wasn't no one cared enough to come and see if her body was at the cabin or not. They wasn't interested. I done taken Sissy off and wasn't no man wanted her back now that she had been with me, which considerin' the kind of women they was usually with didn't make no sense, but then there ain't much about Wood Tick that does make sense.

"And then you come along, and you know the rest from there."

CHAPTER 3

The Thing Down There

The sun was starting to slant to the west, but there was still plenty of daylight left when they arrived on horseback. The house was built of large logs and it looked solid. The chimney appeared sound. The shingles were well cut and nailed down tight. It was indeed a good cabin and the Reverend understood the attraction it held for those who passed by.

Norville slipped off the back of the horse and hurried around behind the cabin. After the Reverend tied up his horse, he too went out back. Norville stood over an empty grave, the cross turned over and broken. Norville and the Reverend stood there for a long moment.

Norville fell to his knees. "Oh, Jesus. I should have taken her off somewhere else. He's done come and got her."

"It is done now," Reverend Mercer said. "Stand up, man. None of this does any good. Let's look around."

Norville stood up, but he looked ready to collapse.

"Buck up, man," Reverend Mercer said. "We have work to do."

No sight or parcel of the body was found. The Reverend went to the well and bent over and looked down. It was deep. He took out a match and struck it on the curbing and dropped it down the shaft, watched the little light fall. The match hissed out in the mud below.

"Do you believe me?" Norville said, standing back from the well a few paces.

"I do."

"What can I do?"

"Whatever you do, you will not do alone. I will be here with you."

"Kind of you, Reverend, but what can you do?"

"At the moment, I'm uncertain. Let's look inside the house."

The cabin, though not huge, had two rooms. A small bedroom and a large main room with a kitchen table and a rocked-in fireplace and some benches and a few chairs. There was blood on the floor and on a rug there, and on the walls and even on the ceiling. The Reverend paused at the rocked-up fireplace. He bent down and looked at the rocks. "Did you notice a lot of these rocks have a drawing on them?"

"What now?"

"Look here." Reverend Mercer touched his finger to one of the stones. There was a strange drawing on it, a stick figure with small symbols written around it in a circle. "It's on a lot of the rocks, and my guess is, if you were to pull the ones without visible symbols free, you could turn them over and the marks would be on the other side. They came from inside the well, correct?"

"Nearly all of them. It's a very deep well."

"As I have seen. Did you not notice the marks?"

"Guess I was so anxious to get those rocks out of there I didn't."

"It is only visible if you're looking for it."

"And you were?"

"I was looking for anything. This is my business. When you said you hit this thing with a rock and it fled after shooting it and hitting it with an axe had no effect, I started to wonder. I believe these are symbols of protection."

The Reverend began walking about the house. He looked under the bed and at the walls and checked nooks and crannies. He bounced himself on the floor to test the boards. He stood looking down at the bloodstained rug for a while. He picked up the edge of the rug and saw there were a series of short boards that didn't extend completely across the floor.

Sliding the rug aside, the Reverend used his knife and stuck it under the edge of one of the boards and pried it up. There was a space beneath and a metal box was in the space. The Reverend removed a few more boards so he could get a good look at the box. It had a padlock on it.

"Find the axe," the Reverend said.

Norville went outside and got the axe and brought it back. It was a single edge, and the Reverend turned the flat side down and swung and knocked the lock off with one sure blow. He opened the box. Inside was a book.

"Why would someone put a book under lock and key?" Norville said.

The Reverend went to the table and sat on the long bench next to it. Norville sat on the other side. The Reverend opened the book and studied it. He looked up after a moment, said, "Whoever built this house originally, their intentions for us were not good."

"Us?" Norville said. "How would they, whoever that is, know we would be here?"

"Not you and I. Us, as in the human race, Norville. They, meaning the ones who possess this book, called *The Book of Doches*. The ones who find it or buy it or kill to possess it always believe they will make some pact with the dark ones, the ones darker than our god, much darker, and they believe that if they allow these dark ones to break through, they will be either its master or its trusted servant. The latter is sometimes possible, but the former, never. And in the end, a trusted servant is easily replaced."

"What are you talkin' about?" Norville said.

"There are monsters on the other side of the veil, Norville. A place you and I can't see. These things want out. Books like this contain spells to free them, and sometimes the people who possess the book want to set them free for rewards. Someone has already set one of them free."

"The sucking thing?"

"Correct," the Reverend said, shaking the book. "Look at the pages. See? The words and images on the pages are hand-printed. The pages, feel them."

Norville used his thumb and finger to feel.

"It's cloth."

"Flesh. Human flesh is what the book says."

Norville jerked his hand back. "You can read this hen scratch?"

"Yes. I read a translation of it long ago, taught myself to understand the original symbols."

"You have the same book?"

"Had. One of them got away from me, the one adapted into English. The other I destroyed."

"How did it get away from you?"

"That's not important to us today. Whoever built this house may have brought this copy here. But their plans didn't work out. They released something, one of the minor horrors, and that minor horror either chased them off or did to them what they did to your poor Sissy. This thing they called up. The place where it is from is wet, and therefore it takes to the well. And it is hungry. Always hungry. A minor being, but a nasty one."

"But if this beast is on the other side, as you call it, why would anyone bring it here?"

"Never underestimate the curiosity and stupidity and greed of man, Norville."

"If the book set this thing free, then burn the book."

"Not a bad idea, but I doubt that would get rid of anything. In fact, I might do better to study the book. My guess is whoever first brought the book loosed the creature. They then decided they had made a mistake, made the marks of power on the stones and sealed the thing in the well where it preferred to reside—it liked the dampness, you see. And then, someone, like you, took the rocks from the well and the thing was let loose. One of the other survivors, the preacher, for example, may have figured out enough to seal the thing back in the well. And then you let it out again."

"Then we can seal it back up," Norville said.

The Reverend shook his head. "Then someone else will open the well."

"We can destroy the well curbing, put the rocks in, build a mound of dirt over all of it."

"Still not enough. That leaves the possibility of it being opened up in the future, if only by accident. No. This thing, it has to be destroyed. Listen here. It's light yet. Take my horse and walk it and take off its saddle, and then bring it inside where it will be safer."

"The house?"

"Since when are you so particular? I do not want to leave the horse for that thing to kill. If it must have the horse or us, then it will have to come and get the lot of us."

"All right then."

"Bring in my saddle and all that goes with it. And those rocks from the well. Only the rocks from the well. Start bringing them in by the pile."

"Aren't there enough here in the fireplace?"

"They are in use. One may cause this thing to flee, but that doesn't mean one will destroy it. I have other plans. Do it, Norville. Already the sun dips deep and the dark is our first enemy."

When the horse was inside and the stones were stacked in the middle of the floor, the Reverend looked up from the book, said, "Place the stones in a circle around us. A large circle. Make a line of them across the back of this room and put the horse against the wall behind them. Give him plenty of room to get excited. Hobble him and put on his bridle and tie him to that nail in the wall, the big one."

"And what exactly will you be doin'?"

"Reading," the Reverend said. "You will have to trust me. I'm all that is between you and this thing."

Norville went about placing the stones.

It was just short of dark when the stones were placed in a circle around the table and a line of them had been made behind that from wall to wall, containing the tied-up horse.

Reverend Mercer looked up from the book. "You are finished?"

Norville said, "Almost. I'll board up the bedroom window. Not that it matters. It can slip between small spaces. But it will slow it down."

"Leave it as is, and leave the door to the bedroom partially cracked."

"You're sure?"

"Quite."

The Reverend placed one of the rocks on the table, removed the bullets from his belt and took his knife and did his best to copy the symbols in small shapes on the tips of his ammunition. The symbols were simple, a stick man with a few twists and twirls around it. It took him an hour to copy it onto twelve rounds.

Finished, he loaded six rounds in each of his revolvers.

"Shall I light the lamp?" Norville asked.

"No. You have an axe and a shotgun lying about. We may have need for both. Recover them, and then come inside the ring of stones."

Chapter 4
The Arrival

While they waited, sitting cross-legged on the floor inside the circle of stones, the Reverend carved the symbols on the rocks onto the blade of the axe. He thought about the shotgun shells, but it wouldn't do any good to have the symbols on the shells and not on the load, and since the shotgun shot pellets, that was an impossible task.

Laying the axe between them, the Reverend handed the shotgun to Norville. "The shotgun will be nothing more than a shotgun," he said. "And it may not kill the thing, but it will be a distraction. You get the chance, shoot the thing with it; otherwise, sit and do not, under any circumstances, step outside this circle. The axe I have written symbols on and it may be of use."

"Are you sure this circle will keep it out?"

"Not entirely."

Norville swallowed.

They sat and they listened as the hours crept by. The Reverend produced a flask from his saddlebags. "I keep this primarily for medicinal purposes, but the night seems a little chill so let us both have one short nip, and one short nip only."

The Reverend and Norville took a drink and the flask was replaced. And no sooner was it replaced than a smell seeped into the house. A smell like a charnel house and a butcher shop and an outhouse all balled into one.

"It's near," Norville said. "That's its smell."

The Reverend put a finger to his lips to signal quiet.

There were a few noises on the outside of the house, but they could have been most anything. Finally there came a sound in the bedroom like wet laundry plopping to the floor.

Norville looked at the Reverend.

Reverend Mercer nodded to let him know he too had heard it, and then he carefully pulled and cocked his revolvers.

The room was dark, but the Reverend had adjusted his eyesight and could make out shapes. He saw that the bedroom door, already partially cracked open, was slowly moving. And then a hand, white and puffy like the petals of an orchid, appeared around the edge of the door, and fingers, long and stalk-like, extended and flexed, and the door moved and a flow of muddy water slid into the room along the floor.

The Reverend felt Norville move beside him, as if to rise, and he reached out and touched his shoulder to steady him.

The door opened more, and then the thing slipped inside the main room. It moved strangely, as if made of soft candle wax. It was dead white of flesh, but much of the skin was filthy with mud. It was neither male nor female. No genitals; down there it was as smooth as a well-washed river rock. It was tall, with knees that swung slightly to the sides when it walked, and there was an odd vibration about it, as if it were about to burst apart in all directions. The head was small. Its face was mostly a long gash of a mouth. It had thin slits for eyes and a hole for a nose. At the ends of its willowy legs were large flat feet that splayed out in shapes like claw-tipped four-leaf clovers.

Twisting and winding, long-stepping and sliding, it made its way forward until it was close to the Reverend and Norville. It leaned forward and sniffed. The hole that was its nose opened wider as it did, flexed.

It smells us, thought the Reverend. Only fair, because we certainly smell it.

And then it opened its dripping mouth and came at them in a rush.

As it neared the stones, it was knocked back by an invisible wall, and then there came something quite visible where it had impacted, a ripple of blue fulmination. The thing went sliding along the floor on its belly in its own mud and goo.

"The rocks hold," the Reverend said, and it came again. Norville lifted the shotgun and fired. The pellets went through the thing and came rattling out against the wall on the other side. The hole made in its chest did not bleed, and it filled in rapidly, as if never struck.

Reverend Mercer stood up and aimed one of his pistols, and hit the thing square in the chest, and this time the wound made a sucking sound, and when the load came out on the other side, goo and something dark came with it. But it didn't stop the creature. It hit the invisible wall again, bellowed and fell back. It dragged its way around the circle toward the horse, tied behind the line of stones. The terrified horse reared and snapped its reins as if they were nonexistent. The horse went thundering across the line, and then across the circle of stones, causing them to go spinning left and right, and along came the thing, entering the circle through the gap.

The Reverend fired again. The thing jerked back and squealed like a pig. Then it sprang forward again, grabbed the Reverend by the throat and sent him flying across the room, slamming into the side of the frightened horse.

Norville swung the shotgun around and fired right into the thing's mouth, but it was like the thing was swallowing gnats. It grabbed the

gun barrel, used it to sling the clutching Norville sliding across the
floor, collecting splinters until he came up against the bedroom door,
slamming it shut.

It started forward, but couldn't step out of the circle. Not that way.
It wheeled to find the exit the horse had made, and as it did, Reverend
Mercer, now on his feet, fired twice and hit the thing in the back, causing it to stagger through the opening and fall against the line of rocks
that had been there to protect the horse. Its head hit the rocks and the
creature cried out, leaping to its feet with a move that seemed boneless
and without use of muscle. Its forehead bore a sizzling mark the size
of the rock.

"Get back inside the circle," the Reverend said. "Close it off."

Norville waited for no further instruction. He bolted and leaped
into the circle and began to clutch at the displaced stones. The
Reverend put his right leg forward and threw back his coat by bend-
ing his left hand behind him; he pointed the revolver and took careful
aim, fired twice.

Both shots hit. One in the head, one in the throat. They had their
effect. The horror splattered to the floor with the wet laundry sound.
But no sooner had it struck the ground, than it began to wriggle along
the floor like a grubworm in a frying pan; it came fast and furious and
grabbed the Reverend's boot and sprung upright in front of him.

Reverend Mercer cracked it across the head with his pistol, and it
grabbed at him. The Reverend avoided the grab and struck out with
his fist, a jab that merely annoyed the thing. It spread its jaws and filled
the air with stink. The Reverend drew his remaining pistol and fired
straight into the hole the thing used for a nose, causing it to go toppling
backward along the floor, gnashing its teeth into the lumber.

Reverend Mercer ran and leaped into the circle.

When he turned to look, the monster was sliding up the wall like
some kind of slug. It left a sticky trail along the logs as it reached the
ceiling and crawled along that with the dexterity of an insect.

The horse had finally come to a corner and stuck its head in it to hide. The thing came down on its back, and its mouth spread over the horse's head, and the horse stood up on its hind legs and its front legs hit the wall, and it fell over backward, landing on the creature. It didn't bother the thing in the least. It grabbed and twisted the horse over on its side as if it were nothing more than a feather pillow. There was a crunch as the monster's teeth snapped bones in the horse's head. The horse quit moving, and the thing began to suck, rivulets of blood spilling out from the corners of its distended mouth.

The Reverend jammed his pistol back into its holster, bent and grabbed the axe from the floor and leaped out of the circle. The thing caught sight of the Reverend as he came, rolled off the horse and leaped up on the wall and ran along it. As the Reverend turned to follow its progress, it leaped at him.

Reverend Mercer took a swing. The axe hit the fiend and split half-way through its neck, knocking it back against the wall, then to the floor. Its narrow eyes widened and showed red, and then it came to its feet in its unique way, though more slowly than before, and darted for the bedroom door.

As it reached and fumbled with the latch, the Reverend hit the thing in the back of the head with the axe, and it went to its knees, clawed at the lumber of the door, causing it to squeak and squeal and come apart, making a narrow slit. It was enough. The thing eased through it like a snake. The Reverend jerked the door open to see it going through the gap in the window. He dropped the axe and jerked the pistol and fired and struck the thing twice before it went out through the breach and was gone from sight.

Reverend Mercer rushed to the window and looked out. The thing was staggering, falling, rising to its feet, staggering toward the well. The Reverend stuck the pistol out the window, resting it on the frame, and fired again. It was a good shot in the back of the neck, and the brute went down.

Holstering the revolver, rushing to grab the axe, the Reverend climbed through the window. The monster had made it to the well by then, crawling along on its belly, and just as it touched the curbing, the Reverend caught up with it, brought the spell-marked axe down on its already shredded head as many times as he had the strength to swing it.

As he swung, the sun began to color the sky. He was breathing so hard he sounded like a blue norther blowing in. The sun rose higher and still he swung, then he fell to the ground, his chest heaving.

When he looked about, he saw the thing was no longer moving. Norville was standing nearby, holding one of the marked rocks.

"You was doin' so good, I didn't want to interrupt you," Norville said.

The Reverend nodded, breathed for a long hard time, said, "Saddlebags. If this is not medicinal. I do not know what is."

A few moments later, Norville returned with the flask. The Reverend drank first, long and deep, and then he gave it to Norville.

When his wind was back and the sun was up, the Reverend chopped the rest of the monster up. It had already gone flat and gushed clutter from its insides that were part horse bones, gouts of blood, and unidentifiable items that made the stomach turn; its teeth were spread around the well curbing, like someone had dropped a box of daggers.

They burned what would burn of the beast with dried limbs and dead leaves, buried the teeth and the remainder of the beast in a deep grave, the bottom and top and sides of it lined with the marked rocks.

When they were done chopping and cremating and burying the creature, it was late afternoon. They finished off the flask, and that night they slept in the house, undisturbed, and in the morning, they set fire to the cabin, using *The Book of Doches* as a starter. As it burned, the Reverend looked up. The sky had begun to change, finally. The clouds no longer crawled.

They walked out, the Reverend with the saddlebags over his shoulder, Norville with a pillowcase filled with food tins from the cabin. Behind them, the smoke from the fire rose up black and sooty and by nighttime it had burned down to glowing cinders, and by the next day there was nothing more than clumps of ash.

"Starlight, Eyes Bright" is an outlier. It came to me in a flash, and although I didn't know intellectually what it represented, I could feel exactly what it represented.

On some level, I knew it was about dissatisfaction with this world, and there's that old, scary proverb, often attributed to the Chinese, about being careful what you ask for. Finding the piece of glass changed the character's life—but for the better or the worse? Is he this or is he that in the end?

I felt it had that Lovecraftian feel of something beyond our world that we can only glimpse now and again, but we fear its entry into ours. The story was also influenced by Bradbury's poetic prose as well as the classic H. G. Wells story "The Crystal Egg," a story that's influenced many a creator in all manner of media. It's a story that is a bit like the powder on a butterfly's wings—don't handle it too much, or it disappears. That's how I wanted it, just barely there, but within the reach of the emotions, if not the intellect.

STARLIGHT, EYES BRIGHT

EARLIER SHE HAD been in the kitchen, putting dishes in the washer, and she could hear the TV in the living room. The news.

After awhile, Jim came into the kitchen and grabbed her from behind and put his arms around her waist, pushed aside her hair, and kissed her on the back of the neck.

"That feels good," Connie said.

"It's supposed to," he said.

He let her go and went to the refrigerator and took out a pitcher of iced tea and poured a glass.

"Anything interesting on the news?" she asked.

He shook his head. "All bad," he said. "I think I'll take my walk."

The curtains were drawn and the lights were out and it was night outside the window. But when the wind blew, the curtains moved and showed not only a patch of night but a glitter of stars and the blush of a bright half moon. The wind came and went, and when it came, it was cool.

They lay in bed and Connie could hear Jim breathing, slow and even, and she thought he was nearly asleep, when he said, "I found something odd on my walk."

He always took a walk after dinner, and tonight when he came back from his walk, she had been in the bath, and outside of a peck of a kiss, like a chicken bobbing for a corn kernel, and the words *good night*, they had discussed nothing and had pulled the slick sheets over them and turned out the light and stretched into position and curled around pillows. Some nights, after his walk, they made love, and others they said little because they liked to go to sleep and wake up early. And tonight she thought was that kind of night, but she had been wrong.

"I thought you were asleep, or close to it."

"No. I'm not really sleepy. I wanted to tell you what I found." She rolled over in bed and faced him, but all she could see in the dark room was his outline, and then the wind blew and the curtains moved again, and she could see him clearly for a moment. He was lying on his side with his elbow on the bed and his hand holding up the side of his head. The moonlight made him look pale as a gravestone.

"I found the oddest piece of glass," he said.

"That's it? You're keeping me up about finding a piece of glass?"

"It was broken."

"Now we're talking tragedy."

"I've never seen anything like it, and it got me to thinking."

"A piece of glass got you to thinking?"

"I don't think it's an ordinary piece of glass. When I first saw it, I thought it was stained glass, but when I picked it up, it was too thick for that, and the colors were far brighter and less even, and inside you could see the colors were like globs, and the globs moved when you turned it."

"A piece of a child's toy. A lava lamp."

"No. It's not a lava lamp. It's nothing like a lava lamp. It's not a piece of a child's toy either. I think it's not really glass . . . not the way we think of it. I just don't know how else to describe it, but I had the sudden notion that it had fallen from space at one time, maybe long ago, and time and weather and years and men working, changing the landscape, earth being shifted and heaved, had caused it to work itself out of the ground."

"That's assuming a lot."

"I know. But I felt that way when I held it in my hand. I felt maybe it was waiting for me, for some reason."

"Waiting?"

"That's what comes to mind," he said. "More I think about it, the more thoughts about it fill my head."

"That's a little odd, Jim."

"I suppose so."

"You're more tired than you think. You can show it to me in the morning."

He ignored her invitation to sleep, said, "The moon is why I saw it. It was lying beside the road, and the moonlight, or the starlight, or both, seemed to be falling down right out of the heavens and into it. It was like there was some kind of connection between it and the rays of the moon and the stars, the vastness of space, and me. I suppose it could have been, or would have been, that way with someone else, but I think it was because everything was right. The night, the moon, and me."

"The vastness of space? The night? The moon and you? That's a funny way to talk."

"I know, but it's how I feel. It's what comes to me when I think about it. This thing lying on the ground, maybe thousands, maybe millions of years old, drinking in the moonlight."

"You can't know it's older than yesterday."

"True. But when I saw it . . . no, when I touched it, that was my first thought. That it's old, very old, and that it was here when dinosaurs roamed, and maybe even before that. That it was either heaved up out of the ground or fell here from the stars. That's what I really think happened. That it fell, or that it was sent here, and that it doesn't belong here because we're all wrong. It's better than us. It fell long ago and was lost to time, and that maybe when it came, something came with it."

She had started to feel uncomfortable with all this talk, but she couldn't help but say, "What do you mean?"

"That it's not like you or me, and it doesn't exist like you or me, and that maybe it's imprisoned in the glass, or whatever that fragment is, glass, rock, something unknown. Maybe, somewhere out there, spread all over the ground for miles, and deep down, too, is the rest of it. I think what I found was a piece of its eye."

She sat up in bed. "You're talking very strange."

"Am I?"

"You never talk like this. You're odd . . . your language . . . you . . . kind of distant. It's . . . well, it's strange. You've been working too hard."

"No. I'm hardly working, really. Work is going fine."

"All right, say you did find something unique. You couldn't know all the things about it you claim to know. Like it being a piece of something's eye. Do you know how that sounds?"

"I know. And I'm not saying I know all there is to know, but . . . I get sensations. I was walking, and then I saw it, and picked it up. When I looked at it, a golden glob of something moved inside it, and then there was a blip of something red inside the gold, and I felt . . . something. Something moved in the thing, and I felt it in my hand, and by the time I was home with it, I had begun to get sensations. I've been sorting them out ever since."

"Sensations? You got sensations? Well, I got one too. You need a really good night's rest. Tomorrow's Saturday. We can sleep in. We can skip the garage-sale crawl and just sleep. Make love, go back to sleep. But now, just go to bed. It'll be okay."

"But nothing's wrong."

"You're tired."

"I'm not tired at all."

"But I am."

"I keep thinking about the poor thing."

"Poor thing?"

"Yes. I feel that it's trapped inside that glass, or some piece of it is, and it wants the other pieces of it found and brought together, and . . . I can feel something else. . . . It's very close to me now."

"Close."

"The thing that it is," he said, "It's very close."

"The thing that it is. . . . That's enough, hon. Lay down and go to sleep, and you'll feel silly about this in the morning. Damn silly."

There was a pause.

"I feel as if I'm no longer of the human race," he said.

"That could be a good thing," she said.

"Yes. I think so."

"I was joking."

"It's no joke. I think we were meant to be like light. The way it feels when you're lost and lonely and way out there in the deep dark, and then suddenly, someone shows, first from a distance, with a light. And we perk up. Maybe a little afraid. Then comes a voice we know. A friendly voice, and the light bobs our way. It should always be that way, a moment of excitement that never becomes fear, because there's the light. A time and a place where we feel safe and wanted, and there's the light. And the closer it gets, the more we become a part of it."

Connie rolled over and looked at him.

"Are you sure you haven't been drinking?"

"I'm not drinking. But I'm drunk. The glass made me drunk. It showed me that once there were good forces in the universe, and they crashed. They crashed like we humans crashed. The good that was is down deep in the ground, and it's bright, and it's colorful, and it's ours for the asking, for the wanting, but not enough of us ask or want."

"The glass? The glass is there for us, and all we have to do is take it?"

"I can't explain it. Not really."

"Who could?"

"I can feel it, but I can't explain it. Talking about it is like talking about the other side of the sky. Like telling someone how love feels when it's fresh. Why a flight of ducks will cause you to lift your eyes."

"You know, Jim, maybe tomorrow, you feel this way . . . you really should see somebody."

"The glory of what IT was, what THEY were, before they crashed, it had no name. No language. No singular connection to anything to which something could be connected. They, if *they* is the correct word, it, this structure of color and life and everything precious, was a hive of joy because there was no reason to be otherwise because it's the only sensation they/it have. Humanity, as we know it, all the whats and ifs and buts did not apply. It just was, and what it was is part of what I feel.

"It was pure happiness, and then something went wrong. Some steering through space, or mechanism, powers outside of itself. Sunspots. A rocket blast from our tired old Earth. A rift in time and space . . . I don't know. But down it went, and it's trying to come back. It wants to come back."

Jim lay back on his pillow and stared at the ceiling.

"We are our own destruction," he said. "They are the joy of the air and the sky and the earth and the beyond."

"Of course," Connie said.

"When I go," he said, "you should come with me. It's only done by choice. The glass is telling me. It wants me to be its rocket, its freedom. It wants me to bear it out and away. Come with me when I go, Connie. Link up with the pieces and let them ride you. Come with me."

"Ride me?"

"They need a host to hold their soul."

Connie was actually scared now.

"Sleep," she said.

"A third of life," he said, "lost in the bed and a dream. For them, it's always life, and it's always full of light, and happiness, things I can't explain with words."

"I've never heard you talk this way ever, Jim."

"I've never been this way. I opened a door tonight. I found one piece, and it found me, and now all the others are easy to find. All the others will want me, and I will become one of many that are one of the same."

He rose up again and put his hand under his head and rested on his elbow and looked at her in a way she thought was different than any way she had ever seen before.

Yes, she thought, *drunk, or maybe some kind of drug. A trip. That's it. He got something from work and hid it, and when he took his walk, he took it. But a night's sleep and he's better. He's gone and done something he shouldn't do, and tomorrow he'll be all right, and we'll talk about it sensibly, and he'll never do it again. It's like that. It has to be like that.*

Almost convinced, Connie lay down, shifted in bed, slid under the sheets, turned her back to him, and closed her eyes. She hadn't felt him move, and she visualized him in the same position, elbow on the bed, hand against his head, watching her.

"When they call," he said. "When I go, don't make me leave without you. Don't let yourself be you. I'm no longer me. Let us be one."

She pretended not to hear him. She closed her eyes. She tried to think of pleasant things. Finally, she felt him lie down. She thought she wouldn't sleep after all that had been said, but perhaps, as a bit of respite from the strangeness of the night, the kicking in of an internal protection device, her body relaxed, and in the silence that followed, she slept.

In the middle of the night, she awoke. She was uncertain why. She had been very tired, but now she was wide awake, and she didn't know if a sound had awakened her or an impulse. She sat up in bed and saw that he was in a chair by the window. The wind whipped at the curtains and light sifted in and fell across his face. It made the eye on the right side of his face bright with shifting light, and then the wind ceased and the curtain fell back and he was in shadow again.

She sat up in bed, said, "What's the matter? Can't sleep?"

"I got up and looked at it again. I held it over my eye. It stayed there."

That was the light she had seen move across his face, moonlight on the piece of glass. She felt a chill move along her spine like a mountain climber wearing cold shoes.

"Take that off and come to bed," she said, like a mother asking her child to remove his play hat and call it a day.

"It won't come off my eye now," he said, tapping at the glass across his right eye, "and honey, I have seen such amazing things inside of it and inside my head. My first sensations were right. It came from outer space, and it came in a ship made of night and light and all manner of matter from the creation of time. It fell here, millions and millions of years ago. Shattered on impact. Some malfunction. And the pieces went deep, lay there for a long time, then festered out of the earth like a splinter from a thumb. I saw it all inside my head, and now this piece of it lives deep inside my eye and inside my brain, and it is a dark place, a very dark place, and it moves in there, and it knows about all manner of horrors because of being here on our world. It knows horrors it never knew, and it seeks the light."

"You need rest. Come to bed."

"No. You keep saying that. I don't need rest. There are things I need, but rest is not one of them."

He moved his hands in the dark as if measuring something huge, and the hands appeared puffy, like oversized Mickey Mouse gloves. "Oh, the misery that we make. When really, all the world is waiting to be anew."

Connie went to the bathroom and put the lid down on the toilet and sat there with the light on, thinking. She didn't know what to say to Jim, and she didn't know what to do. But one thing was certain: The desire for sleep was gone. Like a sailor too long at sea, it had mutinied, and now she was wide awake and nervous.

Jim had been working a lot, so maybe it was the stress of the new accounts at work. And then again, there was the glass, and it was over his eye, held in place by no visible means of support.

Of course it has support of some kind, she told herself. *I just couldn't see it.*

But why in hell would a grown man place a piece of colored glass over his eye and sit by the window and talk about spaceships and aliens and poor sad creatures made of glass from another world?

After awhile, she got up and washed her face, went back to the bedroom. The chair by the window was empty, and he wasn't in bed.

She moved through the house in search of him, but he was nowhere to be seen. When she came to the kitchen, the back door that led to the porch was open, and there was a pleasant night breeze blowing in. She went out on the screened-in porch and looked for him, looked in the rocking chair where he liked to sit sometimes. He wasn't there. She glanced out toward the field that connected to the creek on their forty acres, and she could see him out there in the moonlight, just off the little rough path where he liked to walk. He was down on his hands and knees, digging in the grass with a trowel.

She started walking toward him, and then, perhaps through some motion of his body that gave her alert, or some hidden instinct wrapped up in her brain like a wet dog in a towel, she shivered and stepped behind a sweet gum tree, watched through a fork in the trunk.

He found something. He paused. He reached down, and a light jumped up, covered his face as if with a gel, and then the gel hardened and he shook his head, which looked like the globe of a kerosene lamp, well-lit and the color of amber. More light came from the ground, and

Connie saw it turn solid and pop against him and stick there like shards of glass, and then the glass writhed and rolled and stretched. More leaped up from the earth. More landed on Jim. The glass wrapped around him, and then he was off his knees and on his feet, spinning, stumbling. The glass spread and made scabs on his flesh the colors of cherries and lemons and oranges and apples.

Jim froze as the fragments flew up from the ground, came to roost on his flesh. He stood with his arms spread and his head drooping toward the ground.

The night crawled on. The insects ceased to buzz. The moon hazed with cloud cover. Somewhere, a dog barked. Way, way out on the highway, far beyond, she heard a car hum like a bee in a jar.

Then Jim moved, and the way he moved, it was like the night had come undone and the morning had slipped out in a flash, and then Jim spread his arms high, flapped them rapidly up and down, and the movement radiated colors across the night. Jim's feet came unstuck. He skipped and flittered over the grass, stepping in such a way, it was as if he were trying to avoid piles of dog doo. He flapped his arms and skipped and hopped. He resembled a big butterfly made of stained glass, bright and eager, but Earth-bound. His arms kept flapping, and the light from the flapping became solid, like wings, and the wings fluttered, and up he went, rising into the sky, covered in all the colors of the rainbow, and some that were not in the rainbow, and way up he rose, bright in the night, a palette of colors against the gold of the moon.

Connie felt something then. Things he had said suddenly made sense to her, and like he said, there were no words for it. She felt it because there was light from where he had leaped upward, and she could feel its warmth, taste what it was, and realize what she could have been with him.

She ran to the rainbow of color, screamed at the darting colors across the sky: "Come get me, Jim. Take me with you."

But the rainbow went away, and with it the light, and the streaks in the sky.

And so went, she realized in a hard, cold instant, her chance to be something other than what she was.

Her chance to be more than, and better than, human.

This one I'm quite fond of. Like some of the others, it has a potpourri of influences. Lovecraft, of course, but also Algernon Blackwood, Arthur Machen, "The Captain of the Polestar" by Doyle, as well as true tales about arctic explorations. The sinking of the Titanic *has its place here as well, or a ship like it. There's a bit of Philip José Farmer lurking in the fabric of the story. I think it is sufficiently creepy and has a pure Lovecraftian ending. Put on something warm while you read.*

"Slept, awoke, slept, awoke, miserable life."

—Franz Kafka

"Reality is that which, when you stop believing in it, doesn't go away."

—Philip K. Dick

"The oldest and strongest emotion of mankind is fear, and the oldest and strongest kind of fear is fear of the unknown."

—H. P. Lovecraft

THE MOON WAS bright. The sea was black. The waves rolled and the bodies rolled with it. The dead ones and the live ones, screaming and dying, begging and pleading, praying and crying to the unconcerned sea.

Behind them the great ship tipped up as if to give a final display of its former magnificence, its bow parting the night-waters like a knife through chocolate, pointing its stern to the sky, slipping slowly beneath the cold waves, breaking in half as it rode down into the bottomless sea. Boilers hissed, the steam coughed up a great white cloud. The cloud pinned itself against the moon-bright sky, then faded like a fleeting dream.

The lifeboats bobbed and the survivors in the water swam for them, called to them. One of the boats, Number Three, stuffed full of human misery and taking on water, tried to rescue more survivors, and when it did it tipped, ejected two of its riders, then righted itself again. A man in nightclothes, and a woman wearing a fur coat, fell out. The coat took on water, grew heavy, and dragged her down. A shark rose up close to the boat with its mouth wide open, its teeth gleaming as if polished by rags. Its eyes rolled back in ecstasy, and then the man was in its jaws. The shark's teeth snapped together and blood blew wide and into the boat, along with a soft bed slipper. The shark took half of the man down under, the other half of him bobbed, and then another shark drove up from below and bit the other half, carried it down and away into Davy Jones's locker.

Those that had swam for it, those remaining near Lifeboat Number Three, were taken by the sharks. The water grew thick with fins and an oily film of blood, the sounds of cries cut short. Then a wave caught Lifeboat Number Three and those still in it, pushed it forward, leaving the other lifeboats and the struggling swimmers near them far behind, bobbing like fishing corks.

There was a great strike of lightning in the distance, splitting what had been a clear sky with an electric crack of fire. When it flashed, those in Lifeboat Number Three saw a great iceberg, a cold but beaconing mass; something solid, waiting in the distance, lying jagged and white against the tumbling sea. Far beyond was an irregular rise of what appeared to be mountains. Out of the formerly clear night sky came a dark cloud, wide and thick as all creation. It sacked the moon. For the occupants in Lifeboat Number Three there was a sensation of being wrapped in black cotton.

The lightning flashed again and everything was bright, and then it was gone, and all was dark and empty again. They rode like that on the waves in the darkness, lighted now and then by bolts of lightning, cold rain driving down from the churning sky. They cupped the water that collected in the bottom of the boat with their hands and drank from it, parched. There was water all about them, water full of salt that would make them choke, sicken, and die, but this water was fresh, and their bodies called out for it.

They went through an eternity of jumping sea, darkness, and lightning-torn sky, and then they bumped against the iceberg, and then the boat was pushed back out into the sea. Then eternity ended and there was light and the storm passed and the sun peeked shyly over the waters and showed the survivors that there were still fins visible in its wide expanse. The sharks were waiting.

An iceberg was in sight, perhaps the one they had glimpsed before and bounced off of, possibly another, perhaps even the one their great ship had struck. Certainly it was a different view of the ice, because to their surprise they could see great ships of times long past pushed onto and into the berg, sometimes completely housed by it, like flies trapped and visible in blue-white amber. Attached to the berg, and somewhat in the distance, they could again see a flat expanse of ice, and that became their destination.

There were six oars in the boat and twelve survivors, eight men and four women. One of the men, a young fellow named Gavin, took charge without asking, called out for rowers, and soon six men held the six oars and cranked them, shoving Lifeboat Number Three toward an icy shore. One of the men, an older gent, collapsed at the oar and a young woman took it and began to row.

A gap in the flat ice was their destination, and they were able to row the boat to that spot and land it as if it were a beach. They climbed out of the boat—except the man who had collapsed—and onto the ice, and with fingers and feet aching from the cold, were able to pull the lifeboat out of the water, at least far enough for everyone to disembark.

The man who remained in the boat couldn't be roused. By the time they were able to lift him out and onto the ice, he was dead. Ice had formed where his nose had ran, and around the corners of his mouth and eyes. They stretched him out and pulled his arms across his chest.

Gavin said, "We have to leave him here, for now."

Another man, English, about Gavin's age, said, "Seems less than appropriate."

"You can carry him on your back if you like," said another of the men, middle-aged, an American.

"I suppose not," said the Englishman. "The women must be our first concern."

"Looks to me like we've come to a state of every man and woman for himself," said a younger American.

The young woman who had rowed said, "Seems to me it would be wiser if we all stuck together, helped one another. I think, as a woman, I can help the others as much as you."

"All of you do what you like," said the younger American. "I'm not bound to anyone."

Gavin said, "Very well then. Let's see who wants to stick together."

A quick poll was taken. Only the young American was not in agreement. "Very well," the young man said. "I'll strike out on my own."

"To where?" said Gavin. "Seems to me that we'll all end up in the same places."

"Could be," said the young American, "but I prefer to bear responsibility for me and no one else."

"Good luck to you then," Gavin said. "What's your name in case we have to say a few words over you, lower you into the water and such?"

"If that's the case, leave me where I fall," said the man, "but just for the record, the name is Hardin."

"First or last?" the woman asked.

"It'll do for both," said Hardin, and he started out walking across the ice in the direction of one of the great, frozen ships not encased in an iceberg, but instead pushed up on the ice.

The others watched Hardin for a while. He passed the ship and kept walking. The Englishman who had spoken before, said, "He isn't much of a team player, is he? Very American."

"I'm American," Gavin said.

"So you are," the Englishman said. "No offense. James Carruthers is my name."

"I'm Amelia Brand," said the woman who had rowed and suggested they stay together. "Also American."

An older woman, English, said, "They call me 'Duchess,' but we can introduce ourselves later. Seems to me it would be wise to search out some sort of shelter, and one of the ships appear to be our only possibilities."

No one else seemed even the least bit interested in talking, or giving their names. They looked defeated and ready to collapse.

"True enough," Gavin said, and looked out across the ice at the ice-captured ship. Hardin was still visible, but far away. Considering the ice, he was making good time.

Gavin started out across the ice. Amelia walked beside him. The others fell in line behind them. Glancing back, Gavin saw the wild water had lifted Lifeboat Number Three off the ice and carried it back out to sea.

They kept walking, and came to the first ship.

After a bit, Amelia said, pointing, "Right there. At the stern. I think we can board it the easiest. We'll just have to go easy."

It was a large and ancient ship of dark wood. It looked surprisingly sturdy, and the back end, with its rise of ice against it, appeared to be their way in.

"Might as well," said Duchess. "In an hour it's likely we'll all be dead, and if I can find a way to become only slightly warmer, I'd prefer to die that way."

The side of the ship was high and there were tatters of sails, partly encased in ice like damaged butterfly wings. They made their way up the slope of ice that led to the stern, but it was slick beyond the ability of all but Gavin, Amelia, and the Englishman, Carruthers.

The three of them worked up the slope, finding pocks in the ice they could use to climb. When they made the summit and boarded the ship, they cautiously made for the wheelhouse. The view glass in the wheelhouse was frosted over and the door was jammed with ice, but the three of them leaned up against it and nudged it loose, knocking it back with an explosion of shattering ice and a surprising feeling of warmth, if for no other reason than the wind was blocked by the walls and the glass.

It was short-lived comfort, for in the next moment they saw a body hung up in the wheel. It was a man in a thick coat. His face was not visible, and for a moment it appeared he had been hung there with his back against the wheel, but within an instant they saw that this was not the case. It was the face that was misplaced. His neck was long and twisted, and his head had been wrenched about to face the opposite direction. His legs had collapsed beneath him, but his arms, caught up in the wheel, held him in place. There was a large gap in the top of his head, crusted with frozen blood.

Gavin stood where he could see the man's face. His mouth was wide open and so were his eyes, and they were glazed with ice; the eyes looked like two marbles in the bottom of a glass of water, his top lip was curled back from his teeth, and the teeth looked like stalactites, cracked and broken as they were.

"My god," said Carruthers.

"How could this happen?" said Amelia. "What could have done this?"

"Let's consider later," said Gavin. "It might be best to see if we can get the others up."

Gavin unfastened the latches on the cabinets and looked inside. Eventually he found a thick coil of rope.

"This should do for starters," he said.

They pulled the others up. It took some time, and the old woman, Duchess, had the hardest bout with it, but they got her on board with only a slight sprain to her ankle and some problems with her breathing. She heaved the cold air in and out like a bellows. After everyone was on board they removed the dead body at the wheel, took it out on deck and slipped it over the far side. It was a sad thing to do to what had once been a living human being, but Gavin and the others could see nothing else for it. Leaving it there was demoralizing.

The body was stiff as a hammer and went sliding over the rise of ice like a kid on holiday, making a kind of scratching sound as it glided along. Finally it drifted off the rise and shot out onto the ice and lay there like a sunning seal. Gavin said that later he'd try to get the body out to sea, which seemed more fitting than just letting it lie on the cold ice, but he knew, as the others did, that it was a lie. He figured, as they all did, that they would soon be dead. Already their wet clothing had turned icy.

In the galley section they found a door had been knocked down, and with enough force to shatter it into several pieces. Not far beyond that they found a man's body with a large hole in his head, the blood around the wound frozen over so that it looked like someone had scooped a large chunk out of a ripe tomato with a spoon. The revolver that had killed him was still clutched in his right hand.

Obviously the scoop in his head had been made after he had shot himself, but by whom and why?

His body had to go over the side too, but it was becoming so cold, one of their number, a little middle-aged man they later learned was named Cyril, tried to get the gun out of the man's hand to use on himself, but the weapon was frozen in the dead man's fist, firm as if it were part of his fingers.

Gavin and Carruthers wrestled Cyril away from the gun that he was trying frantically to tug from the dead man's hand. They wrestled him to the floor, pulling the dead man along with them, yanking on the gun and taking two of the dead man's fingers with it, snapping them free like frozen asparagus sprouts.

"Kill me, but get off of me," Cyril said. "The cold, it's too much."

That ended the fight, and when it was done, Gavin and Carruthers were too weak to care anymore. Together, all of the survivors wandered off across the galley and down steps and into the hold below the upper deck. They found blankets there, and clothes, jackets, gloves, scarves, and wool hats. A veritable stockpile of items. They each peeled off and redressed. The women rid themselves of their wet clothes and dried on the blankets and wrapped themselves in them so that they might dress beneath them, though anything to be seen had been seen. Amelia was the only one that didn't follow that path. She boldly removed her clothes and dried in full view, and then dressed, in full sight of the men who had thrown modesty completely out the window.

Gavin took note of Amelia. What he saw he liked, though beyond that note of admiration, he was too cold for biological consideration, too eager to dress in dry and warmer clothes.

A few minutes later, with all of them dressed in the dry clothes and wearing thick, hooded coats taken from the larder, fat gloves on their hands, blankets draped over their shoulders, the world seemed slightly brighter, even if lit up only by a crack of fading sunlight through a split in the roof of the ship. Cyril, who moments before had been ready to shoot himself in the head, seemed happier and more secure. A bit of warmth had lifted everyone's spirits.

When they were dressed, they went back up the steps and found a storage room off the main section of the galley, and in there they found a man hanging from one of the meat hooks on the wall. A short piece of rope was tied about his neck and he had his hands stuck down through his belt. His head had been broken open like the others, again, most likely after death. He hung like smoked meat.

Actual smoked meat dangled on either side of him, and like the man with the gun in his hand, they left him there, but took one of the smoked hogs down and carried it back below where it was warmer.

They made it warmer yet by tying ropes across the length of the hold, finding plenty of them about, and from the ropes they dangled thick blankets and made a series of crude tents.

It was much warmer that way, and when Amelia found a small grate stove, they moved it to the side of the ship where there was a crack in the wall, and busted up some odds and ends they found, crates and an old chair, and built a fire. There were plenty of working matches that had been wrapped securely in waxed paper and then stuffed into leather bags, and there was tinder to get a fire started. When it was lit and burning, the smoke rose up through the split in the ceiling, drifted out through the wheelhouse and away. They cut strips of the hanging meat with Gavin's pocket knife. It was as fresh as the day it had been frozen. They warmed it at the fire and ate like starving wolves. Even with all that had happened to them at sea, the sharks, the cold rain, the dark toss on the waves, the dead bodies, for a moment they were hopeful.

When they were strong enough, Gavin and Amelia and Carruthers went to and dropped the other bodies down the slide of ice, and out onto the flat of it. Finished with that disconcerting chore, they returned to the hold and ate more meat.

Amelia, after eating, said to Gavin, "How old do you think this ship is?"

"1800s, I guess. I don't really know, but that seems right. An old sailing ship that went latitude when it should have went longitude. That's me trying to be cute. I don't know one from the other."

"Nor do I."

"I suppose it tried to enter an opening in the ice, tried to survive here, but things went wrong."

"What do you think happened here, besides things went wrong?"

Gavin shook his head. "I don't know. Someone on board must have went crazy and killed the men we found. As for the other sailors, no idea."

Gavin and Amelia moved to the far side of the hold and gathered up between two barrels, sitting close together for warmth.

They could see the others nearby, in the tents or just outside of them.

"What do you think of our chances?" she said.

"Grim."

"I think you're right, but believe it or not, I'm optimistic."

"Are you now?"

"I am now. We have warmth and food, and maybe we'll be found. And if not that, maybe we can find a way to leave."

"That would be a neat trick," he said. "I have no idea where we are, and I have a feeling that our ship didn't either. It all looks wrong out there."

"Wrong?" Amelia said.

"Yeah. I don't know exactly. Stars and moon, even the sea and the sky. Even in the daylight, it all looks odd."

"Have you been at sea in a lifeboat before?"

"No," Gavin said. "I admit I haven't, and could have gone my whole life without it."

"Maybe everything looks different when you're in a small boat at sea."

"I suppose," he said. "But it all seems so odd. The ship was lost before we hit the berg. I overheard a crew member say something about being lost, that the stars weren't right."

"You think he meant the constellations?"

"I guess."

"But what about the navigational equipment? You don't need stars to guide anymore."

"Sailors still depend on them, though. I think the equipment went south, and then they tried the stars, and the stars were wrong."

"Or the sailors were out of practice."

"Maybe. But even the air tastes funny."

"When it's cold, and you're in an old ship, I think the air would taste funny."

"You're right, of course, but it seems so odd."

Amelia was thinking the same, but unlike Gavin, she wasn't yet ready to admit it.

They watched as the crack of light in the ship grew darker, then was relighted as the moon rose.

"Sitting and waiting to run out of food doesn't appeal to me."

"There's a lot of food. I saw canned goods as well. The cold has probably preserved them. Water we can manage by melting ice."

"Still, there's an end to it. It's best to find a way to leave, a boat we can manage."

"It won't be this one. It's got splits in the sides. And it's too damn big."

"I don't know how we leave," Amelia said. "Only that in time, we have to, by boat or by discovery, or by death."

They slept, and when the morning light came, Amelia awoke. Gavin was gone. Bundled in her found navy coat and with a blanket draped over her shoulders, she went exploring and discovered upstairs that the others had heated up the galley stove. It was a big stove, and they were roasting the hanging meat in it. There was a tremendous amount of warmth from the stove. It felt good. The fuel for the fire had been made from coal in a bin in the galley. There was still quite a bit of coal left. That alone was reassuring.

Gavin was supervising the cooking. As it turned out he had been a chef in a large hotel in New York City. He told them about it while the meat cooked. He told them his mother was an heiress, his father was in oil and gas and loved airplanes. No one else volunteered their history, not even Amelia.

When the meat was done, they ate. There was a lot of meat, and it was determined then that they needed to stretch it out as far as possible until another plan could be hatched. Cyril suggested they eat as much as they wanted and then go out and lay down on the ice and wait for death, who would most likely show up wearing a heavy coat and carrying an ice cutter.

"Don't be silly," Amelia said. "We need to see if we can find fishing equipment for more food. The other ships can provide wood for fuel when the coal runs out."

"And when the wood runs out. What then?" Duchess said, her old skin having grown tight in the cool air.

"Perhaps we'll be rescued," Amelia said. "Perhaps we can rescue ourselves. Perhaps if this is the edge of a continent, or even some icy island, there will be someone living here. Somewhere."

"Like Eskimos?" Duchess said.

"Like anyone," Amelia said.

"Aren't you the hopeful one," Carruthers said.

"I am at that, and I'm more hopeful if we do what we can to survive for as long as we can, have a purpose. I saw lifeboats on the deck, and we might cast to sea in one of those."

"I've told you how I feel about that," Gavin said.

"We had a lifeboat," Cyril said. "We were glad to get out of it."

"If we provision, take warm clothes, and perhaps prepare a sail, we might have a chance," Amelia said.

"Are you a sailor?" Cyril said.

"No, but I prefer to try something other than giving up."

"Die here in this ship, out on the ice, or at sea, makes no difference," Cyril said. "We're going to die. Have you forgotten the dead sailors? Someone killed them."

Gavin laughed. "Yeah, but not yesterday, not fifty years ago, but well over a hundred years ago. I doubt the murderer is alive and waiting on the ice, ready to sneak back on the ship and chop holes in our heads."

"Maybe it was some kind of animal," Cyril said. "Could be that. Like a polar bear. Another one could be around."

"Bears bite and claw," Duchess said. "They don't hit you in the head with some kind of weapon, an axe perhaps."

"One thing that would be helpful in your case, Cyril," Gavin said, "is if you're going to die, and constantly talk about it, go ahead and get it over with. That leaves more food for us. That gun probably wouldn't have worked anyway. Who knows? But you can always strip and lie on the ice like you suggested. That was your idea, wasn't it? Die on the ice? I've come to think that's not a bad idea for you at all. Anything to shut your negativity up. I mean, hell, I know things are bad, and I may not want to go to sea, but I'm not ready to throw in the towel just yet, even if I'm not sure we have a towel to toss."

The others, none of which had much to say before, and hadn't even given their names, chimed in with agreement. "Yeah, shut up about dying all the time," one of the older men said. "Go out and die, but shut up."

Cyril, now that he was warm, and in spite of his words, seemed a little less inclined to follow his own suggestion. He said, "Well, I'm just saying, things aren't looking too good."

"You think you're the only one that's made that observation?" Amelia said. "What we need to do is first decide how much food is to be provided to each of us, how far we can stretch it. No midnight snacks."

She looked around at the others. They nodded in agreement.

"Then," she said, "we need to find fishing equipment and put some sort of fishing crew together. After that, we can think about the boat, the sail, and for those who want to stay, they can. For those who would like to leave, we can try. The boats, I saw two. That way we can have two crews."

"Some crews we'll be," Carruthers said.

"I saw nautical books on board," Gavin said. "I'm good at learning things from books, maybe I can figure something out."

"Somehow," Cyril said, "I doubt there will be among those nautical books one about basic sailing."

"We can find out," Gavin said.

Amelia and Gavin discovered the sick bay on a search of the ship, and found that the table used for patients was folded out from the wall and covered in blood. Something had happened on board besides being marooned. The dead sailors were proof of that. Their wounds didn't seem to fit any type of available weapon. Duchess was right. Bears and other animals seemed unlikely. Did they turn on one another in claustrophobic fury? Cannibalism? There was food, so why resort to such? And here in the sick bay, had someone been wounded due to fighting? Had someone tried to help them, and if so, where were the rest of the bodies? Why weren't they frozen on board?

The general consensus among the group was that there had been some kind of mutiny, perhaps after the ship was marooned, and a blood bath incurred. Where the survivors, if any, had ended up was unknown, but certainly the ship had sailed a crew larger than the dead men they found. Perhaps they had struck out to find what they could discover, or escape whoever, or whatever, was killing them in that head-smashing fashion.

In another part of the ship, fishing tackle was located and fishing expeditions were sent out to cast heavy lines in the cold water, using small pieces of meat for bait, and in time, the intestines from landed fish, or smaller fish, were hooked and put back in the water as bait.

Fish near the ice seemed ravenous, and they successfully pulled large catches from the icy waters, cut them up, and cooked them in the great galley stove. With a reasonable supply of renewable food somewhat assured, the spirits of all involved increased.

This went on for a few days, the meals alternating between the meat in the galley and the fish from the sea, and then Amelia said she wanted to explore, see if there were other things they could use from the ice-locked ships, and so after a night of high wind and blowing snow, she and Gavin started out on an expedition. The daylight sky seemed as odd as the night sky had been, though the storm had long blown out. The sunlight was somewhat green on the horizon and cool yellow above them, like a light doughy crust on the sky.

Another point of contention, which had first been addressed by Carruthers, was the fact that there was day and night. It seemed logical, considering the ice, that they might well be at a point on the globe where night reigned for long periods before giving way to daylight for equally long stretches. But that wasn't the case here. Day came with its strange green and yellow tints and an anemic red-hazed sun that soon turned egg-yolk yellow. Day gave it up within hours to thick, blue-black darkness with a greasy moon that appeared to wobble when not being observed directly. The stars moved in great swirls, as if the earth and all the darkness and pulsing orbs were slowly traveling toward an exit by cosmic drain. None of this fit the fact that they had been crossing a calm and warm ocean the night before, but another weird factor was no one could remember ever having boarded the ship, and they could only remember vagaries of the trip, some events on board, drinks and dancing. Trying to discuss this led to a lot of quiet moments. No one remembered where they were going, or why they had chosen to be at sea, or for that matter, none could even remember if they were crossing the Atlantic or the Pacific. Atlantic seemed more likely to lead them to ice, but still no one knew for sure. It was a distressing fact that could only be discussed briefly. It was like trying to remember what had happened in the womb.

Gavin carried the pistol with him, though he wasn't sure it worked. He didn't see any reason to need it, but it made him feel better somehow. They looked where they had dropped the body of their comrade over the side of the ship with the long-dead sailors, but no bodies were there. Something had taken them away. Polar bears? So far nothing of the sort had been seen. There were no tracks and no drag marks, but considering the constantly blowing wind and renewing ice, as well as blankets of snow, there was nothing unusual about that.

After walking for a time, they began to feel certain they were not on an iceberg at all, but a large mass of ice that stretched far to the horizon. There were ships locked into it here and there, and some of the ships were more modern. Dogsleds were found, buried in the ice, and finally they came upon a prop airplane, blood-red in color. It seemed to have landed smoothly and sat there as if ready for takeoff. The exception being the wheels, which were sunk into the ice. Its nose was lifted upward, the tail was resting on the ice. In the far background, mountains, tinged puke-green by the light, rose up high and misty. As they stared at them, they seemed to move, ever so slightly.

"How can that be?" Amelia said. "Moving mountains?"

"A mirage," Gavin said. "The movement part, anyway."

"Sure looked like it moved. It was subtle, but I saw it."

"Me too, but mountains don't move. Has to be a trick of the light. . . . But the plane, it's here. It's an Electra. Late thirties or forties, I'm reasonably sure. My father owned one. Or one very similar. No expert, but I'm a little knowledgeable on recognizing a few of them. My dad also had models of a lot of other kinds of planes. So I was aware of certain things about them without really being highly knowledgeable."

"Can you fly?"

"I only have a general idea how it's done. You know, from listening to my dad. Besides, the plane would only comfortably carry a couple. Of course, that couple could be us. But then there's that whole almost knowing how, and if this plane has sat here for very long, the engine is certainly ruined by the weather. If it flew, I'd probably manage, at best, to run it into the sea, or take it up and have it come down too fast and on the nose."

Amelia let the thought of flying away with Gavin run around in her head. She owed the others nothing. Still, it seemed like a rotten thing to contemplate.

She examined the plane, saw that the hatch door was flung open. It had steps leading from the door to the ground. She walked up the steps and stuck her head inside.

"Jesus," she said. "It's warm in here. How could that be?"

Gavin climbed the steps and looked in. He stepped inside beside her. "It's more than warm, it's been flown. The motor has only been off a short time, that's why it's warm in here, even with the door open. Engine heat."

"That means someone just left it," Amelia said.

They went outside and looked around. No sign of anyone. They prowled the outside of the plane, gently touched its underbelly. No doubt. Gavin was right. The engine was warm.

"How can that be?" Amelia said, moving her hand away from the plane.

"Just because it's from another era doesn't mean it hasn't been kept in good condition, even flown recently by some plane enthusiast. But how anyone would end up way out here in a small plane like that is hard to guess."

"Where's the pilot?" Amelia said.

"They may have force landed here, fuel or weather reasons. A number of possibilities. Engine trouble, perhaps. They went outside to look about, trying to figure things out, same as us, or deciding to pee, the storm hit. Remember how fast that storm came? I was looking at that crack in the ship. The sky was clear. I could see the moon. And then there was a moan of storm and a blow of snow, and the sky went white. It happened in the time it takes to blink. The pilot could have been trapped outside and unable to make it back to the plane. They might have been covered by snow, iced over. Hell, we could be standing on them. Or they stumbled off blind, walked into a snowbank or the sea. It would be easy to become lost in a storm like that."

"Could be," Amelia said. "Think about how we ended up here. We were fine on our ship one minute, and the next, we weren't."

"Warm, clear seas, and then some place full of ice," Gavin said.

"Exactly. And we don't even know why we were on the ship, how we got there."

"I thought it would come back to me. Thought we were all in shock. Now, I'm not so sure. What I am sure of is things aren't right here, Amelia. All these ships and planes. It's as if they all went through some hole and ended up here. Maybe a hundred years ago, maybe five minutes ago."

The wind swirled particles of snow. It seemed chill enough to freeze an open flame.

Amelia tugged her scarf tight over her mouth and the tip of her nose. "Why are we standing here? Let's get inside the plane for a while."

They stepped inside, closed the door against the wind and the cold. Already the warmth was dying.

Prowling the front of the plane, in a pocket by the controls, Amelia found a small revolver. It was loaded with five rounds.

"Now we're both armed, in case we're attacked by a sea bird," Amelia said.

"I think there's a lot more than sea birds to fear out here," Gavin said. "At first I didn't think so, but now I wonder. More I think about it, the more worried I am. Maybe those ships haven't been here as long as it seems."

"The hole in time idea?"

"Something like that."

"Right now I'm not ruling anything out," Amelia said.

They looked about. There were a few clothes in the plane and a small mattress. They looked for anything usable, but found nothing other than the gun, and a sweater that Amelia took with her as they left, slipping it on and then putting her coat back on over it. It gave her a bulky appearance, but the sweater was flexible beneath the coat, and she was warmer. They found a flight manual, a couple of hardback books, but nothing else. They left it all.

At the view glass, they looked out at the sky. It had turned azure and there were strange strips of yellow and gold leaking into it, and even as they watched, those gave way to blue then black. Amelia said, "The sky's colors are always changing."

"Nothing seems right here," Gavin said.

The moon appeared like a blister, high and full, ready to pop. The stars were plentiful, but it was as if a hand had stirred them into new formations. They were of varying sizes, like coins and pinheads tacked to the heavens. There were large numbers of jetting streaks, shooting stars, red, blue, and green, and variations of those colors. Amelia was reminded of schools of bright darting fish in an inky pond.

They decided it was best to return. The night was bright, and in time the plane would grow cold. So out they went, carefully stepping onto the moon-glared ice.

Using ships and sleds they had passed before as their guides, they made their way back to the ship where their companions waited. The wind kicked up, and the already intense cold became nearly unbearable. Tugging the collars of their coats tight around their necks, wrapping their scarves around their heads like bandages, leaving only their eyes visible, they continued. Snow was as thick as exploded goose down blown loose from a pillow.

They stumbled forward, trying their best to keep an eyeline, back to their ship. Now and then there was a gap in the snow, and it gave them an occasional glimpse of a recognizable ice formation, but those kinds of things could change quickly, reshaped by snow and wind.

Amelia tripped over one of the dogsleds they had encountered earlier. As she was rising, the wind and blowing snow shifted, and she saw moving in the brief gap of white a naked man wearing a strange and oversized headdress. The headgear was flapping and blowing in the wind with the frantic movements of a bird with its feet tied to the ground. It was visible for an instant, then gone.

"Did you see that?" Amelia said.

"Hardin," Gavin said. "It was Hardin."

"Naked? Wandering through snow? How could that be?"

"How could it be anyone?"

They tried to see Hardin again, but the snow had wrapped him up and hidden him away.

"What was he wearing on his head?" she asked.

"No idea."

"Should we try and find him?"

Gavin shook his head. "We are lost ourselves. And remember, he didn't want to be found. Maybe he stripped down to die quicker."

"But he's been out here for days now."

"Perhaps he holed up somewhere for a while before he made his final move."

"So he hung out, then today stripped naked, put on a weird headdress, and wandered out in the snow?"

"Hell, I don't know, Amelia. I know what you know."

They found themselves, without discussing it, moving away from where Hardin had been seen, heading away from the direction he had taken. Trudging on for some distance, they ran up against the wall of a ship. They immediately knew it was not their ship. Its wood was black and tarred where there had been repairs. They found it too high to access by normal means, but near the bow they discovered there was a crude ladder, and though it was slippery, they managed it, and climbed on board.

The interior of the ship was a brief respite from the blowing wind and snow.

They combed the ship. No food supplies or frozen bodies were found. The crew had obviously abandoned the sailing rig, taking whatever was edible with them, as well as stripping it of furniture and the like. Most likely to make sleds to drag their goods, or to provide firewood. The vessel seemed to be from a similar era as the ship where their group had ended up. The lifeboats had been removed, and Amelia wondered if they had made it to somewhere safe by sea, or were they dead on the ice, preserved like frozen sardines with the tops of their heads torn open? And how long ago did this ship arrive here?

"You know what's odd," Amelia said. "In the back of my mind I feel like I know the answer to this, or a piece of it, but I just can't get that answer to surface."

"I know exactly what you mean," Gavin said.

In the back of the ship's hold they found a mass of blankets, and they covered themselves in them, pulling them over their heads, and then they lay on others and listened to the snow blast about outside.

Cold air came through cracks in the ship and licked at them, but the stack of blankets warmed them, and they lay there reveling in the warmth.

They were snuggled close together, and without suggestion, they touched noses. They lay in silence for a while, and then Amelia reached out and touched Gavin, and then Gavin touched her, and then their lips pressed together. They pulled at one another's clothes, and for a time they were all right beneath the mass of blankets, wriggling into each other, as if trying to be absorbed by the other's warmth.

When they were finished they lay panting beneath the blankets, snug and comfortable as they had been since landing in the wet ocean, and then on the ice.

"Guess we needed that," Amelia said.

"Needed and wanted," Gavin said.

Amelia lay in Gavin's arms. He was strong. She could feel the muscles in his arm beneath her neck.

"The wind has stopped," Amelia said.

"Now we're back to living in the real world. Or the unreal world. Whatever the hell kind of world we are in. Look, I think the smartest thing would be, when the storm calms, we go back to our ship, bring rope, use one of the dogsleds to drag lumber back for firewood. You know, chop it out of this one with the axe. We can mount expeditions that can take us farther, the way you suggested. Figure out some way to make tents, devise heating vessels to take with us. Go as far as we can, using our ship as base."

"We will need to make snowshoes to travel long distances," Amelia said. "I think we can figure out how to do that. There's a lot of odds and ends on board our ship. And to go back to my theme, seeing what's out there is better than waiting to freeze, or eventually starving."

"I've come to agree," Gavin said. "Especially now that I have another reason to live."

Amelia touched his face and kissed him. "You mean me, right?"

Gavin laughed. "Of course. But listen, girl. I'm willing to try and see what we can find, but to be honest, I don't expect that within a few miles we will come to green grass and cows grazing in a pasture."

"We could try my other plan, use one of the lifeboats, rig a sail of some sort. Try and find land. Land that isn't freezing. Land where someone lives and things make sense. I know. I've suggested it before, and no one has been keen on the idea, but it's still something to consider."

"I'd rather die on the ice than in some boat on a black-ass sea."

"I'd rather not die," Amelia said. "Period."

"A fine sentiment," Gavin said. "But for the time being we have food at the ship, and we can carry some of these blankets with us to add to our store there. Later we can come back for more, bring some of the others so we can tote more supplies."

"Provided we can get them to leave the ship to do anything but fish."

"Food from the sea has proven reasonably certain," Gavin said. "What's out here beyond the ships, toward the mountains, there's nothing certain about that."

The snow quit swirling and the wind ceased to howl. Moonlight speared through the cracks in the ship. They dressed and climbed off the ship and started walking again. The night was clear and bright, so bright it was as if they were walking under a giant streetlamp. The wind had left snow piled on the ice. As they walked, they came across footprints—bare footprints.

Amelia said, "Hardin?"

"Possibly."

They went surely in the direction of their ship, able to see landmarks now—ships and sleds and juts of ice they recognized that were close to their destination. Before long they came to a broad snowbank, and lying in it was Hardin.

He was facedown and there was blood on the snow; it had crystallized like ruby jewels and smears of strawberry jam.

Amelia bent down and looked close at Hardin. Finally, with help from Gavin, she rolled him over. It was difficult, and Hardin made a ripping sound as the ice tore away from his flesh. His mouth was open; his eyes were wide as well. He had died with his nostrils flared, like a horse blowing air. High on his forehead was a tear in his skull, wide and deep.

"He looks terrified," Gavin said.

"Yes, and look here."

There were drag marks in the blood. There were places in the snow that gave the impression of an octopus wriggling, and then the places grew larger, and finally there was a great shape in the snow. It was a cylindrical shape with a large star-shape at the top. There were thrash marks in the snow all around it. They could see marks where it had crawled off across the snow, its size swelling.

"Whatever it was," Amelia said, "it grows rapidly."

"And it came out of Hardin's head."

"Or attached itself to him. What in hell does that?"

"I don't know, but here's another thing," Gavin said. "He walked."

"Perhaps not on his own power," she said.

"That's insane."

"You saw what was on his head. Some kind of parasite. He may have been dead for days, moving around, but not truly alive, being fed on and articulated like a puppet by that monster."

"All right, but the question has to be, what does this parasite feed on normally if humans aren't in supply?"

"Seals. Sea life. Maybe it's sea life itself, comes on shore from time to time, but exists in the waters as well. Maybe it eats what it eats because it's there to eat, not because it needs it for sustenance. Something left that imprint, and whatever it is, is certainly not human."

They traveled on, tingling with unease. They felt as if they were being watched, but when they looked, nothing was there, just mounds of snow, a few juts of ice in the peculiar moon and starlight. Still, the persistent feeling of being observed moved with them, and with it came a strange feeling of nausea, as if they were breathing air that had been disgorged by something foul, a primitive perception that something primal and dangerous was nearby.

"Suddenly I'm hoping this pistol works," Gavin said, pulling it from his pocket and holding it in his gloved hand.

Amelia followed suit with the pistol she had found in the plane.

They trudged along with their pistols, and walking near the waterline, they saw a lifeboat banging up against the ice.

"It's Lifeboat Number Three," Amelia said. "It washed up here."

"Well, I never want to be in it again," Gavin said. "I hate water."

"And you took a trip on a ship?"

"Thought I might meet women."

Amelia laughed. "That part worked."

As they watched, the dark waters caught up the boat and moved it out into the night. The moonlight coated the lifeboat in silver paint, and they watched until it bobbed up and down and out of sight, as if hiding behind the waves.

They continued until their ship was in sight, then tucked their guns away. When they climbed the ice at the stern and stepped on board, they found a sheet of dark ice running from the bridge to the stairs that led to the hold. The ship was as quiet as a snail's progress.

"That looks like blood," Amelia said, pushing back her jacket hood, unwinding the scarf over her face. Gavin pushed his own hood back, pulled down his scarf.

They pulled their pistols again, followed the dark trail, crept down the stairs, trying not to slip on the ice. At the bottom of the stairs they encountered cold, though not freezing cold. There were remnants of warmth from human bodies and a near-dead fire in the small stove below. The coals glowed weakly through ash and semi-devoured chunks of wood formerly belonging to what might have been a chifforobe.

There was a clank toward the back of the hold, in the shadows, and Amelia and Gavin hesitated, then eased in that direction, pistols at the ready.

Movement.

Something running in the dark.

Gavin said, "Hey, folks. It's us."

A flash of shadows, something whirling in the dark, catching moonbeams from a crack in the hold. A flutter of rubbery movement atop something, and then it was gone.

Amelia turned to the right where she heard a faint sound, saw nothing, then turned completely around.

That's when a shadow broke loose and darted into the moonlight, came for Amelia with a shriek and a flash of tentacles.

It was Duchess, or what she had been. Her head was broken open and a great mass of writhing tentacles flapped from her skull. A bladder shape dangled out of a wide crack in her forehead, and the bladder almost covered her eyes. She was stripped of clothing. Her saggy breasts flapped like something skinned. Her hands were reaching, her mouth was screeching.

Just as Duchess reached her, Amelia lifted the pistol and shot her in the face, right above the bridge of the nose, right below the wide crack in her skull. Duchess's hands brushed Amelia's shoulders and a black mess came from the bladder inside her skull, squished out and into the moonlight in one long squirt. The beast in Duchess's head tore loose from its cranial house, flipped through the air, smashed against the deck, began to puff and swell like a bagpipe. Duchess's lifeless body collapsed in a heap at Amelia's feet. The thing on the floor hissed, then squeaked, and then revealed an extended torso that slid slickly out of the bladder like a fat rat from a greased pipe. Its body was tubular and long with a starfish head. It swelled as it slithered. Sucker-covered tentacles extended from the cylindrical portion of its body, slapped at the floor and waved in the fat slit of moonlight as if trying to grab the moon's attention.

Amelia stepped close and shot the star-head. Tentacles snapped out, smacked the top of her hand, nearly knocking the gun loose, leaving a circular welt, red and inflamed, just above her thumb. It made a gaseous sound and slid greasily across the flood as if pulled on a rope, collapsed, tentacles falling and flailing like electrified noodles.

Amelia heard Gavin's gun snap without firing, snap again. Amelia turned and shot at what was charging across the floor at them—Cyril, his head broken open, giving ride to one of the tentacle-bearing bladders. She shot again, directly for the bladder this time, and when she did, the black goo went up and out, darker than the shadows around it. Cyril stumbled as if he had stepped into a hole, fell facedown, his naked ass humping up in the air once, then collapsing, his pelvis slamming against the floor. The creature detached from Cyril, scuttled away. Amelia was about to shoot again, but Gavin stopped her.

"Save the shot," he said. There was an axe near the stove, one they had used to shatter wood for burning. Gavin grabbed it, swung it into the creature, chopping the star-head loose, causing a dark mess to gush across the floor.

"Jesus," Amelia said. "What are those things?"

Gavin trembled. "I'm going to guess nothing known to science."

Gavin made his way to the stove, picked up the matches that lay on the floor nearby, scooped out a partly lit stick of wood from the stove, waved it about in the cold air until it flamed slightly. Amelia, all the while, was turning with her pistol, watching. She had one shell left, as the revolver had only housed five loads. Gavin's gun was useless, packed as it was with ineffectual loads.

Gavin wagged the small torch about. In the shadows they saw a heap of nude bodies. The remains of their lifeboat companions. Cautiously, Amelia and Gavin moved nearer. All of the heads were broken open, but none contained their former passengers. Carruthers lay on top. All of them were nude. Either their clothes had been ripped from them by the creatures, or they had torn them loose themselves, as if the things made their bodies boil.

Something clattered in the dark.

They turned. Gavin lifted the small torch. Creatures fluttered in the light and hustled away. Nothing was seen distinctly.

"They're all over the place," Gavin said.

"We have to go," Amelia said. "Right now."

Gavin dropped the torch, and carrying the axe at a battle-ready position, he and Amelia rushed up the steps, onto the deck, and over the side where the ice was high. They scrambled so quickly they fell into one another and slid down the ice in a tumble. At the bottom of their fall, they looked up. There, on the deck, were the things, tentacles waving about like drunks saying howdy. The creatures pushed together. At first Amelia thought it was for warmth, and then she thought: *No, they live here. They endure here.*

As they watched, the things came together, tighter. There was a great slurping sound, and then they hooked together and twisted and writhed and became one large bulbous shape with a multitude of heads and an array of tentacles. It started to edge over the side of the ship.

Amelia and Gavin began to run.

They ran along the snow-flecked ice, falling from time to time, and when they looked back, they saw the thing dropping off the side of the ship, falling a goodly distance, striking the ice heavily, and then rolling and gliding after them.

The snow began to flurry again. It blew down from the sky in a white funnel. It spread wide and wet against them, pushed them like a cold, damp hand. They wound their scarves around their mouths as they ran, pulled their hoods down tight, only looked back when they feared it might be at their very heels, but soon it was lost to them, disappearing within a swirling surge of blinding snow.

Winded, they began to trudge, having no idea where they were heading. Without snowshoes, it was a hard trek. Eventually they came to the plane, its bright red skin flaring up between the swirling flakes of snow. They stood and stared at it.

"I'm so cold I don't care if that thing catches up with me," Gavin said. "I've got to get warm. If only for a little while."

Amelia nodded. "Yeah. That thing can have me, but only if I get a bit warm first."

They slipped inside, having to really tug the door free this time, the whole machine having been touched with frost. They closed the door and locked it. They moved to the cockpit and looked out. There was nothing to see. Just snow. It had ceased to flurry as violently as before, but it was still blowing. After a brief rest, Amelia looked around the plane, more carefully this time, found a few more rounds of overlooked ammunition, enough to fill her pistol. There was a flare gun they had not found in their initial search, and there were four flares in a box beneath the cockpit. Gavin took the flare gun and loaded a flare in it. It wasn't a perfect weapon, but it was something. Gavin stuck the remaining flares in his coat pocket. Finally, exhausted, they laid down on the mattress together and, without meaning to, fell asleep.

At some point, much later, Amelia thought she heard a kind of coughing, and then a loud growl. She tried to wake up, but exhaustion held her. If the things were on her, then they could have her. She was warm and exhausted by fear. She couldn't move a muscle. Shortly, the growling ceased, and Amelia drifted back down into deep sleep. Down in that dark well of exhaustion she sensed a darkness even more complete. Things moved in the dark, bounded about inside her head. Images struck her like bullets, but then they were gone, unidentified. It was a sensation of some terrible intelligence, a feeling of having a hole in the fabric of reality through which all manner of things could slip. She slept deep down in that crawling dark, but yet it was still a deep sleep and in time even the horrors down there in her dreams let her be.

When Amelia awoke, Gavin was missing.

Or so she thought. She sat up. He was sitting in the pilot chair in the cockpit. It was daylight. She went to join him, sat in the co-pilot chair. Gavin had a manual in his lap and was reading it.

"No monsters yet?" she said.

"I think we lost them, confused them, or they're taking a nap. I don't know. You know what? I can fly this. Theoretically, anyway."

"Will it fly?"

"The engine was warm not that long ago. It hasn't been ruined by the cold yet. While you slept, I tried it. After a few false starts it fired."

Amelia realized this was what she had heard while sleeping. Not the roar of some monster, but the roar of a machine.

"I think the pilot was driven down by a sudden storm. Nothing in the sky one moment, the next a storm. They probably flew here through some dimensional gap, the way we sailed here in the ship. Slipped right through, like a child's toy through a crack in the floor."

"Then why haven't you flown us out, you're sure you can do it?"

"I'm not all that sure, actually. Like I said, theoretically, I can fly us out. I cut the engine because I could tell it was stuttering. I wanted it to warm a bit more, or rather I have plans to warm it, and running it before its warmer would just use up gas, and I couldn't see to fly anyway. I couldn't see six inches in front of me. I got started, though. While you slept I used a board and dug around the wheels, freed them. Wore me out. I'm going to build a fire out front of the plane to warm it more. It might ruin things, catch the damn plane on fire, or it might improve things. I don't know. But if the storm passes, as the daylight comes, the sun will warm the engine and then I'll warm it with a bit of fire."

"A bit of fire might be too much fire. Why not just let the sun warm it?"

"It will be warmer, but it won't be warm," Gavin said. "The sun will need some help."

"That would be the fire," Amelia said.

Gavin nodded. "It's warm, then, we might fly out. For all I know I won't be able to fly it at all. Or I'll manage to get it up, only to have it come right back down. Or say I get it up and we fly away. Where are we flying to? How much fuel do we have? Still, what else is there? You with me?"

"Get us up, and fly us out," Amelia said. "You can do it. Any place is better than here."

It seemed like a long time, sitting in the cockpit waiting for daylight. Sitting there expecting the monsters to arrive and break through the plane and knock holes in their heads, cause them to tear off their clothes and turn them into naked staggering corpses. They sat back and waited for light, but it was a nervous wait.

The wind died down, the snow blew out, and the daylight finally came. The sun looked at first like a gooey hot-pink lozenge. It turned slowly from pink to orange, spread light like a hot infection across the horizon.

Amelia and Gavin dragged the mattress outside, under the front of the plane, cut it open with the axe. The cotton stuffing inside sprang up through the splits. They piled debris from inside the plane on top of that. They tore pages from the books they had discovered inside, and used them for tinder. Gavin used the matches he had taken from the ship to light the pages. Gradually the flames caught, sputtered, began to eat the tinder and the pages. They watched the pile burn, and watched for any tentacle-bearing visitors that might show.

When the fire was licking at the bottom of the plane, they went inside and waited. Gavin said, "Here's to no unfortunate explosions."

"I agree," Amelia said.

They touched their fists as if they held drinks in their hands.

They watched as the flames grew and licked up around the nose, saw the paint start to bubble and flake.

"I think it's time," Gavin said.

Gavin tried turning the engine over.

It did nothing at first. And then it coughed, and then it died, and then Gavin tried again. It coughed again, started to die, but clung to life, blurted and chugged, and then began to roar. Eventually, it began to hum.

Gavin took another look at the manual, which he had again placed in his lap, said, "Let me see now."

"That does not inspire confidence," Amelia said.

"All right. I got this. Mostly."

Gavin touched the controls, managed to move the plane, rock it along on its wheels, veer it to the right, away from the direction of the fire and the sea. Then he gunned it. It rolled and slid on the ice.

As they rattled forward on the icy surface, it seemed as if the plane might come apart.

But there were worse things happening. They saw it coming across the ice, the star-heads united into one fat star-head, a hunk of dark meat coated in sun-glimmered slime with pulsing bladders and thrashing tentacles. Somehow it had found them, heard them perhaps, seen the fire. It was directly in their path.

"Ah hell," Gavin said.

He worked the controls, turned the plane a little, moving to the left of the creature.

Now Gavin turned again, placing the creature at the rear of the plane. The plane slipped and wobbled, but continued to rush over the ice.

"I forget how to lift," Gavin said.

"What?"

"I forget how to lift off. Damn. I just read it."

Amelia grabbed the manual. "All right, let me see. . . . No, that's how to land."

"The ice ends."

"What?"

Amelia looked up. The ice sheet had a drop-off, and the drop-off was jagged and deep.

"Turn," she said. "Turn the goddamn plane."

Gavin turned to his left, the wheels managing to stay on the ice, but not without sliding. They could see the creature again from this position, out the side window. It was rising up and smashing down on the ice, throwing up crushed sparkles like fragments of shattered glass, then it inched forward with the flexibility of a caterpillar, rising up again, smashing down, repeating the method, traveling at surprising speed. The plane was moving away from it, though, gaining speed and gaining space.

"Okay. The throttle," Amelia said. "Listen to me, now. Do what I say."

Slowly and loudly she read out the instruction booklet. Gavin following them as well as he understood them, the machine lifting up, then coming down on the wheels, bouncing, slipping, yet moving forward. Not too distantly in front of them were large snowbanks.

"It's now or never," Gavin said.

Amelia read from the manual, and Gavin, listening intently, did as he was told, trying to be careful about it, trying to cause the plane to rise.

The plane jumped up into the frosty air like a flame-red moth, into the richly dripping sunlight. Below, the white face of the earth shimmered and the montage monster hastened across it, lifted its great starred head toward the vanishing plane, its shadow falling down behind it to lie dark on the ice. It cried out loud enough to be heard even inside the speeding plane, then the beast fell apart. The creatures from which it had been constructed came unstuck and collapsed against the ice, their multitude of shadows falling with them.

The plane sailed on.

For a time, Amelia and Gavin coasted in the sun-rich sky, over the ice, toward a green haze drifting above jagged mountain peaks.

Gavin tipped the wheel, the nose lifted, and the plane sailed up. When he was as high as he felt he could comfortably go, he leveled out. The mist, white and foamy as mad-dog froth, parted gently.

Below them were wet mountaintops, and straight before them were higher mountains tipped by clouds. To the right of those peaks was a V-shaped gap.

"There," Amelia said, pointing at the gap. "Go there."

"You know I don't really know how to fly, right?"

"You know enough," Amelia said. "You learned more from your dad than you thought, and that manual. We're up here, aren't we? Go there."

Gavin tilted the plane to the right, then settled it, set a nose-aligned course for the gap in the mountains. Shortly, they were in the center of the gap, mountains on either side of them. When they came to the other side of the gap there was a valley of ice and snow, and far to the left there was the darkness of the great waters. Directly before them were more mountains, and above those a green mist shimmered with sunlight. They saw something on the ice directly below them that took their breath away.

There were spires, golden and silver, and what could have been thick glass or ice, great structural rises of wicked geometry. Littered before the structures, in a kind of avenue, were what looked to be white humps of stones.

"My god," Gavin said. "A city. The place is enormous."

"How could those things build this?"

"Most likely they didn't," Gavin said. "But whoever built it, built it while drunk."

And on and on the city stretched, toward the blue-black mountains tipped by what looked like a green fungus.

As they neared them, Amelia felt as if a great presence was moving behind the sky and sliding down and into her thoughts. It was the same as during her sleep in the plane, but more intense. In fact, it was

painful, even nauseating. She felt stuffed with thought and information she couldn't define.

They flew above the irregular city, watching with awe. When they
finally passed over it and the rocky avenue, Gavin turned the plane
for a return pass, and when he did, the plane coughed, sputtered, and
started going down.

"Out of fuel," Gavin said.

"Priceless," Amelia said.

"I'll try and glide it."

There was a stretch of ice beyond the avenue, and as the plane
began to spit and sputter and hurry down, Gavin leveled it, cruised
over the avenue toward the ice. It was not a perfect plan, but they were
less likely to catch the wheels in the rocks and flip.

Gavin said, "I'm pretty sure I can land it." His hands trembled at
the controls.

"No doubt, one way or another you will," Amelia said.

The plane's engines sputtered and died.

Gavin did his best to glide it down and smooth it out for a landing,
but the plane was moving fast and he was uncertain what to do. Amelia
read frantically aloud from the instruction manual. She was reading it
when they came within twenty feet of the ice. She stopped reading
then. There was nothing else left to say, and no time to say it.

The plane came down on the ice and the wheels touched. The plane
bounced, way up, then back down, went into a sideways skid, and then
Gavin lost control and the nose dipped and hit the ice, and the plane
spun and started coming apart.

The cold brought Amelia around. She could see the sky. It was odd,
that sky. She thought she was seeing reflections off the ice, but instead
she was looking as through a transparent wall. She could see people
walking, riding horses, clattering about in wagons, cars of all eras
driving, boats sailing and planes flying. There was depth to her view.

People stacked on top of one another as they walked, drove, flew, or sailed. People floated by, sleeping in their beds, and there were the star-head things, and monstrous, unidentifiable visions, and all the images collided and passed through one another like ghosts. She was flooded with the soul-crushing realization that she was less than a speck of dust in the cosmos. The knowledge of her insignificance in the chaotic universe overwhelmed her with sadness and self-pity. Whatever was out there not only had a physical presence, it had a powerful presence in her unconscious, a place where it revealed itself more and more.

She awoke with something warm and wet running down her face. She lifted her hand and opened her eyes. She saw blood was on her gloved fingers. There were tears in her eyes. She touched the wound on her head. Not bad, she determined, a scrape.

The sensation passed. She tried to sit up, only to realize she was in the plane seat, and it was lying with its back on the ice, and she was lying in it. It had come free of the plane and she was sliding along the ice with it.

She rolled out of the chair, put her gloved hands on the ice, got her knees under her and stood up. She wobbled. There was wreckage strewn across the ice. There was a vast churn of black smoke on the ice. Gavin came walking out of the black smoke and into the clear carrying the axe he had taken from the ship, and now recovered from the wreckage of the plane. His face was bloody and blackened from smoke, he had a limp, but he was alive.

As they came together and embraced, Gavin said, "Told you I could land it."

They both laughed. It was a hearty laugh, a bit insane really.

"What now?" Amelia said.

"I think we have no other choice than the city. Out here we'll freeze. The wind is picking up, and it's damp, so if nothing else we have to get out of the wind."

"It's chancy."

"So is being out here. No shelter. No food. No plane."

They looked toward one of the buildings, a scrambled design of spires and humps, silver and gold, or so it had seemed from the sky. Now they could see that the light had played on it in a peculiar way, giving it a sheen of colors it did not entirely possess.

"Very well then," Amelia said, and holding hands they started toward the structures.

They came to the rocky, white road, discovered the lumps were not stones, but skulls and bones, all of the skeletal parts pushed into the ice by time. There were animal skulls and bones amidst human bones and skulls, long and narrow skulls, wide and flat skulls, vertebrae of all manner were in the bone piles, many impossible to identify, some huge and dinosaur-like.

Amelia glanced at the city buildings, which stretched to one side as far as the eye could see, and to the other until they reached the sea. She stared at the building before them, saw it was connected to others by random design. It was hard to figure a pattern.

The wind whistled and hit them like a scythe of ice.

"You're right," she said. "We have to go inside."

They made their way inside the city.

It was warmer inside. No wind, and there seemed to be a source of heat. They didn't notice that until they were well inside and found the path beneath the structure divided and twisted into a multitude of narrow avenues, like a maze. The floor was smooth, but not slick, and the walls were the same.

Gavin marked the walls with the axe as they went, forming a Hansel and Gretel escape path. Soon they unwound their scarves and let them hang, they removed their gloves and stuffed them in coat pockets and loosed the top buttons on their shirts. It was comfortably warm.

They were eventually overtaken by exhaustion. Amelia said, "We should rest while we have the opportunity. I think I may be more banged-up than I first realized."

"We don't know what's inside this place," Gavin said.

"We know that right this minute we are okay. There is nothing more we can know in this place, and I don't know about you, but being in the cold, flying in an airplane with an untrained pilot, crash landing on the ice, has tuckered me a little."

Gavin chuckled. "Yeah. I'm pretty worn."

They stopped and leaned against the wall, stuck their feet out. The warmth inside the structure was pleasurable. It was like a nice down blanket, though there was a faint foul smell.

"I had this vision, of sorts," Amelia said. "Or maybe I actually saw something."

"Vision? Worlds and animals and people and things stacked on one another, flowing through one another. A feeling of . . . miasma."

"You too?"

"Yeah. I don't know what I was seeing exactly, but when I awoke it was in my head. I feel better awake than asleep, like out here I can see what is happening, but inside of my dreams I can feel what is happening, and it's worse."

"Like a truth was trying to be revealed?"

"Yeah," Gavin said. "Like that, and it was like my primitive brain understood it, but my logical brain couldn't wrap itself around it. Like the answer was in sight, but on a shelf too high for my mind to reach."

"Oh, I think I know. I think you know. Our minds know what's there on that shelf now, they just don't want to reach up and take hold of it. Don't want to know that truth. You see, Gavin, I think we saw a glimpse of the in-betweens."

"In-betweens?" he said, but she could tell it was mostly a rhetorical question. He knew exactly what she was talking about. She could see it in his eyes.

"Talking out loud," she said, "it's like finding a footstool and being able to reach that high shelf. What if there's a crack in our subconscious that allows us, from time to time, to slip from what we perceive as our

own life into a nightmare of sorts. One that's real. Not dream logic altogether, but a real place that we perceive as nightmare, but sometimes it's
more than that. A dimensional hole, like you suggested. We sometimes
pass through it, like the people and things you saw in your dream. Not
by choice, but by chance. The hole is there, and the right dream and the
right time, well, we fall through. Or we're pulled through."

"Yeah," Gavin said, picking up where she left off, really feeling it
now. "We get pulled in. Our world, the one where we're lying in bed, is
now the dream, and we can't get back. The hole closes, or we just can't
find it. Maybe in our old world, we're one of those who unexpectedly
dies in their sleep. But what is us now, the us in this dimension, we stay
here, and we experience whatever it is we find here, and our other self
truly dies. We have left the building back home, so to speak."

"Exactly," Amelia said. "The things that people see in nightmares,
monsters. Perhaps they really see them. At a distance sometimes. See
them, and then the dreamer slides back to where they belong. Sometimes
they don't. And perhaps, sometimes it works the other way. What's on
the other side seeps into our world like a kind of cosmic sewage."

Gavin interrupted her before she could speak another word.

"And us, and all the people on the ship, the others who came here,
the pilot of the plane, we all fell through the same hole. We were
having different dreams, but we all fell through, and then we were all
having a similar dream. Some of us dreamed of a ship, and we all were
on board, and the dream ship slipped through. Same for the plane,
the other ships and dogsleds. Say someone was traveling over the ice,
an explorer, for example, pulled by sled dogs, and that night he makes
his tent and he dreams. Dreams himself into another dimension, this
dimension, and the dogs go with him. Imagination becomes flesh and
blood because he and his dream have passed through that dimensional
hole. We've collectively dreamed ourselves into another reality. We've
fallen into our subconscious and we can't get out. We have all found
the same pit on the other side of the hole."

Amelia was silent for a long time before she spoke.

"As much as it can be explained, that's it. I feel it in my bones. Whatever is here in this horrid world is not just those star-heads, but something else of greater intelligence. Something that stands here waiting at the hole in our dreams, waiting for something or someone to slip through."

"To what purpose?"

Amelia reflected a moment, then, "It's like we're experiencing some eternal truth, and the horrid thing about it is, it's nothing wonderful. It's merely a place where we go and suffer. A sort of hell inside the mind that becomes solid. The Christian hell may not be Christian, but it may not be myth. And in our case, it's not fire on the other side, but ice."

"Maybe we can dream ourselves out," Gavin said.

"Do you feel that you can?"

Gavin shook his head. "No. I feel the gap to the other side has winked closed, and dreaming doesn't open it. Dreaming just makes you susceptible when the gap is open, is my guess. Dreaming here you just get tapped into by this intelligence, as you called it. It wants us, for whatever reason, but the reason isn't reasonable."

Amelia laughed. "That makes no sense."

"Because it isn't within our concept of logic. It wants what we can't understand. Things that would make no sense whatsoever to us. It feels hopeless."

"It's giving us the knowledge it wants us to have," Amelia said. "And only because it's a knowledge that fills us with defeat. And here's another thing, who says that knowledge is real? That may be part of its powers. It affects the mind, lets you imagine what it wants you to imagine. You can control it to a certain extent, but the closer you are to it, and we must be right on top of it, the stronger that power is. We have to decide not to let it defeat us with negative thoughts and uncomfortable revelations, because they may all be projection, and not reality."

"All right," Gavin said. "All right. We won't let it win."

They rested awhile, and without meaning to, they slept. It came over them as if they had been drugged. They fought it but it won, and they dreamed. A dream of great darkness rising up to overwhelm them, swallow them down and take them away, chewing up flesh and sucking out souls, their little sparks of life-force being sucked away into some horrid eternity even worse than where they were.

When they awoke, they saw no remedy to their problem other than to explore, plotting together to see if they could find and kill this thing that was wiggling in their brains. That was the plan. They would kill it. They had a gun and an axe, and Gavin still had the flare gun and flares in his coat pocket. They had something to fight with, and that meant they had a chance.

There was an array of irregular pathways that twisted and turned, and there were spears of light coming in through gaps in the structure, and the sunlight lit the halls and walls with enough intermittent illumination they could see clearly. They chose one of the pathways and followed it. It became narrow and low, and to exit it, they had to crawl on their hands and knees for some distance before it opened into a larger chamber. A smell like all the death and rot that had ever occurred wafted toward them in a hot, sticky stench. Gavin was overwhelmed by it, and threw up against the wall.

"Might want to step around that," he said, wiping his mouth.

"May have some to add to it," Amelia said.

They pulled their scarves around their noses and mouths and kept going. The chamber went wide, and then it went small. The stink intensified. They came to narrow halls again, and they kept going, not searching for anything in particular, but searching.

They arrived at a great drop-off, wide and deep and full of stink, lit by cracks of light from above. Hanging over the pit, fastened there by a scarf to what looked like a dry hose running above her, was a woman. She was wearing khaki pants and a leather jacket. She wore pilot gear, goggles pushed up on her head, and tight on her skull was a leather cap with ear flaps. Her skin was yellow, and her neck was long. The meat was beginning to rot, speeded up by the hot stink rising from the pit beneath her. Her feet dangled over the great and stinking pit, and one boot was slipping free of her rotting flesh, soon to fall into the pit below.

"The pilot," Gavin said. "Has to be. She ended up here somehow, and it must have been too much for her. The things we felt she must have felt, that damn presence, force, whatever. She didn't have anyone to bolster her and give her strength. She was on her own, so she just quit."

Amelia nodded, looked down into the pit.

"What is that?"

There was very little light now, just a split of gold through a crack here and there, so Gavin put a flare in his gun, fired it downwards. It glowed bright, and then it hit something below and sputtered with red light. The pit was full of blackened meat and rotting guts and all manner of offal.

Slowly Amelia's face paled.

"What?" Gavin said, staring at her face in the rising glow of the flare.

"I've got it figured, Gavin, and it's worse than we thought. This isn't a building. This place isn't a city. Above, those aren't hoses. They're veins, or arteries. Down below, that's afterbirth. We're inside a corpse, a drying one. Like a huge mollusk. Don't you see, Gavin? Down below, that's a womb. The star-shaped things. They were born here. Look around. There aren't any corridors. Those are artery paths that we've walked through, chambers for organs. Not human-like organs, but organ housings just the same. And this is the birth canal, and down below, the womb. The bones we saw outside, they're from this thing's digestive system, crapped out and onto the ground where they were dried by time and cold wind. Bones of humans and all manner of creatures that have ended up here. Those star-heads, they link up and grow, become solid at some part, don't separate anymore, and then they give birth and die, leaving these shells."

"You're sensing this?" Gavin asked.

"No. I'm speculating this, or you'd feel the same thing. Perhaps they're hermaphrodites. Once birth is completed, the host for the children dies. The replacements feed on what they can find. Maybe their mother, or whatever this thing can be called. And then they feed on whatever comes through the dream hole. These aren't buildings in a city. These are the remains of dead creatures, and they have given birth and left their remains, and the cycle continues."

Gavin looked about. "Maybe," he said.

"I can't be absolutely sure I'm right, but close enough, I think. What I am certain of is, I don't think being here is a good idea. We are too close to whatever that primal power is, the thing we sense, the thing that pulls us in from our dreams, it's nearby. And that can't be good. We have to find food, drinkable water. And most important, I can't stand this stink anymore."

They went back the way they had come, following the axe scratches, seeking the exit, fearing the arrival of the star-heads.

The cold was almost welcome.

They moved along the bone walk, toward the mountains, choosing a central range that looked dark with dirt and green with foliage, but no sooner had they started out, then the central mountain range trembled. The stretch of the horizon trembled. The green mist that floated above the mountains was sucked back toward the peaks, as if inhaled, and then the mist was blown back out in a great whirling wad, as if by a sleeping drunk.

And then they understood.

There were no cities, and there were no mountains. Only giant, irregular-shaped shells of creatures. Old ones that had given birth. Some larger than others.

Some as big as mountain ranges that still lived and were most likely stuffed tight with new life being baked inside a womb, and in this case, a womb much larger than any of those that had made up the false city. For before them was a beast. Not a mountain, but an impossible slug. The flesh had yet to harden. It trembled like Jell-O and it was vast.

The mountain trembled again, and then moved. Ever so slowly, but it moved. It was easy to outrun, of course. It inched its way. It would take days for it reach where they now ran. But they soon came up against the coal-black sea, stood on the shore with nowhere to go. Waves crashed in against the ice, flowing up to the toes of their boots. Gavin began to cry.

"It's all insane," he said. "That pilot was right after all."

Amelia touched his shoulder.

There was a banging to their left. It made them both jump. It was their old friend, Lifeboat Number Three. It had drifted away and back again, sailing crewless along the stretch of icy shore.

"Fate doesn't hate us after all," Amelia said.

Gavin laughed. He turned and looked back toward the mountain. It was difficult to tell it had moved. It seemed in the same place, but he knew it had. Tentacles, the size and length of four-lane highways, lifted off of the beast and snapped at the sky. They had appeared like rows of rock and dirt, but now they were revealed for what they were. The ice screeched with the monster's glacial progress.

Amelia ran to the boat, slipped on the ice, struggled to her feet, and grabbed at it. The back end of it swung around, banging against the hard ice. Another few minutes and they would never have known it was there. It would have washed out to sea again.

Amelia held the boat and looked at Gavin.

"The oars are still in it."

Gavin hurried to join her. He smiled at her. She smiled back. And then the smile dropped off her face.

Coming much closer than the mountain were the star-heads that they had outdistanced. They were as one again, larger than before, but smaller by far than the mountainous monster. They moved much faster than their creator, slurping over the ice, tentacles flaring, mouths open, showing multitudinous teeth, licking at the air with a plethora of what might have been tongues.

"This can't be real," Gavin said. "It's a mad house. One mad thing and then another. I have to wake up."

"I'd rather not stay here and find out if it's a dream, Gavin. Come on. We have to go. Now."

They pushed the boat into the water and climbed aboard, pushed at the ice with the oars, shoved out into the dark and raging waters.

They began to row savagely.

The star-head thing moved to the edge of the water and broke apart and its many bodies spilled into the waves.

Amelia and Gavin rowed wildly. The star-heads swam fast, cruising through the water, tentacles tucked. On they came, and soon Amelia and Gavin knew there was no chance of outdistancing them. They clutched their oars, ready to fight. The star-heads loomed out of the sea, tentacles flashing, attempting to clutch.

Amelia and Gavin were sitting at different ends of the boat, and they positioned themselves on their knees, swinging the oars, batting back tentacles, slamming down on star-heads as they peeked up over the rim of the boat. Tentacles slapped about like limbs whipped by a violent storm. Amelia felt them brush her, burning her with their sucker mouths, but they failed to manage a solid grip. She frantically wiggled free and swung the oar, knocking them aside.

"Oh god," she heard Gavin say. She glanced back. One of the star-heads had risen up beside the boat and whip-snapped its tentacles around Gavin and his oar, causing it to lie against his chest; the paddle part of the oar pointed up as if in sword-like salute. The star-head dropped completely back into the water, its tentacles stretched out, and lifted Gavin up like a mother holding a young child on display.

Gavin stared down at Amelia as he was hoisted out of the boat and dangled above the water. Amelia leaned out and swung the oar, struck the tentacles with it, but they were too strong, their grip too tight.

Gavin's face was as bland and white as the ice. He ceased to struggle, dangled in the monster's grip. The tentacles coiled him close and pulled him away, took him down under with little more than a delicate splash.

Amelia began to scream at the beasts, as if bad language might frighten them. She continued to struggle, whipping the oar through the air, contacting other star-heads. They came in a horde now. Tentacles flashed everywhere, popped at her legs, snapped against her arms. The black water turned greasy with blood. Star-heads were grabbing at the boat from all sides, shaking it with their tentacles, as if they might tear it apart or pull it down under. Gavin's head, minus his body, surfaced, rolled, and then was taken by a star-head's wide-open mouth. As it started to jerk Gavin's head below, fins broke the surface of the water.

Sharks. A mass of them.

A great white leapt out of the water, rolled its black eyes up inside its head as it snapped at the star-head's tentacle, pulled it and the remains of Gavin down with it. Sharks began to jump from the waves as easy as flying fish. They grabbed the star-heads in their toothy mouths, crunched them like dry toast, then pulled the remains of their squirming meals into the deep.

More sharks came and went, like a pack of wolves, cutting through the blood-slick waters, snapping at the star-heads quickly, darting away and under, only to rise and circle back and strike again.

And then the battle ceased. The sharks had won. Both sharks and star-heads were gone. One to eat, one to be eaten.

The night rolled in and a ragged moon floated up out of the sea, found a place to hang against the night. The waters churned and the boat jumped. Tired, Amelia lay down in the boat and was eased into sleep by exhaustion. The dark things moved inside her head.

When Amelia awoke the next morning it was still dark, but light was bleeding in with squirts of red, and in short time the sun trembled up and turned bright gold. She thought of Gavin, almost expecting to see him when she had the strength to rise from the bottom of the boat, but his fate was soon sharp in her memory. All she could think about was how he had been taken away by different monsters of the sea. Yet the sharks had been her saviors, and after a long time with the sun warming the boat and the sea, she found a dead shark floating on its back in the water, the bottom half of its tail eaten off in what had probably been a continued and cannibalistic shark frenzy from the night before. She paddled up beside it and saw that its belly was ripped open, and strings of innards hung out of it. A meal abandoned for whatever reason. She reached down and pulled the creature's insides loose, tugged them into the boat, snapping them off, tossing them on the floor of the craft like enormous tomato-sauced noodles. The guts were filled with offal. She shook that out as best she could, washed it clean with the waters of the sea, then ate it raw. It tasted good at first, but then when she was past her savage hunger, it made her stomach churn. Still, she scooped more out of the shark and tossed it in the bottom of the boat for later.

She had no idea what to do. Perhaps the only choice was to try and see if she could find a place farther down on the slate of ice where the mountainous monster and the star-heads didn't dwell. If such a place existed.

It was surprisingly warm, considering the ice. From way out she could see the mountainous creature. It took up all her eyeline when she looked to the shore. It had moved ever closer, changing the landscape in an amazing way, slipping along on a monstrous trail of slime that oozed out from under it and greased its way toward the sea.

It was massive. She would have to sail for days to get around it, if that was even possible.

Amelia ate some more of the shark, but the guts had gone bad in the sunlight. She vomited over the side.

Amelia counted four days at sea, and then she lost count. She had been lucky. A fairly large fish had leaped into the boat, and she had bashed its head with an oar. She ate its brains where the oar had broken its skull, ripped it open with her bare hands and used her teeth on the soft belly, biting off chunks, wolfing it down. It was far more palatable than the shark had been, and when she finished, she was refreshed. It was all she would have that day, and by next day she was hungry again, but no prize fish presented itself. She did manage to nab a few floating chunks of ice and suck on those for water.

She sailed hungry through a day and night. She wasn't sleeping. It was too dark down there in her dreams, so she tried to stay awake. Inside her thoughts the creature continued to come to her.

It didn't speak to her, but it communicated with her nonetheless. It was a terrible communication that made her dreams scream and her skin crawl.

Her hunger helped keep her awake.

Another fish might present itself, and that was something to think about instead of the monster that stretched for as far as she could see. Earlier in the day she had seen a seal, or something quite like one, swimming near the boat, not too far underwater, quite visible when the sun hit the waves just right. She hoped she might come across another, one more foolish, willing to rise up and present its head to be banged with an oar. It amazed her that animals she knew existed here amongst things her world had no idea existed.

By midday the boat had actually caught an underwater current of some sort, and it drifted out and away from the shoreline. But then an odd thing happened. It was discernable, but only a little, and near impossible to assimilate mentally. The mountain had reached beyond the shoreline. It was about to enter the water. And that's what happened. The entire icy shoreline cracked with an ear-piercing sound, and the great mountain dropped straight into the water, part of it disappearing like the fabled continent of Atlantis. Monstrous tentacles writhed from it.

It was so insane Amelia began to gulp air, like a fish that had been docked.

As the mountain slipped into the water, the sea rose up and the boat rose with it. The weight of the mountainous monster, a small continent of sorts, swelled the sea level. The impossible creature kept drifting down into the waters, and then abruptly it ceased to drift. It had hit bottom, but still the peaks of it rose out of the sea and the tentacles, as big as redwood trees, thrashed at the air and smacked the water like an angry child. The broken ice popped up before it and along its impossible length in iceberg chunks, bobbing like ice cubes in a glass.

The boat was borne toward the shoreline, which was entirely taken up by the behemoth. And then, all along the visible part of the beast, there was a horizontal fissure. The fissure spread wide with a cracking sound so loud Amelia covered her ears. The fissure spread for miles. There were jagged rows of teeth inside of it, each the size of mountain-tops, and there was spittle on the teeth, running in great wet beads, as if it was tumbling snow from an avalanche, and rising out of the great mouth was a sudsy foam, like white lava from a volcano. The teeth snapped together with an explosion so loud it deafened Amelia. When the impossible mouth opened again, it became wider yet; the bottom of it touched the sea. The water flowed into it with the briskness of a tsunami, and in the drag of it, the lifeboat jetted toward the mouth.

Amelia grabbed the oars and tried to use them, but it was useless. The rush of the water toward the open mouth of the creature was too strong and too swift; it could not be denied.

She saw the great fissure of a mouth tremble, and then the boat came closer, flowing now with even greater speed.

"Why?" she yelled to the wind and water. "I am nothing. I'm not even an appetizer."

Amelia began to laugh, loud and hysterical. She could hear herself, and it frightened her to hear it, but she couldn't stop.

And then the little flyspeck of a boat, with its smaller laughing speck inside, entered into the trembling, foam-flecked mouth that was a length beyond full view of the eye, and tumbled as if over a vast waterfall. The boat banged against one of the jagged teeth like a gnat hitting a skyscraper, came apart, and it and Amelia, who gave one last great laugh, were churned beneath the water and carried into the monster's gullet, along with creatures of the sea.

About Joe R. Lansdale

JOE R. LANSDALE is probably the only person in the International Martial Arts Hall of Fame who has received the Edgar, ten Stokers, the Raymond Chandler, the British Fantasy, the Spur, the Golden Lion, the Grinzane Cavour Prize, the Herodotus, and the Inkpot Awards. Lansdale has also been designated as a Grandmaster of Horror by the World Horror Association. His acclaimed works have landed him in the Texas Literary Hall of Fame and the Texas Institute of Letters.

Lansdale's extraordinary output includes mysteries, Westerns, horror, pulp fiction, science fiction, and thrillers. He has written more than 40 novels, 400 shorter works, numerous comic books, and a handful of screenplays as well as creating the Shen Chuan Martial Science. His novels include *Dead in the West* (1986), *The Magic Wagon* (1986), *The Nightrunners* (1987), *The Drive-In* (1988), *Cold in July* (1989), the Edgar Award–winning *The Bottoms* (2000), *A Fine Dark Line* (2002), *Flaming Zeppelins* (2010), *The Thicket* (2013), the Spur Award–winning *Paradise Sky* (2015), *More Better Deals* (2020), *Moon Lake* (2021), and *The Donut Legion* (2023). Beginning with *By Bizarre Hands* (1989), Lansdale's short stories have been collected in several volumes, including *The Best of Joe R. Lansdale* (2010), *Terror Is Our Business* (2018, with Kasey Lansdale), *Things Get Ugly* (2023), and

The Senior Girls Bayonet Drill Team and Other Stories (2024). He has edited fifteen anthologies, including *Dark at Heart* (1992, with Karen Lansdale), *Weird Business* (1995, with Richard Klaw), *Retro Pulp Tales* (2006), *Crucified Dreams* (2011), and *The Urban Fantasy Anthology* (2011, with Peter S. Beagle).

Lansdale's most famous creation is the unlikely duo of Hap and Leonard. Hap Collins is white, liberal, and even-tempered. Leonard Pine, who is quick to anger, is Black, conservative, and gay. In a series of 14 novels, spanning *Savage Season* (1990) through *Sugar on the Bones* (2024), and several novellas and short stories, the best friends encounter violence, racism, and adventure in their East Texas haunts. The often-humorous tales have garnered much praise and a legion of devoted fans. Many of the Hap and Leonard novellas and shorter tales are collected in *Veil's Visit* (1999), *Hap and Leonard* (2016), *Hap and Leonard: Blood and Lemonade* (2018), *Of Mice and Minestrone* (2020), and *Born for Trouble* (2021). For three seasons, the pair were featured on the television series *Hap and Leonard* (2016–18), starring James Purefoy and Michael K. Williams.

Lansdale's works that have been adapted for film treatments include *Bubba Ho-Tep* and *Cold in July*; "Incident On and Off a Mountain Road" for *Masters of Horror*; "The Dump," "Fish Night," and "The Tall Grass," for the Netflix series *Love, Death & Robots*; "The Companion" for *Creepshow*; and *Christmas with the Dead*, which Lansdale produced with a screenplay by his son, Keith. He has written many screenplays and teleplays, including episodes of *Batman: The Animated Series*. He has also written graphic novels for DC, Marvel, Dark Horse, IDW, and others. The documentary *All Hail the Popcorn King* explores the enduring legacy of Lansdale and his creations.

Lansdale also possesses multiple black belts, and he is the founder of the martial arts system Shen Chuan: Martial Science and its affiliate, Shen Chuan Family System.

Joe R. Lansdale lives with his wife, Karen, in Nacogdoches, Texas.